"Gritty and raw, *Blackbirds* sports a unique heroine in the form of Miriam. Both sympathetic and pitiable, she dances through Chuck's brilliant turns of phrase and crisp writing to an illuminating ending which begs the question: Are we truly masters of our own fate?"

Allison Pang, author of A Brush of Darkness

"Chuck Wendig unloads with both barrels and *Blackbirds* hits you like a shotgun blast to the torso at close range."

Matthew McBride, author of Frank Sinatra in a Blender

"Everyone dies eventually and the way it happens isn't fair; the way you check out is the way you check out. Wendig appeals to the slightly nasty part of us that we don't want to admit to but know is there. Who amongst us doesn't secretly want to know how it all ends for us? And who amongst us doesn't want to know how others die so that we can hope for something a little easier for ourselves?"

Graham's Fantasy Book Review

"*Blackbirds* is a high energy, whisky-fuelled ride, that will pull you along for the journey and have you questioning whether we can change destiny. A must-read book by an author who is worth watching."

Fantasy Faction

Also by Chuck Wendig

Blackbirds

Double Dead

Dinocalypse Now

Irregular Creatures (short stories)

Shotgun Gravy (novella)

Non-Fiction

250 Things You Should Know About Writing

500 Ways to be a Better Writer

500 More Ways to be a Better Writer

Confessions of a Freelance Penmonkey

Revenge of the Penmonkey

CHUCK WENDIG

MOCKINGBIRD

ANGRY ROBOT
A member of the Osprey Group

Lace Market House,
54-56 High Pavement,
Nottingham,
NG1 1HW, UK

4402 23rd St., Ste 219,
Long Island City,
NY 11101
USA

www.angryrobotbooks.com
The future is killing me

An Angry Robot paperback original 2012

Cover Artist: Joey HiFi

Distributed in the United States by Random House, Inc., New York.

ISBN 978-0-85766-233-0
eBook ISBN 978-0-85766-234-7

Printed in the United States of America

9 8 7 6 5 4 3

PART ONE

THE CAGE-TRAINED GIRL

She's only a bird in a gilded cage,
A beautiful sight to see.
You may think she's happy and free from care,
She's not, though she seems to be.
'Tis sad when you think of her wasted life
For youth cannot mate with age;
And her beauty was sold for an old man's gold,
She's a bird in a gilded cage.

Bird in a Gilded Cage
Arthur J. Lamb, Harry von Tilzer

ONE
SHIP BOTTOM

Boop.

Suntan lotion.

Boop.

Pecan sandies.

Boop.

Tampons, beach towel, postcards, and, mysteriously, a can of green beans.

Miriam grabs each item with a black-gloved hand. Runs the item over the scanner. Sometimes she looks down and stares into the winking red laser. She's not supposed to do that. But she does it anyway, a meager act of rebellion in her brand new life. Maybe, she thinks, the ruby beam will burn away that part of her brain that makes her who she is. Turn her into a mule-kicked window-licker, happy in oblivion, pressed up against the walls of her Plexiglas enclosure.

"Miss?"

The word drags her out of the mind's eye theater and back to checkout.

"Jesus, what?" she asks.

"Well, are you going to scan that?"

Miriam looks down. Sees she's still holding the can of green beans. Del Monte. She idly considers braining the woman standing there in her beachy muumuu, the worn pattern of hibiscus flowers barely covering a sludgy bosom that's half lobster red and half wood-grub white. Two halves marked by the Rubicon of a terrible tan line.

Instead, Miriam swipes the can across the scanner with a too-sweet smile.

Boop.

"Is something wrong with your hands?" the woman asks. She sounds concerned.

Miriam waggles one finger – a jumping inchworm dance. The black leather creaks and squeaks.

"Oh, these? I have to wear these. You know how women at restaurants have to wear hairnets? For public health safety? I gotta wear these gloves if I'm going to work here. Rules and regulations. Last thing I want to do is cause a hepatitis outbreak, am I right? I got Hep A, B, C, and the really bad one, X."

Then, just to sell it, Miriam holds up her hand for a high-five.

The woman does not seize the high-five opportunity.

Rather, the blood drains from her face, her sunburned skin gone swiftly pale.

Miriam wonders what would happen if she told the truth: *Oh, it's no big deal, but when I touch people this little psychic movie plays in my head and I witness how and when they're going to die. So I've been wearing these gloves so I don't have to see that kind of crazy shit anymore.*

MEET MIRIAM BLACK

"Think *Six Feet Under* co-written by Stephen King and Chuck Palahniuk… Wendig's surefooted prose means that this ride is well worth sticking your thumb out for."

SFX Magazine

"Visceral and often brutal, this tale vibrates with emotional rawness that helps to paint a bleak, unrelenting picture of life on the edge."

Publishers Weekly

"Balls-to-the-wall, take-no-prisoners storytelling at its best."

Bill Cameron, author of County Line

"Truly the dark fantastic. *Blackbirds* is one of the most amazing, gritty, gruesome, witty, terrifying, wonderful books I've been lucky enough to read this year."

Kat Richardson, author of the Greywalker Chronicles

"Chuck Wendig has raised the bar of the urban fantasy genre and introduced a dynamic new character who, if left to her own devices, will most likely steal more than just your heart."

New York Journal of Books

"*Blackbirds* is dirty, filthy, nasty… fantastic. If you can stand the sight of some awfully ugly stuff, you're exceedingly likely to love it."

The Speculative Scotsman

"Wendig has taken the American roadside story and turned it into a tale supernatural terror. This is a treat for those of us who like their horror vampire-free and swearword heavy."

Starburst

"Trailer-park tension, horrified hilarity, and sheer terror mixed with deft characterization and razor plotting. I literally could not put it down."

Lilith Saintcrow, author of Night Shift

"*Blackbirds* is a horror story, a traveling story, a story of loss and what it takes to make things right. It's a story about fate and how sometimes, if we wrestle with it hard enough, maybe we can change it. *Blackbirds* is the kind of book that doesn't let go even after you've put it down."

Stephen Blackmoore, author of City of the Lost

"Mean, moody and mysterious, *Blackbirds* is a noir joyride peppered with black humour, wry observation, and visceral action."

Adam Christopher, author of Empire State *and* Seven Wonders

"A gleefully dark, twisted road trip for everyone who thought *Fight Club* was too warm and fuzzy. If you enjoy this book, you're probably deeply wrong in the head. I loved it, and will be seeking professional help as soon as Chuck lets me out of his basement."

James Moran, Severence, Doctor Who *and* Torchwood *screenwriter*

Or the deeper truth behind even that: *I wear them because Louis wants me to wear them.*

Not that the gloves provide perfect protection against the visions. Nobody but Louis is touching her anywhere else, though. She keeps covered up. Even in the heat.

Behind the woman is a line seven, eight-people deep. They all hear what Miriam says. She's not quiet. Two of the customers – a doughy gentleman in a parrot-laden shirt and a young girl with an ill-contained rack of softball-sized fake tits – shimmy out of the queue and leave their goods on the empty checkout two rows down.

Still, the woman hangs tough. With a sour face, she pulls a credit card out of nowhere – Miriam imagines she withdraws it from her sand-encrusted vagina – and flips it onto the counter like it's a hot potato.

Miriam's about to grab it and scan it when a hand falls on her shoulder.

She already knows to whom the hand belongs.

She wheels on Peggy, manager here at Ship Bottom Sundries in Long Beach Island, New Jersey. Peggy, whose nose must possess powerful gravity given the way it looks like the rest of her face is being dragged toward it. Peggy, whose giant sunglasses call to mind the eyes of a praying mantis. Peggy with her gray hair dyed orange and left in a curly, clumsy tangle.

Fucking Peggy.

"You mind telling me what you're doing?" The way Peggy begins every conversation, it seems. All in that Joisey accent. *Ya mind tellin' me what y'doin'?* The lost

Rs, the dropped Gs, *wooter* instead of *water*, *caw-fee* instead of *coffee*.

"Helping this fine citizen check out of our fine establishment." Miriam thinks but does not say, *Ship Bottom Sundries, where you can buy a pack of hotdogs, a pack of generic-brand tampons, or a handful of squirming hermit crabs for your screaming shit-bird children.*

"Sounds like you're giving her trouble."

Miriam offers a strained smile. "Was I? Not my intention."

Totally her intention.

"You know, I hired you as a favor."

"I do know that. Because you remind me frequently."

"Well, it's true."

"Yes. We *just* established that."

Peggy's puckered eyes tighten to fleshy slits. "You got a smart mouth."

"Some might argue my mouth is actually quite foolish."

By now, the line is building up. The woman in the floral muumuu is holding the green beans to her chest, as though the can will protect her from the awkwardness that has been thrust upon her day. The other customers watch with wide eyes and uncomfortable scowls.

"You think you're funny," Peggy says.

Miriam doesn't hesitate. "I really do."

"Well, I don't."

"Agree to disagree?"

Peggy's face twists up like a rag about to be wrung

out. It takes a moment for Miriam to realize that this is Peggy's happy face.

"You're fired," Peggy says. Mouth twisted up at the corners in some crass facsimile of a human smile.

"Oh, fuck you," Miriam says. "You're not going to fire me." It occurs to her too late that saying *fuck you* is not the best way to retain one's job, but frankly, the horse is already out of the stable on that one.

"Fuck me?" Peggy asks. "Fuck *you*. You bring me nothing but grief. Come in here day after day, moping about like someone pissed in your Wheaties–"

"Do people even eat Wheaties anymore? I mean, seriously."

"–and I don't need a grumpy little slut like you working in my store. Season's over after this weekend anyway, and you're done. Kaput. Pack up your crap and get out. I'll send you your last paycheck."

This is real, Miriam thinks.

She just got let go.

Pink-slipped.

Shit-canned.

She should be happy.

Her heart should be a cage of doves newly opened, the free birds flying high, fleeing far and away. This should be a real *the hills are alive with the sound of music* moment, all twirling skirts and wind in her hair. But all she feels is the battery acid burn of rage and bile and incredulity mingling at the back of her throat. A rising tide of snake venom.

Louis always tells her to keep it together.

She is tired of keeping it together.

Miriam yanks her nametag off her chest – a nametag that says "Maryann" because they fucked it up and didn't want to reprint it – and chucks it over her shoulder. The muumuu lady dodges it.

She goes with an old standby – her middle finger thrust up in Peggy's juiced lemon of a face – and then storms outside.

She stops. Stands in the parking lot. Hands shaking.

An ocean breeze kicks up. The air brings with it the smell of brine and fish and a lingering hint of coconut oil. Serpents of sand whisper across the cracked parking lot.

A dozen gulls fight over bread scraps. Ducking and diving. Squawking and squalling. Drunk on breadcrust and victory.

It's hot. The breeze does little for that.

People everywhere. The *fwip-fwip-fwip* of flip-flop sandals. The miserable sob of somebody's child. The murmur and cackle of endless vacationers smelling a season drawing to a close. A thudding bass line booms from a car sliding down the slow traffic of Long Beach Boulevard, and she can't help but think how the beat sounds like *douche-douche-douche-douche* and how it echoes her hammer-fist heartbeat dully punching against the inside of her breastbone. And Walt the "cart boy," who's not really a boy but in fact a developmentally handicapped fifty-year-old man, gives her a wave and she waves back and thinks, *He's the only one here who was ever nice to me.* And probably the only one she was ever nice to, too.

She thinks, *Fuck it.*

She peels off one of her gloves.

Then comes the other.

Miriam pitches both over her shoulder – her hands are freakishly pale, paler than the rest of her body, the fingertips wrinkled as though she's been in a long bath.

If Louis wanted her to keep it together, he'd be here. And he's not.

Miriam goes back inside the store, cracking her knuckles.

TWO
THE LIBERATION OF MIRIAM BLACK

Peggy has taken over from Miriam at the second check-out counter in from the end, and Miriam marches right up to her, taps her on the shoulder, and offers her a hand – ah, the fake handshake, that old trick to get people to touch her, to get one tiny moment of that skin-to-skin contact necessary to get the psychic death-visions a-flowing. She's itching to see how this woman bites it. *Hungry* for it. Desperate like a junkie.

Miriam's hoping for some kind of ass cancer.

"I just wanted to say thank you," Miriam lies through clenched teeth. *Thank you with ass cancer.* "Wanted to do this the honorable way and shake your hand."

But Peggy, she's not buying it. She looks down at Miriam's hand as though it's not a hand but rather a big stinking tarantula.

Take my hand, lady.

I need this.

I need to see.

It's been so long. Her hands are practically tingling.

Once she hated her curse.

She still does. But that doesn't change the need.

Shake my fucking hand.

"Get lost," Peggy says, pulling away.

The buzz, killed.

Peggy turns her back. Continues checking people out. *Boop, boop, boop.*

"Please," Miriam says. Urgent now. Tremble twitch. "C'mon. Let's leave this as professionals."

Peggy ignores her. The customers stare.

Boop. Boop. Boop.

"Hey. Hello. I'm talking to you. Shake my damn hand."

Peggy doesn't even bother turning around. "I said, *get lost.*"

Miriam's hands are practically aching. She feels like a dog watching a man eating a steak – the desire, the hunger, it lives in the hinge of her of jaw, a tightness before salivation. She wants nothing more than to pop this cork. "All right, you insufferable twat, I'm going to have to do this the hard way."

Feet planted firmly on the point of no return, Miriam grabs Peggy, wheels her around, and smacks her with the–

Peggy screams. She runs but staggers over a dead body lying face-down on the sand-swept tile of Ship Bottom Sundries. The dead body is Walt, the cart boy. Blood pools beneath Peggy's hands, blood that isn't her own, and out of her throat comes a cry that sounds like the bleating of an animal just before the knife drags across its neck. But Peggy's cry doesn't rise alone; the whole store is people screaming, ducking down aisles, running for the door. And then a thin man parts the crowd – he doesn't belong, what with the dark sunglasses and the black V-neck T-shirt and the khaki pants stained with food or motor oil or who-knows-what – and he raises a pistol, a boxy Glock, and the pistol barks and the bullet peels a piece of Peggy's orange-haired scalp off her skull, and then another bullet punches like a train through her lung and she draws one last guttering gasp.

–back of her hand, and Peggy's head snaps back, but it's not her who's left reeling. Miriam can hear the blood rushing through her ears, and it makes her dizzy. The world swoons and she doesn't believe that this could possibly be real, that this could really be what she's seeing.

Peggy has three minutes left to live.

Three minutes.

Here. Now. Today.

Oh, god.

The doors open and Walt struggles to bring in an unruly herd of shopping carts, but he whistles a happy tune just the same.

Peggy gapes. "I'm calling the police."

Miriam hears her but the words are a distant echo, like they're being spoken by someone underwater. Instead her eyes rove to the back of the line just as a man steps into the queue. A man in dark Ray-Bans. And a V-neck T-shirt. And dirty khakis.

The gunman.

Two-and-a-half minutes.

It's then that Miriam sees movement above. A crow in the rafters, shuffling from foot to foot. The crow has one eye. The other eye is a ruined, featherless crease.

The bird clacks its beak and, in her head, Miriam hears: *Welcome back, Miss Black.*

She blinks and the bird is gone.

Peggy tries to restrain her, tries to grab her wrists, but Miriam doesn't have time. She shoves the woman back into the cash drawer with a *ding.*

Miriam has no idea what she's doing. She feels lost. Unmoored. And yet somehow, that wild and wobbly uncertainty feels like home.

She heads around the back of the line. Like she's on auto-pilot. Buckled into a ride she can't stop. Peggy shouts at her. Miriam can barely hear.

Those in line ogle her. They move away from her as she gets close. They don't want to give up their place in line but they don't want to be near her, either.

Two minutes now. Maybe less.

She sidles up behind the killer. The killer doesn't move. Doesn't blink. Doesn't care.

Peggy stands aside, looking stunned. Calling for someone to call the cops. Mumbling something about assault. She asks the customers for help. Help restraining Miriam. No one offers. They just want to buy their shit and get out.

Some set their stuff down and escape. *Too awkward for my blood,* they're probably thinking. Miriam isn't thinking about anything but the killer, the gun, and death.

"You have a gun," Miriam says to the man in front of her. Her voice croaks when she speaks, her tongue so dry it sticks to the roof of her mouth.

He turns halfway, cocking his head like a confused

dog, like he couldn't possibly have heard what he just heard.

At the front of the store, Walt sees her again. And waves.

She waves back.

The man registers what she said.

"They want me to kill everyone."

"They who?"

"The voices."

You can't," Miriam says, a hollow plea. A minute-and-a-half left. She knows begging won't help. Nothing she says will matter. That isn't how it works. The rules have been clear ever since she put a bullet in a drug kingpin at the Old Barney lighthouse over a year ago. "Don't. Please."

What fate wants, fate gets.

Unless. *Unless.*

Unless she pays the cost. A cost of blood. Eye for an eye, tooth for a tooth, a life for a life. Only an act *that big* will sway fate. To change the course of a raging river, you need a big-ass motherfucking rock.

"Did the voices send you, too?" he asks

Miriam shakes her head. "No." She doesn't know who he's talking about, but she sees the way his lips form words he's not even speaking, sees the way his fingers work at the air like the legs of an overturned beetle, can *smell* the stink of sweat and gun oil on the man, and it's all too clear: He's nuts, crazy, a real farking moonbat.

But he's a moonbat on a terrible mission.

Before she knows what's happening, he's got the gun out. The Glock.

His hand moves fast and clips her across the top of the head with it. She sees bright white starbursts behind her eyes as she tumbles backward and falls on her butt-bone.

The chance to do what must be done is slipping away as she sits dizzy on the floor.

Everything seems to go slow. She's a flitting mosquito caught suddenly in a blob of tree sap.

A line of blood runs down the side of her nose.

She can barely find her feet to put them beneath her.

The man raises the gun straight up in the air and fires.

Screams. Movement. Chaos.

He levels the gun. Another shot. The front door shatters.

Miriam stands, head pounding, colorful flashes of light dancing in her vision. She's behind him. Her gaze drifts down the man's arm and to the sights of the gun as the weapon tracks Walt behind his row of shopping carts.

It's now or never.

Will fate get what fate wants?

She knows this store. She's been working here since before the beach season started. Who hasn't looked around their work environment and played the, "What around here could be a weapon?" game? Maybe she's alone. Maybe it's just her game. Miriam Black isn't most people. Not anymore.

She turns. Grabs something off an end-cap.

A long, stainless steel, two-pronged fork.

For barbecuing.

She stabs it into the side of the man's neck as the gun fires.

Walt screams and falls. A cart drifts away.

Blood burbles up around the fork like the water in a bubbler fountain. It begins soaking the gunman's neck and T-shirt collar.

The killer wheels on Miriam. A clumsy pirouette, the fork sticking out the side of his neck, looking like a lever you could pull to power him down.

She finds herself staring down the barrel of the Glock.

"You're the one always messing with things," he says, his lips wet with red. The words aren't angry. Wistful, maybe. Sad. Definitely sad.

A flash from the muzzle. She doesn't even hear it.

She feels it though. Her head rolls – a burning sensation in the deep of her skull like the searing gaze of Satan himself.

The man collapses sideways into a rack of shell-jewelry, faux pirate *tschotskes*, and beachy snow-globes filled with swirling sand instead of snowflakes. They shatter as they hit the floor.

Miriam tries to say something.

Finds her mouth is no longer connected to her brain.

For the world, that may be some kind of mercy.

But for her, it's a certain terror.

A deep and wretched darkness reaches for her and grabs hold.

INTERLUDE
THE TRESPASSER

Miriam sits on the beach, her butt planted on a cheap white plastic chair, her hands steepled on a patio table made of the same, her toes burrowed into cold sand like a row of ostrich heads.

Sitting across from her is her first boyfriend, Ben Hodges, the back of his head blown out from the shotgun he ate so long ago. Back when they were both dumb horny teenagers in high school. They fucked. She got pregnant. He killed himself. And his mother took out her lonely mother rage on Miriam with a red snow shovel.

That day. The day Miriam was really born. The now-Miriam. The Miriam with this curse, this gift, this thing-that-she-does.

Ben clears his throat.

A pair of dark-winged birds – blackbirds, each with a dime-sized splash of red on each wing – picks at his exposed brain like they're looking for worms.

The sea slides in, the sea slides out, the ineluctable susurration of the tides.

"I knew you couldn't stay away for long," Ben says.

Except Miriam knows this isn't Ben. Once upon a time she would have said he was a figment of her imagination, a shape-shifting tormenter of her own devising, and that may still be true. But now she's not so sure. Maybe she was never sure.

"I am who I am."

"That's what we're counting on."

She unsteeples her hands and leans forward. "We. That's not the first time you've said that word."

"We are legion. The demons in your head."

"So this is all just a hallucination? You're just some asshole I made up?"

Ben says nothing. His eyes flash with mischief.

Just then, one of the blackbirds yanks its head upward, and in its beak is something that looks like a stringy tendon. Ben's left arm jerks up in the air. When the bird drops the tendon, the arm plops back at his side.

The birds, working him like a puppet.

Cute.

And then a shadow passes over Miriam. She looks up, sees a Mylar balloon floating up in the sky, moving in front of the pale disc that passes for the sun here, and when she looks back at Ben he's no longer Ben. Instead, he's the gunman. The one from the store. Replete with bloody mouth and a barbecue fork sticking out of his neck.

"So. How does it feel?"

"How does what feel?" she says, but she knows what he's really asking.

"Don't be coy. Your second kill." Again, mischief glimmers. "Or third, if you want to count your dead baby."

That hits her like a fist. She tries not to show it but just the same she leans back in her chair, looks away, stares out over the gray ocean, over the foam-capped waves.

The gunman shrugs. "Guess we won't count the baby, then."

"You need a name," she says to change in conversation. "You may not have a face but I want you to have a name."

"Will I be Ben? Louis? Mommy?"

"I'm not calling you Mommy. Fucking sicko."

"When was the last time you saw her, by the way?"

She doesn't bother saying anything. He – or she, or it – already knows the answer.

"I should call you the Intruder," she says finally. "Because that's what you do. You intrude. Here I should be drifting through the darkness before my death, all peaceful and shit, and then you come along. Trespassing on my mental property. Actually, I like that. Trespasser. There we go."

"Don't pretend like you don't invite me in."

"I do no such thing."

The gunman smiles. A blackbird lands on the neck-stuck BBQ fork.

"Besides," the Trespasser continues, except now it's not the gunman who's speaking but the blackbird perched on the fork's handle. Still with Ben's voice. "You're not dead. You're just in shock."

"I'm not dead?"

"Not yet. Soon, maybe. You have work to do first. We can't let you off the hook that easy, little fishy. This meeting is just our little way of saying we're glad to have you back."

"You should've brought cake," she says.

"Next time, maybe."

THREE

JUST A FLESH WOUND

She has to give her statement to three different cops and each of them urge her to get in the goddamn ambulance already.

As she sits on the curb, smoking like a cancer factory, the cops tell her that she might have a concussion. And that the bullet graze along the side of her head – that's what it is, a line of parted flesh and lost hair where the bullet dug a burning furrow through her scalp – might get infected.

Miriam tells them she's not getting in the ambulance.

She's not going to the hospital.

She's fine.

She doesn't have health insurance, and she doesn't have the money to compensate for not having health insurance. The last time she was in the hospital, she got walloped with a bill that had so many zeroes she thought she was at Pearl Harbor. (That bill – and all the others that followed – ended up in the trash).

The statement she gives isn't all that far from the truth. In fact, she tells them everything – even the part where she backhanded Peggy – except for that mess about psychic visions. It's not that Miriam is averse to sharing that with people. But she's tried it in the past, and it turns out the cops don't care much for the "I had a psychic vision" defense.

No reason to go kicking over hornet's nests.

Instead she tells them that she saw the bulge of the gun and saw the man start to pull it out. Nothing that happened contradicts the story.

Peggy doesn't want to press charges. Peggy doesn't even want to see her or talk to her, which is fine by Miriam.

She tries to find out more about the gunman. But nobody knows anything. Or they're not talking. Either way, it's Ignorant City, population: Miriam.

And so hours later, Miriam is free. They give her the old warning: "Don't leave the state just in case we need to talk to you again."

She hears them. But she doesn't really *hear* them.

She needs another cigarette.

She needs to go home.

If only she knew what that really meant.

FOUR

HOME AGAIN, HOME AGAIN, FUCKITY-FUCK

The LBI causeway is a nightmare because it's always a nightmare, the island constantly binging and purging vacationers. During the summer, the causeway – a white bowing bridge over the gray-and-brown froth that is the Manahawkin Bay – is blocked like a plaque-clogged artery.

It's the one way on and off the island.

But Miriam doesn't drive. And that means she can move. The Schwinn 10-speed, the frame pockmarked with syphilitic sea-born rust, carries her past the cars – a swish of colors, a Dopplerian effect of radio stations and conversations.

The wheels turn with a flywing hum.

Her head-wound stings in the salt air.

She smokes as she rides, the cancer plume lost behind her.

It was a year ago that she first came over this causeway, heading to the island to save Louis from a fate she'd inadvertently assigned him. He was tied to a chair at the top of a lighthouse. Tortured by a monster.

She saved him before he lost his second eye – and, subsequently, all brain function – and in turn learned that one special exception to her abilities.

The only way to divert death is to give it a life.

Like she did today, with the gunman. *Fork him, that motherforker*, she thinks, the joke pinballing around the inside of her skull. But it doesn't get funnier with each echo. Instead, it makes her feel sicker, stranger, more unstable.

You have work to do.

She shudders even in the heat.

Finally, the end of the causeway. Bay Ave gives way to Barnegat Road. Pine trees thrust up out of sandy mounds. She never thought pine trees belonged at the beach but here they are. Of course, she never thought medical waste belonged at the beach either, but that's New Jersey for you.

She ducks down Green Street, past the little surf shop, then past the dinky bait shop, all to avoid the traffic circle. That's another New Jersey thing: the traffic circles. Can't just be a regular intersection. Oh, no. Around and around. A hellish carousel of traffic that would make Dante fall down in a pile of his own sick.

You could just ride one of those circles forever, she thinks.

Swirling the drain.

That's how she feels as she heads home. Like that's all she's doing. Treading water, doggy-paddling, waiting for sharks to come or for her arms to give out or for a boat to come along and suck her into the propeller.

Home. *Home*. Ugh.

Home now is a 1967 Airstream Trade Wind trailer parked at the Bayview Trailer Park just outside Tuckerton. The name of the park is a bit of a misnomer, though she eventually discovered it's not a *total* lie – if you climb on top of one of the trailers and then scamper up the nearby telephone pole, sure as shit you can see the murky gonorrhea tides of the bay.

The trailer park is the standard assortment of miscreants and deviants. Over there, a nice older couple with a fetish for vintage Hawaiian shirts and a pair of the Chattiest Cathies she's ever had the displeasure of meeting. Next to them, a duo of college drop-outs who sell ditch-weed to other college drop-outs. At the other end of the park is a seedier contingent: a guy who makes either meth or bombs (or maybe both), a hoarder who hoards not stuff but Jack Russell terriers (the barking, *the barking*), and a middle-aged divorced guy who always wears flannel shirts even in the heat and who Miriam is pretty sure is a big ole kid-toucher.

A real friendly crowd.

A crowd to which she belongs. She knows this. She doesn't like it, but there it is.

Miriam waves at the nice older couple – the Moons – but is sure not to stop, lest she find herself trapped in a conversational gravity well from which there is no escape but to hack off an arm with a nearby garden trowel.

She grabs her crotch at the two pot dealers – Scudder and Nils, the former a gangly surf-bum version of Ichabod Crane, the latter a pot-bellied man-boy with a hipster beard and black-rim eyeglasses. They wave back with big dumb smiles. As is the tradition.

Then: home.

"Home."

Whatever.

Dead marigolds sit out front in a planter made of crooked bricks. Next to them stands a ceramic lawn gnome with a cracked hole in his forehead, a hole she put there with a rusty mini-golf putter she found behind the Airstream. A putter she uses for a variety of purposes: to whack pebbles off the Airstream roof, to scratch her back, to threaten both meth-heads and cockroaches alike.

The putter lays nearby, in high weeds and grass.

Crossing the threshold of that trailer cinches her stomach into tightening knots every time.

"Lockdown," she says.

Into the belly of the silver whale.

Metal walls. Shore décor: all pastel and wood paneling and 1980s fixtures. She hasn't touched a thing. The only thing she's done to decorate in here is to hang a bird skeleton above the kitchen sink. She guesses it's a crow. She found it dead about three months back, most of its meat eaten by ants, a few feathers still clinging to dead bones.

Doing any more than hanging that one thing would feel like she owns the place. Like she actually *lives* here.

She does, of course. But reality has never been her strong suit.

"Hullo, bird," she says in her best Mister Snuffleupagus. She taps the crow skeleton – which she crucified on to some popsicle sticks with fishing line and twist-ties. The dead bird spins lazily in the afternoon light.

Louis assured her that the bird skeleton was disgusting and that it did not belong in the trailer, much less above the kitchen sink where they wash dishes.

She told him it's the only thing she wants in this place, it's the only thing she really *has* in this place, and that were he to try to remove it, she would sit on his chest while he slept and smash his balls flat with a ball peen hammer. Miriam further assured him that this was *why* that hammer earned that name, because it was for smashing both *balls* and *peens*, so he should take great caution.

They haven't been getting along.

They'd been lovers. He was gentle and sweet. He convinced her to stay in Jersey. He used some of his saved-up money to buy a place, said they could live there, said it'd be fine because he wasn't here all that often what with his long hauls up and down the East Coast and oh, hey, she could get a job and start to settle down and and blah blah blah normalcy–

Miriam doesn't want to think about it.

Her head gash throbs. She touches it with a finger. Sticky. Mealy. Pink fluid, not red, wets her fingertip.

Can't help poking the wound.

Once, hope bloomed that she and Louis could make a real go of it. But hope turned to resentment and it wasn't long before the Airstream felt less like a place to settle down and more like a tin-can tomb.

Now they're roommates. And friends. And enemies. And every once in a while she still gets that urge and she climbs on top of him like a little girl in a big saddle and they share a mercy fuck. Maybe the mercy's for him. Maybe it's for her.

Who knows. Who cares.

Louis is gone two weeks out of every three.

This is one of his "gone" weeks. But it's ending now. He could be home at any point. She smells the air. No Old Spice – the old Old Spice, not the new Old Spice, which smells to her like the urinal cake in a Ukranian bathhouse.

The longer he stays gone, the less that smell lingers.

Just when it's all gone she knows it's time for him to return.

She goes outside to have a cigarette.

No smoking in the house, he said to her.

It's not a house, she replied.

But it's a home, was his response.

Her answer to that was a gagging noise, finger thrust deep throat.

FIVE
TWEAK

Miriam sits next to the dead marigolds, smoking cigarette after cigarette, thinking that just one more will cure her of the tightness in her chest, will help her breathe a little easier. She flicks ash into the gnome's broken head.

Hours pass.

Evening comes. Still light out. Cicadas give way to crickets. A breeze stifles her sweat.

It isn't long before the first scavenger – an ugly human dingo, a mangy man-coyote – comes sniffing around. One of her neighbors. One she hasn't yet met.

He's lean, rangy, got a funny tilt-and-bounce to him like he's hearing music nobody else can hear. Long brown hair pulled tight at the sides and bound with a rubber band at the top.

She sees the marks up his arms where he's been picking. Notes the teeth; none are missing but, judging by their color and consistency, it won't be long before they start breaking off like icicles.

The cat piss smell is hard to miss, too.

He's one of the tweakers. She doesn't recognize him, but that's normal – they've got a rotating bunch coming in and out of there.

"Sup," he says, shuffling over.

He probably thinks he's going to get some trailer-trash pussy. Either he heard about her from the others and thinks he can conquer the unconquerable, or they're fucking with him and told him she's easy. They're probably watching from the tree-line. Jokers.

"Ahoy," she says.

"You look nice." It's an almost sweet thing to say. But then she catches his thousand-yard stare, which looks clean through her.

"*You* look like a human-shaped pile of scabs."

"That's not a very nice thing to say."

"There's that word again. *Nice*. You don't know me very well."

He steps closer. Fingers rubbing together. "But I want to."

"Dude. This is not a good night for me," she says. "I don't know what your basehead buddies told you, but this girl's legs are closed to the likes of you."

"Fuck you, bitch." His eyes flash with anger.

Now he starts walking toward her, his hands balled up into twitchy fists.

Seems we're gonna do this, she thinks.

He lunges.

With spidery fingers he grabs at her wrists–

The needle goes in what looks to be an old man's arm, dead in the center of a spider-web tattoo the nexus of which is already a cratered mess of track marks, skin like the surface of the moon. He lets the needle hang there over the bunched-up blaze-orange sleeve of his prison jumpsuit, and his head lolls back, gray hair draped over shoulders, toothless lower jaw creaking open, a slow and happy hiss leaking from the back of his throat. The heroin-horse goes stampeding through his arteries and galloping over his heart and then to his brain and the drug-beast stomps the gray matter flat. One last convulsion, a blob of pukey mouth froth, and a final slump of the head as he dies where he sits.

–but it's not hard for her to twist out of his grip and shimmy to the side.

He swats at her again but she ducks and weaves.

"True story: You die in prison," she says, already panting. Shit, she's out of shape. "Pumping some of that sweet Mexican Brown into your arm."

He kicks at her, but it's not exactly a Kung Fu move. More like a fat-kid-trying-to-hit-a-kickball move. "Fucking what? I don't–" He grunts. "Shoot that shit."

"Not now. But in the future, you will."

He throws a clumsy fist, and she catches it, pivots, and jams the arm into the small of his back. The tweaker cries out more in frustration than pain.

"Funny thing is, when you die, you look like you're, what, sixty, sixty-five years old. But this happens in fifteen years, my man. Meth ain't milk, buddy. It does *not* do a body good."

She underestimates him and, frankly, is basking in the glow of her own amusement. It gives the basehead an opportunity, and he takes it. The fucker is squirmy like a snake – a snake cranked up on a powerful methamphetamine – and he tosses back an elbow that happens to hit her smack dab where the bullet carved a small trench in the side of her head.

Fresh blood runs straight into her eye.

The tweaker shoves her. Hard. Knocks her down.

Sand at her elbows. Grass tickling her neck. Blood in her eye. The basehead is laughing now. He tries to spit on her, but it mostly just dribbles up over his chin and hangs there. He kicks dirt.

Scabby grabs at her ankles. She doesn't bother kicking. Part of her thinks, *This could be it, this could be my last day here.* After all, it's not like she knows. She can find out how anybody else is going to die, but her own doom remains a mystery. A mystery that gnaws at the ends of her fingers.

Earlier today she thought the gunman had her. Now some meth-junkie.

Only problem: She doesn't want to go out like that.

"I killed a man today," she hisses through closed teeth.

This gives the tweaker pause. Her hand closes around something in the grass, not far from the dead marigolds, near the trepanned gnome.

"You ain't no killer," he says, grinning.

She lashes out with the golf putter. The weapon cracks him hard across the forearm – he howls and lets go of her – but she's not done. She springs up and swings with the putter, again bringing it down across his forearms. He's not even yelling anymore. Now it's just a whimper, like a blubbering kid paralyzed by a swarm of yellow jackets stirred. The addict's ankle catches on a mound of uneven ground – out here, with the sand and tree roots, it's *all* uneven ground.

His turn. He falls.

"Fuck away from me," he says, still simpering.

"*You ain't no killer,*" she repeats, mocking him. "Who knows what I am? You sure don't."

She raises the putter over her head. Miriam's the hand of fate. She saw his death: heroin overdose. But the power is in her hands to change that. Putt his ass off this mortal coil, that's one less tweaker rapist asshole in the world. She'd be doing everybody a favor.

He cries out. Blows a big old snot bubble.

The putter falls from her hands.

"Get out of here," she mumbles, nudging him with her toe.

It's like he doesn't recognize a reprieve when he sees one.

She kicks sand in his ear. "I said get the fuck out of here!"

The tweaker yelps, crab-walks away until he can manage to stand, then ducks between a pair of double-wide trailers.

Miriam goes inside. Lights another cigarette. Hears Louis' voice inside her head, chastising her not to smoke in here, but right now, she doesn't care. She *can't* care no matter how hard she tries.

She finds herself in the bathroom, or what passes for one. It's so cramped you can barely turn around. The door isn't even a door, just an accordion you pull closed. Beneath her, a carpet the color of diarrhea. If you're going to carpet the bathroom, at least going with a shit-color has a practical side.

The blood is sticky on her brow. Like a pawing cat, she spins the toilet paper roll until she's got a bunched-up heap of tissue on the floor. *Rip.* She uses it to dab at her head, looking at the black and red crease across her hair.

Hair that once was a different color depending on the day. Blue purple blonde green whatever. Blackbird black. Vampire red.

Now just chestnut. Her original color.

Trimmed down the side by a bullet's furrow.

It's then the walls feel tight. Tighter than usual. She can barely breathe, so she stubs out the cigarette in the sink.

"Fuck it," she says to nobody but the dead bird. Her voice quavers, rain on a tin sheet. Palms slick. Stomach sick. "I'm done."

She goes and packs a bag.

SIX

THIS WAY TO THE GREAT EGRESS

A long stretch of Jersey highway – highway 72, Barnegat Road – where the heat vapors lick the gray macadam, the yellow dotted line melting between them like pats of butter.

Two-lane road. Cars pass. Going to the shore. Coming from the shore. Families packed in minivans. Frat fucks hooting out of open-air Jeeps, bad music blasting. Someone on a bike dressed in tight lycra emblazoned with endless corporate logos as though he's a sponsored cyclist rather than just another asshat with delusions of significance.

She sees the first bike and thinks, *Ah, right. Bike. Should've ridden my bike.* But then she thinks, no, that's not the plan. The plan is, go back to the old way. The normal way. The Miriam Black way.

All she needs is her hitchhiking thumb and her getaway gams.

Time to say goodbye. To be rid of the anchor that is Louis and this life and once more become a free radical churning thorough the arterial byways and circulatory highways of the United States of America. A cancerous mote.

Except, for some reason, she doesn't stick out her thumb.

She just walks.

"I'll catch a ride somewhere ahead," she says, talking to nobody except the black turkey buzzards orbiting overhead on breathy vectors of hot air rising off the roads. Seeing her, they probably think she's going to drop dead here at some point. They'll pick her bones the moment she hits the ground.

She doesn't intend to offer them the satisfaction. Ugly birds. Bald so they have no problem plunging their shriveled dagger-like heads into the gooey meat of a rotting beast. *You were a vulture once,* she thinks. *You will be again.*

Sweat shellacs her brow. Drips in her eyes. Stings.

To the left and right, trees. Mostly pine. Thin, wispy-needled. Stuck up out of the sand, sometimes whispering in the wind. Power lines overhead like strings of black licorice. Sometimes a house – a mini-mansion here, a rat-hole there. Then back to the pines and their slanting shadows.

Evening twilight starts to bleed night-blood. Sun down, moon up. Soon she sees the pitch pines – stunted and twisted trees that grow here in the dead sandy soil, trees that thrive thanks to the occasional forest fires that burn through, killing the underbrush so that the pines live on, unmitigated by their scrubby competitors.

Pitch pines mean she's in the Pine Barrens. A long stretch of nowhere. Home to the Pineys – the weird off-the-grid inhabitants of this trackless waste. Home too to the mythical Jersey Devil, a donkey-headed chupacabra type with bat wings and a witch mother, at least if you believe the stories.

As night officially takes hold and the cars traveling this route die back, Miriam thinks she might just wander off the road and into the trees where the Pineys or the Devil may take her.

And yet, she keeps on walking.

It was a year ago that she was tortured in a small cabin here in the Barrens.

Her legs ache. Tongue dry. Feet bottoms burning. Old calluses reawakening.

She has a bottle of water. She takes a sip. Then another. Then it's gone.

How many sips has she been taking?

Shit.

She thinks finally, maybe it's time. Time to hitchhike. Time to *commit* to this old life, commit to her lack of commitment. She knows that most of these cars will just take her back to the island, though. Irony of ironies. Like trying to pull yourself out of quicksand and only sinking deeper.

Still, she puts out her thumb as the dark road glows in the light of headlights coming from behind her. Whoever it is, fine. Fate shall play its role. Kindly grandmother? Stoned sorority girls? Jack Torrance from *The Shining*?

Fate has other ideas. Twisted as the pygmy pines.

The rumble of an engine strikes a too-familiar chord. She looks back: the headlights are big, bright, two searing suns fast approaching, burning away the night.

Brakes engage. A hydraulic squeal.

Part of her is saying *no, no, no, NO*.

But between every *no* is a *yes*.

"Miriam?" Louis's voice calls over the truck engine.

She's torn like tissue paper: Her muscles want to run, but her bones want to go to him. The tug-of-war ends when she just sits down. Drops like a puppet with its strings cut, down into the weeds next to the highway.

Eventually she hears the door open, the door close, and then Louis Darling stands behind her, a massive shape – comforting and scary all in a single measure, warm and soft like a bear, but she knows that he could twist her head off like the bloom on a Black-Eyed Susan.

"Come on," he says. And he urges her up and into the truck.

To her own surprise, she goes.

SEVEN
COFFEE & CIGARETTES

"I'm not going back to that fucking trailer," she says, sitting in the passenger seat. The truck rumbles along.

Just the cab. No trailer. Everything inside the Mack looks new. Because that's how Louis keeps it. It stinks of Armor-All and pine scent and, yes, that lingering Old Spice odor.

"Okay," he answers. In that one word, the soft Southern drawl – the accent subtle, not strong like the hard pluck of a banjo – feels comfortable. Like a ratty old pillow.

He looks over at her with that one eye. The other is a ruined eyeless pucker hiding behind a black eye-patch. *My fault,* Miriam thinks.

"I'm also not going back to that fucking island."

"All right."

"In fact, if you take me even remotely back toward the direction of the Jersey Shore, I'm going to take out your one good eye. With my thumb." She runs her hands through her hair, makes a wordless animal sound.

For a little while, he just drives. Looking at her as much as the road. It feels all too familiar. Him the cautious guardian. Her the frazzled lunatic.

"You got shot," he says finally.

"What? Oh." She feels her head. Again the bullet-dug ditch has crusted over: a scabby topography beneath her searching fingertips. "Right. Yeah. Wait. Who told? How'd you even find me?"

The answer crosses her mind before he says it. "Peggy called me."

Right. Peggy. The bane of her existence all summer – not exactly a friend of Louis's but an acquaintance. He met her dropping off, well, who knows what? *Tampons and hermit crabs,* she thinks. Peggy said she had a job opening if he knew anybody. Louis told Peggy he had just the girl. And the legacy of misery began.

"You got *shot,*" he says again. "You okay?"

"Fine."

He draws a deep breath. "You got shot. With a bullet."

"Yeah, that's usually what 'shot' means. This barely counts. Last year I got stabbed in the tit. Deflated my lung like a bike tire. This... isn't anything. Just a flesh wound. So, how'd you find me?"

"Got the call. Went back to the house–"

"Trailer."

"–and you were gone. So was your pack."

"I could've gone anywhere. North to New York. South to Atlantic City."

"Those directions wouldn't have taken you through the Pine Barrens." He watches her, warily. "I took a shot. It paid off. I think I know you pretty well by now."

Something about that galls her.

"You don't know shit," she spits, the words falling out of her like battery acid from an upended bucket. "You really think you know me? Good joke. Wanna know the punchline?" She's not laughing. "If you knew me, you wouldn't think that locking me away in a trailer for a year would be a super idea. You wouldn't think that my ideal job would be scanning postcards and sand pails and fucking Utz pretzels for the greasy coconut-besmirched touristy *throng*."

Louis sighs. "That's what people do, Miriam. They settle down. They get jobs."

She rears back a foot and kicks his dashboard. Not enough to dent it or crack it but enough that it reverberates through the truck cab.

"I'm not people!"

"Miriam–"

"Pull over."

"What? No. Wait. There's something I need to tell you–"

"I said pull the fuck over, you one-eyed sonofabitch."

Louis grits his teeth, slams the brakes. The truck grinds to the side of the road. "There. I pulled over."

"I'm out."

"Again. You're bailing. *Again*."

"Again, yeah, a-fucking-gain."

"You don't want to hear what I have to say."

"No, I do not."

"Fine, then. Go."

"I'm going."

"Doesn't look like you're going."

She grabs her crotch. "What's *this* look like?"

Miriam throws open the cab door. Leaps out into the gravel.

Door, slam. The truck shakes with the force of it.

Louis doesn't hang around. The tires growl on loose stone, and the Mack pulls away in a cloud of dust. It's just greasy, gauzy taillights diffused in a haze hanging low over the nighttime road. A haze that smells of smoke and distant fire.

Good. He's angry. He should be. It's not often Louis gets angry. Always the diplomat. The peacemaker. *Be a fountain, not a drain,* he said once. She said back, *I like to piss in fountains. And you're a real drain.*

The taillights wink and fade and are gone.

Miriam keeps walking.

By now, her dogs are really barking. It's tempting to take off her damn boots and go barefoot, but this is Jersey. Who knows what she'll step on? Or in? Shudder.

After a few hours, she sees a Wawa gas station and market ahead – glowing yellow and red in the Pinelands dark. Her stomach is growling. Her teeth and tongue itch for a cigarette. She's got some cash but not much, maybe not enough.

She passes the pumps. Then she sees the truck parked off to the side. Engine off. Cab dark.

And here he comes. Walking toward her.

Louis has in his hands the biggest coffee cup Wawa makes. A sixty-four ounce thirst-aborter and sleep-destroyer. Under his other arm is a carton of cigarettes.

He thrusts them out.

"For me?" she says, faking demureness. It takes all

her energy and it doesn't come across all that sincere but she does it just the same.

"For you."

"Maybe you know a *little* something about me."

"Maybe just a little."

"Thanks."

"Can we get back in the truck? I have something I want to tell you."

Her radar pings – not a tickle but a painful itch. Like an innocuous mole becoming suddenly cancerous. Just the same, she nods, takes her gifts, and they go back to the truck so she can hear what Louis has to tell her.

EIGHT
STEP THREE: PROFIT

Miriam's waiting for the axe to fall. She's *always* waiting for the axe to fall. Louis and she sit in the truck, still parked in the Wawa lot.

He looks hesitant.

She knows what's coming. Mentally, she's fine with it. He doesn't want to be with her. Why would he? Emotionally... well. Emotionally she's a garage full of cats on fire.

Then he hands her a book. Thin, glossy cover. Portrait-sized. Like a mailer. It's even got the spot for the address on the back.

She turns it over. "The... Caldecott School."

She flips through it.

Glossy photos. Trim text.

Is your daughter achieving her academic potential?

The Caldecott School offers your daughter a New Beginning.

Girls in gray blazers. Navy skirts. High socks. A variety pack of ethnicities, all teens and pre-teens. Studying. Eating lunch. Gazing longingly into microscopes. Happy faces. Eager smiles. All bullshit. No kid is that slack-jawed and zombie-eyed for learning.

Miriam peeks over the edge of the book.

"Are you... trying to send me back to school?" She ill-contains a snorty laugh. "Because I might be a bit too long in the pubes for that."

"What? Oh, no. This is a job."

Miriam swiftly rolls up the mailer and thwacks him on the knuckles. "What did I tell you about getting me jobs? Throwing my ass into a normal 9-to-5 thing is like vinegar and baking soda, sodium and water, like making a cobra and a mongoose live together in a studio apartment and then filming it and putting it on MTV."

"It's not that kind of job."

She makes a jerk-off motion with her hand. Then mimes a cheek-bulging blow-job. "Is it... that kind of job?" She salaciously licks the invisible cock.

"I'm not your pimp. This is a..." He can't seem to find the words. "A psychic job." To clarify, he taps his head.

"Psychic job."

"Yeah. Yes."

"I don't even know what that means. Can I telecommute?"

It's then that Louis explains. He does charity work now and again, making deliveries for those who need them – in this case, donations of school supplies to a series of schools around the northeast. Boarding schools, charter schools, private institutions, small colleges.

Schools including this one. The Caldecott School. For girls.

"I know a teacher there," he says. "Katherine. Katey. Nice woman. Teaches English. Doesn't have any family, not anymore. Not married. She's convinced that she's dying."

There it is. The stink of death crawling up Miriam's nose. The rustle of blackbird wings. The vulture's hiss before it plunges its head into the wound.

"We're all dying," Miriam says.

"That's dark."

"Just biology, dude. Entropy bites us all in the end. What's that poem? Something something, the center cannot hold?"

He stares at her blankly. Not a poetry fan, then.

"She thinks she's dying now. Katey believes she's sick. Her whole family died from some sickness or another. Cancer mostly. A niece from meningitis. A brother from a DVT."

"DVD? Musta been one shitty movie."

"D-V-*T*. Deep Vein Thrombosis."

"Oh. Oooh. Sounds like a great band name."

His nostrils flare. His big fingers move to fidget with the eyepatch. An autonomic gesture he makes whenever he's tired of her shit.

"Point is, she said she was thinking of consulting a psychic. She asked if I'd met any."

"And so you told her about me."

"I did."

"Did you ever think maybe I want that kept private?"

"You tell everybody."

"Not everybody."

"You told the mailman."

That's true. She did. He had a skin thing she said he

should get checked. A black patch that looked like Texas on his neck. He won't get it checked, of course. But sometimes she gets a thrill from yelling at the tides.

She tosses the Caldecott book onto the dash. Grabs her coffee from the cupholder. It's warm in her hands. Comforting. "I thought you didn't want me to do this... thing anymore."

"I never said that."

"You bought me gloves. You strongly suggested I keep them on."

Again with the eyepatch and the fidgeting. "I just thought it might be a problem. With your job."

"At least you let me take them off in bed."

He blushes. After all this time, he blushes.

She decides to be the jackrabbit. Jump ahead of all this nonsense. "So, Miss Teacher is a total hypochondriac. She thinks she's dying. You mention me, tell her about my disturbed gift. When was this?"

"Three months ago. Thereabouts."

"You think she's still interested?"

He nods. "I already called her."

"You sly dog."

"So. What do you think?"

Her hands are tingling. Like her fingertips are hornet wings tapping against a windowpane. She *thinks* that all parts of her want this in ways she doesn't even understand – like she's got this yearning, this deep urge tangled up in all her bodily systems, from her teeth and tongue all the way down to the verdant valley between her legs. She can hear its song in the moist and fetid hollows of her mind: a siren's cry singing once more about death and distant highways, about birds stirring in dark places and gold coins slick with the grease of blood. The body wants. The mind seeks.

Her hunger must be on display. Her face an antenna beaming an eagerness that borders on impatience. Louis studies her.

"I guess that's a yes, then," he says.

"I didn't say anything."

"Just the same." His voice is sad, and she's not sure why. "It's a yes."

NINE
NO TIME FOR LOVE

They crash at a motel that night. Just down the way from the Wawa. The Sugar Sands Motel. The guy who checks them in looks like a true-blue sister-fucker who is himself the son of a true-blue sister-fucker. Eyes too big. Face too small. Fingernails so brittle they look like broken seashells.

The room is nothing to honk at, either. It still carries that beach motif – captain's wheel on the wood-paneled wall, bathroom cast in pinks and seafoams, a shitty acrylic painting of a lighthouse hanging over the twin beds, which lean toward each other as though co-dependent.

It stinks of mold and salt water.

Doesn't matter. Miriam is awake. Alive. Electric. It's not just the caffeine. Nor the nicotine. Her hands throb with a weed-whacker buzz.

It's sick. She knows it's sick. That distant lingering promise of death has her feeling more alive than she's felt in a year.

It's gas for the engine. And she can't help but rev the motor.

Louis sits down on a bed, goes fumbling for the remote control that operates the boxy little TV on the flimsy pine dresser. But she doesn't give him a chance to find it.

She leaps up onto his back. Bites his ear. Makes a monkey sound. Lets her hand drift down across his chest, finds what she hopes is a nipple and not a button and gives it a good twist.

"I want my hands everywhere," she hisses. And she does. It's like they're on *fire*. Part of it is frustrating: She can no longer know how Louis is going to die. She knew, once – stabbed in both eyes atop the Barnegat Lighthouse – but then she went and changed the course of fate and now his demise remains a delicious mystery. As does her own.

Her other hand moves to his hip. Then starts to ease toward his lap. He breathes heavy.

But then he bites that breath and grabs her with both hands. Picks her up like she's nothing – he's got at least 120 pounds on her. He pitches her onto the bed. The bedsprings bray like a mule.

"No," he says. Like he's telling a child to drop that cookie.

Her hand reaches again for him, this time curling a finger around one of his belt loops. He extracts her hand and puts it back on her own lap.

"We're not doing this," he says.

"Seriously?"

"Yes. Seriously."

"But this is what we do," she says. "Maybe we don't work so well on an emotional, touchy-feely huggywuggy level. But we still work. We got gravity, man. Two planets crashing together. Cosmic fist-bumps. Key word: bumps. Like, you know. Bumping uglies. Or maybe the key word is fist? I dunno. All I'm saying is, I feel good. *This* feels good. Being back on the road with you. This is how we work, you and me."

"Not anymore."

There it is. The iceberg that sinks the ship.

"You're pissed," she says.

"I'm not."

"Disappointed, then. Like a parent."

He says nothing. Goes to sit. Finds the remote control sitting on a table between the two crooked beds, next to a blinking clock radio.

She gets it. She tells him so. "You want me to be someone I'm not. You wanted me to make a different choice back there. To say, nah, you know what, I'm done with this thing. I don't want to know how people die. Normal people don't do shit like that. Do they? That's why you didn't tell me about this three months ago. Even though you knew I was in misery back on that island. Caught like a rat in a trap. You knew even then that, you give me the choice, I'll choose the wrong road every time. The one you can't stand. The one that reminds you that I am nothing like a normal person. Nothing like your wife."

Louis' wife. Dead, now. Drowned before Miriam met him.

Mentioning the wife is an electric shock. She knows it and this isn't the first time she's used it. It's the most direct way through to him. Like cracking open his chest with a rib-spreader and letting a rattlesnake bite his heart.

Sometimes it gets him mad. This time, he just shuts down.

He chucks the remote in the table drawer next to a Gideon Bible. Then he goes into the bathroom and closes the door – not with a slam, but with a gentle click.

INTERLUDE
THE DREAM

She does a Russian kick dance against the bathroom door. Water suddenly seeps out from under it – brackish and murky, like the birth water from a swamp monster's womb. It's cold on her bare toes. It stinks, too. Stagnant. Funky. Fungal.

Ah. Yes. This. A dream. A vision. A something.

The door opens, and a woman steps out. Hair matted to a bruise-purple face. Weeds braided in the slough-slick hair. She opens her mouth, and a waterfall of muddy runoff splashes onto her dead bare chest.

"You," Miriam says.

Maggots do squirming laps around the corpse-woman's ruined gray nipples.

"Me?" she belches, more mud-water splashing over her rotten lips.

Miriam snaps her fingers. "Yeah. You. You're supposed to be Louis' dead wife. I get that. I have whatever… prerequisite dream knowledge I need to figure that much out. But I don't know what she looks like so you're just some… face playing the part."

In response, the face changes. Bones and skin to liquid and back to bones and skin. From a dead white woman to a dead... Latina woman? The face darker, grayer, deeper striations like poison ivy threaded beneath the skin.

Then it shifts again. A black woman with shadow-dark eyes. A white woman with blonde ringlets gummy with algae. All drowned.

Then one more change.

The face becomes Miriam's own.

Hair dyed with river water. Capillaries burst in yellow eyes.

"Cute," she says. But it's not cute, and the space between her heart and her stomach goes sour, a caustic curdled pocket.

Her cadaver-self looks old. The wrinkles are from the water, like the way fingers look after spending too much time in the tub. Just the same, those ancient creases do little to ease the rotten knot in her gut.

"You're on the right path," Corpse-Miriam coos. "The path to the river."

"I can tell," she tells her dead self. "If there's one way to make a person feel reassured it's to appear to them in a dream as a drowned dead woman."

"This is a warning."

"A warning. Fine. So warn me."

"You're not alone."

"I'm not alone? What's that even mean? Is that the warning?"

Corpse-Miriam smiles. Slime slides from between her teeth. She opens her mouth wide, wider, widest –

the jaw cracking and snapping and then her mouth becomes a howling tunnel, and in that tunnel Miriam sees onrushing waters, a river-tide of poison. An acid flume like heartburn shoots up her own chest and into her mouth and she tastes vomit and blood and mud and then the dream dissolves like sugar poured into hot coffee.

A whisper, then, as the dream falls apart: "The river is rising, Miriam."

the jaw cracking and snapping and then her mouth becomes a howling funnel and from it [illegible] sees onrushing waters, a [illegible] of poison. An acid thing like [illegible] of her own chest and into her mouth and she tastes vomit and blood and [illegible] and then the dream dissolves like sugar poured into hot coffee.

A whisper, then, as the dream falls apart: "The river is rising, [illegible]."

PART TWO
THE SCHOOL OF BROKEN DOLLS

"You gave me hyacinths first a year ago;
They called me the hyacinth girl."
– Yet when we came back, late, from the Hyacinth
garden,
Your arms full, and your hair wet, I could not
Speak, and my eyes failed, I was neither
Living nor dead, and I knew nothing,
Looking into the heart of light, the silence.

The Wasteland, *T.S. Eliot*

TEN

DISORDER

"So not only is this an all-girls' school," Miriam says, one leg dangling out the truck window, toes constantly adjusting and readjusting the passenger side mirror, "but it's a school for *bad girls.*"

Louis grunts. That's been his response for the last couple days while they've been holed up in the Sugar Sands Motel. They camped out there while he waited for Katey to return his call. She did. School's in session. She's back at Caldecott and eager to meet Miriam.

Beyond the disinterested caveman noises, Louis isn't saying much.

Miriam fills the silence.

"Listen to this," she says, the mailer splayed open in her lap. She reads from the book: "*Some girls benefit from a New Beginning* – New Beginning, that's capitalized, by the way, and you know something's important when needless capitalization enters the picture – *a New Beginning away from family and friends. How do you know if a girl will benefit from a New Beginning at the Caldecott School?* Okay. Checklist time. *Does your daughter: act out in defiance of accepted social norms? Believe that consequences do not apply to her? Become angry and defiant without warning? Engage in wanton promiscuity?* What a great phrase. Wanton promiscuity. If it's so bad, they shouldn't make it sound so interesting. It almost sounds like an appetizer. Won-Ton promiscuity. That's a dude fucking his soup. Just going to town on it. Sure, he's scalding his gonads, but that's the price of forbidden love. Am I right?"

Louis stares out at the road ahead. A grim-faced cyclops.

She poked the bear too hard this time. The wife is a pressure point and she didn't just push on it – she hit it with a fucking sledgehammer.

"Whatever. Anyway." She turns back to the mailer. "They list a number of disorders they try to help 'curtail' – another great word, 'curtail'. A cur's tail. Huh. Anyway. They list, let's see, depression, manic-depression, bipolar disorder, ADHD, anxiety, oppositional defiant disorder – whatever the hell that is – borderline personality dis–"

"It's oppositional defiant disorder." It almost startles her it's been so long since Louis has said more than three words to her. "It's a sign of someone who doesn't play well with authority. Doesn't like being told what to do. Angry, resentful, argumentative. Usually in some kind of trouble. Often does the opposite of what they're told just because that's how they are."

"Ugh." Miriam wrinkles her nose. "Bet those kids are fun to be around. Like hanging out with a cat."

It's then she sees Louis looking at her. That one eye

firing a concentrated laser beam of scrutiny, slicing her apart and inspecting the remains.

"What?" she asks.

"Nothing." He goes back to driving.

"You trying to say something?"

"I'm not."

"I know what you're saying." She gets it now.

"Do you?"

"I don't have oppositional defiant disorder."

Grunt.

"I don't. That's crazy-talk. I was a good girl once. And it's not my fault I'm surrounded by idiots and lunatics half the time. I just go my own way on things. That's what an independent woman does. Right?" She scowls. "Just keep that one eye of yours on the road."

Then, just to tick him off, she cranks down the window, pops a filterless cigarette in her mouth, and brings a lighter flame to its tip. Puff, puff, puff. She blows a jet of cancer outside.

She picks a nit of tobacco off her tongue, flicks it out the window just as they pass a highway sign.

SELINSGROVE, 5Mi
SUNBURY, 7Mi

A hard knot like a calcified clump of hair forms in her throat. "We're in Pennsylvania."

"You were asleep when we crossed through Philadelphia."

Susquehanna River Valley. Three counties. All around the river.

The river is rising, Miriam.

But it's not that. Or not *just* that.

If they're near Selinsgrove, then that means right now, at this very moment, they're only thirty minutes north of where she grew up. Where her high school boyfriend blew the roof of his skull off with a shotgun. Where the boyfriend's mother beat Miriam half to death with a snow shovel. Where her baby died inside her.

Where her own mother still lives.

Miriam hasn't seen the woman since she ran away. Almost a decade now.

Maybe she's dead, Miriam thinks. Once she discovered she had the power to see how people were going to die, she never again touched her mother. By the next morning, she'd already bolted.

Ghosts, restless and sad, stir inside her.

It takes all her effort to tamp them down with a hard mental boot.

She clears her throat.

"Did Miss Katey get my rider?"

Louis grunts. An affirmative sound. Miriam already knew the answer to the question. They stopped off at a Kinkos to fax Miriam's handwritten list of rock-star demands to the school for the teacher.

"Fine," she says. "Good. Great. Let's go to school."

She flicks the cigarette out the window, half-finished. It just doesn't taste good anymore.

INTERLUDE
THE PHONE CALL

Rain hammers the phone booth.

Miriam, sixteen, holds the receiver against her ear. Her jaw shivers.

It rings and rings. She doesn't want anyone to answer. *Go to the answering machine,* she thinks. It's like a prayer. A mantra. *Go to the answering machine. Go to the answering machine. Go to the answering machine.* It starts to sound absurd in the echo chamber of her own head.

Click.

"Miriam?" her mother's voice. Small and afraid. She's never afraid. It's like something's been stolen from her. And maybe it has.

"The baby's dead, mother."

"I know. I know." Of course she knows. She was there at the hospital. "God will take care of him now."

"Mother–"

"Where are you?"

"God can't be real," Miriam says, throat raw, eyes puffy. Every part of her feels like a tooth that's been cracked in half, the nerve ending exposed.

"Don't you say that. Come home to me."

"I can't. Something's wrong." Something she doesn't understand. The baby died inside her but something remained. Some little ghost, some little demon, fragile like the skeleton of a baby bird. It's changed her. Turned her very touch into a sponge, a sponge that draws poison. A sponge that soaks up death the way a gauze soaks up blood.

She doesn't understand it: Every time someone touches her – one of the nurses, a doctor, the security guard outside the hospital – she sees the most awful things. Visions of how they die. And when. They can't be true.

But they feel true.

All the more proof her mind is lost. It's like a moth – touch a moth and a powder comes off the wings, and once that powder's off, the moth can no longer fly.

The powder, she thinks, is off her wings.

"Just tell me where you are. I'll come get you."

"I'm leaving."

"Please, Miriam. God will protect us. He'll help us get through this."

"This. This? This is all proof he's just a... a bedtime story, Mother. To make you feel better about the way you are." She wants to tell her mother how horrible she is, how she's just a bitter pill, a mean little rodent, but she can't muster the words. She wants to yell about how her mother was never nice to her, not until she got pregnant – which means now that the baby's dead the old ways will return, the dismissals and the insults and God's love blinding her like the beam of a too-bright spotlight. By now, Miriam's crying again. She can't believe she has more tears, more spit, more snot, but here it comes, just as the pain of unstoppable grief is again hitting her in the chest like a sledgehammer. She doubles over. "I won't. I won't go back. I won't come back."

"Miriam, I'll do better."

And then she says the final words: "No. You won't. Because I won't give you the chance." She slams the phone down. With her back against the inside of the booth, she slides to the rubber mat and huddles next to the cigarette butts, the candy wrappers, the dead moths.

It's there she stays until morning.

INTERLUDE
SUMMER'S END

The gates – iron, each spiked at the top with a *fleur-de-lis* – look like teeth to Miriam. A hungry mouth with black metal canines. Probably what the Gates to Hell look like. The Devil's own maw. Chompy-chompy, all you sinners, all you dirty-birdy bad girls.

Louis pulls the truck up. A guard at the gate – an old black dude with eyes pinched tight behind rolling slugs of skin and cheeks sprouting a wan, wire-brush beard – gives a palms-out wave. "As I live and breathe. If it isn't Mister Truck Driver, tumbling in off the road after a long haul."

"No long haul this time," Louis says, leaning out the window. "How you doing, Homer?"

The guard gives a dismissive wave. "I could complain, but nobody'd want to listen. Who you got in there with you? Late admission?"

Miriam scrambles up over Louis and thrusts her head out the window. "Do I look like a student to you?"

"Shoot, I dunno."

With one of his bear paws, Louis urges Miriam back

into her seat. "This is Miriam Black. She should be on your list there. She's here to see Katherine Wiznewski."

Homer looks over a clipboard, squinting even harder. So hard his eyes all but disappear and Miriam's not sure how he can see anything at all.

"Uh-huh, uh-huh. Here you go. Miss Black to see Miss Wiz. You hanging around, Louis? Almost lunchtime."

Louis shakes his head. "Just dropping her off."

"Wait, what?" Miriam asks. This is news to her.

He turns. "I have a job."

"Yeah. To be here. With me."

"A real job," he clarifies, the phrase a barb, a thorn, a needle. "You'll be fine. You're meeting Katey out back at the picnic tables. It's all set."

"And then what? Do I go sleep in the woods? How long do you think this is going to take? I'm not harvesting corn. I touch her. I get a vision. I tell her about it. Thirty seconds. Game over. I've spent more time smoking a cigarette."

"You don't want me there."

"No," she says. "*You* don't want you there."

"I've got to go. What she's paying should cover you, but just in case–" He peels a trio of twenties out of his money clip. "Here. Get a cab. Go rent a motel room for the night. I have a quick run up to Erie, and I'll be back tomorrow."

"You're really leaving me. Please. Stay."

"Go on. It'll be fine."

"Fine," she says. "I don't – you know what? I don't need you. This is what I do best. Walk. Wander. Alone. It'll be fine."

"It will be fine."

"It *will*, it totally will. Later, Louis."

"Miriam, I'm sorry–"

But she doesn't want to hear it. She's worked up. Miriam's already hopping out of the truck, his voice lost to the slamming door.

The truck grumbles, reverses, and is gone.

The Gates of Hell remain open. Just for her.

"You going in or what?" Homer asks.

She almost doesn't. Something about this place gives her a bad vibe and she's not even through the gates. She can't see the school yet – it's a winding drive that takes an elbow curve into the woods. All she has before her are the iron gates, the guard's booth, and a brass plaque on pale brick that says *The Caldecott School* in dizzying calligraphic loops and whorls.

Going back to school always gave Miriam the piss-shivers. Even though it's late summer and the Caldecott School starts its year early, the feeling is the same: The days are getting shorter, mornings darker, evenings creep on like a stalker outside your window. With the end of summer comes the start of school, and school was never a good time for Miriam. The classes, sure. Tests. Papers. Lectures. Those were fine. But the other kids. Mean, shitty little fucks. Grade school – elementary and up – is like being dropped in a dunk tank filled with starving piranha.

And they never get full.

Every part of her wants to run away. Even though she's an adult. She doesn't have to do this anymore.

But Homer snaps the fingers on both hands at her. "Come on, now, shit or get out the outhouse."

Miriam jogs through the gates.

They close behind her with a mechanical whine.

Fuck fuck fuck fuck fuck.

Clang. The way is shut.

Still, her fingers tingle. While every other part of her – down to the twisting, thrumming marrow – wants to bolt for the woods, her hands know where they want her to go. They want to feed. They want to taste death.

Five-fingered vampires, they are.

"I... walk?" she asks Homer.

He leans out of the booth, looks up and down the drive, and then scowls at her. "Where the hell else you planning on going? It's one road. It goes to one place. You want a map and a hang-glider?"

"I just figured you had a golf cart or something."

"Oh, I got one up my ass but my doctor says I should keep it up there in case it tears something bad coming out."

"You're funny. You. Are. Funny. You missed your calling, Homer. Should've been a comedian."

"Why'd the chicken cross the road?"

She knows she shouldn't bother, but says anyway, "Why?"

"To peck you in the butthole so you hurry the hell away from my guard booth. Like I told Mister Truck Driver, it's lunch-time and I am goddamn hungry."

"Okay. Bye, Homer."

"See you on the way out, Miss Black."

"How far is the school?"

"Far as it needs to be." He laughs.

Asshole.

She likes him.

Time, then, to go back to school.

The road is paved, no potholes, smooth as a beetle's back. Trees rise up on each side of her, these trees nothing like the scrub pines of Nowhere, New Jersey – these tall legacy oaks ringed in dark wet bark, each a silent sentinel, each a judging spire.

Soon she hears it: the murmur of river water.

The river reveals itself before too long. Five minutes later, the trees give way to a grassy uneven bank, and beyond it the Susquehanna churns and shushes, Ovaltine waters gurgling forth.

The drive bends again, and there she sees the Caldecott School.

Ah, Victorian overindulgence. The middle of the school looks to be an old manor house, three stories high, the grim Gothic windows paired awkwardly with gingerbread trim. Each roof is red like a child's wagon, the walls a kind of gray-green, a clayey painted smudge dull in contrast to the house's red.

To the left and right of the house are the rest of the school – the bulk of it, really, plainly added on long after the original house was built. The two wings are almost prison-like in their austerity. Down to the wrought iron bars on the windows.

The Caldecott crest – eagles, books, a knight's helmet and other bullshit frippery – flies on a flag. The flagpole comes up out of a massive VW-bug-sized hunk of anthracite coal, which itself sits in the middle of the circular drive.

From here, the school looks silent, dead, no movement. No students, no teachers, not even a pair of ugly-ass pigeons.

Again that feeling: a twist, a twinge in her gut.

Like at any moment a big tentacle is going to burst out of the front door, coil around her, and drag her into its depths. Past other kids who mock the way she looks, walks, chews, exists.

Fucking school.

Let's get this over with, she thinks.

Time to find "Miss Wiz."

TWELVE
TRUST FALLS

Miriam passes an art class on the back lawn of the school, kids sitting in a half-circle around some wispy moonbeam teacher in a batik frock, all of them trying to sketch a fallen leaf.

Closer to the river, though, Miriam sees her target – no, that's not it, that's not right. Not target. Not victim. Customer.

How things have changed.

The woman sits on a park bench underneath a red maple, the leaves shuddering and shushing above her head as squirrels bound from branch to branch.

School squirrels are forever unafraid.

The woman is dowdy. Frumpy. Not what Miriam expected. Pink blouse, gray slacks, a build like a linebacker gone to seed. She's got a sweet face. A lullaby face. Were you to go to sleep every night and see that face, you'd feel safe, comforted, snoozy.

As she sees Miriam approach, she stands, offers her hand.

"Miss Wiz," Miriam says. She's not sure how to begin

this exchange, so she snaps her fingers and points a pair of finger-guns at the woman. "Pow pow".

The woman seems taken aback.

Miriam clarifies. "We probably shouldn't shake hands. Because of the thing. You know. *The thing*. The reason I'm here."

"Right. Right. You're, ah, not what I expected."

"Nor you," Miriam responds.

The woman laughs. "Here people always tell me I look like a teacher."

"It's not that. It's just... you know. *Katey*."

"Katey." The teacher doesn't understand.

"Right. Katey is – see, I have a thing for names, names that don't match, and yours is – okay, it's like this. Katey? Total pixie girl name. Katey is a tiny sorority girl who only drinks vodka because she doesn't want to put on weight. Katey dresses up like a slutty witch every Halloween. *Katey* has a bob-cut, wears size zero jeans, marries a banker who was once a quarterback. You look like a..." She gives the woman another good look over. "Kathy. There you go. See how easy that was?"

"Well. My name's Katey." The woman laughs, but it's cagey, nervous. For a moment the only sound between them is the river behind them. The forced smile wilts like a spinach leaf in a hot pan. "Maybe this was a bad idea."

"What?" Miriam asks. "No. No! *No*. It's fine. It's all good. Sit."

They sit. Hesitantly. Miriam drums her fingers. Beneath her hands, the table is carved with girl's names: *Becky Vicki Rhonda Bee Georgia Toni Tavena Jewelia* and on and on. Nothing profane. Just names.

"Oh, here," Katey finally says, pulling out a plastic JC Penney bag. She slides it over to Miriam.

"This my stuff?" she asks.

"Everything you asked for on your list."

"A rider," Miriam says. "It's called a rider. Like a band might ask for, a bowl of all blue M&Ms, or a Longaberger basket filled with heroin and clean needles, or maybe a dwarven sex gimp swaddled in Saran Wrap."

"Yes. Well." Another spike of nervousness. This time punctuated by a pursed frown, a grit of irritation forming a pearl of disgust. "It's all there."

Miriam upends the bag.

Out tumbles: A bag of Utz pretzels. A carton of Native Spirit cigarettes. A jar of Tallarico's hot hoagie spread. Two mini-bottles of booze (one a bottle of Glenfarclas Scotch, the other Patron Silver tequila). A travel-size bleach. And finally, a single box of hair-dye. *Fuchsia Flamingo*. The kind of nuclear pink you might see in the heart of a mushroom cloud. Just before the blast turns your eyes to aspic.

Nice. A good choice.

Miriam says so. Holds up the box. Winks.

Then she starts setting up shop. Opens the hoagie spread. Tears into the bag of pretzels. Uncaps the Scotch.

Pretzel into the spread, then into the mouth. *Crunch crunch crunch*. Mouthful of Scotch. Everything is salt and spice and smooth caramel burn.

As she does this, Katey slides out a stack of money onto the table. Starts to move the money toward Miriam but pulls it back to her chest.

"Whuh's wrong?" Miriam asks, licking booze-soaked pretzel bits out of her teeth.

"This is all... strange. You're very strange, a very strange girl. You're the real deal? You can tell me about..."

Miriam swallows. "Yeah, yes. How you suck the pipe, feed the worms, find yourself on the Holy Shit I'm Dead Express."

Blink. Blink. "How do I know you're telling me the truth?"

"You don't, I guess. Louis knows. He can vouch for me. So if you trust him, then you know I'm on the up-and-up. If you don't trust him, then I guess we don't have much more to talk about."

Katey slides the money across. "Five hundred, you said."

"I did." As Miriam takes the money, Katey quick pulls her own hand away.

"Not going to count it?"

"I trust you. Besides, the count's wrong, I'll cast a hex on you. A pox. A pox-hex on your home and school." She swirls another pretzel into the jar of pepper relish. "I'm just fucking around. I can't curse anybody. I'm the cursed one." *Crunch crunch crunch.*

"You been this way since you were a little girl?" Katey asks.

"This way? What way? A crazy bee-yotch? Or a psychic bee-yotch?"

She's interrupted. A young girl yelling. She turns, sees one of the girls in the art class – a little red-headed freckle-machine, maybe twelve or thirteen years old –

standing up and holding her sketchbook like a mighty Viking weapon.

The girl whacks another girl across the face with it. The other girl – a little blonde thing, probably named Katey – shrieks and goes down, flailing.

After that it's all just a pile of limbs and whipping hair. A sensible brown shoe goes pirouetting up in the air.

"Boy, she nailed that other girl good. Pow. Right in the kisser."

"Par for the course here at Caldecott. These are good girls... for the most part. But many of them are troubled. Or just unwanted. It leaves... well, it leaves a mark. Inside. Sometimes outside, too."

"I hear that."

"My break is almost over," Katey says. Suddenly her eyes narrow. "You know, I don't want to do this anymore." She stands. "You can keep the items but I'd like the money back."

"Whoa, whoa, what? No, hell with that, we're doing this. Louis said you're some kind of raging hypochondriac and so I came all this way and we are jolly well fucking doing this. Give me your damn hand."

Katey's face sags. Her eyes go sad. "Is that what he said? Hypochondriac? Is that what people think of me? I suppose I knew that."

"No, it's not what he said, it's what *I* said. Now shut up and let me do this."

The woman reaches in. Goes to grab the money.

Her hand knocks the Scotch bottle over.

Whisky spills between the wooden boards of the table top. Her fingers touch the stack of cash.

Miriam grabs her arm, quick twists the sleeve to expose the skin.

Fingers encircle, skin on skin–

Katey Wiznewski looks the same as she does now, with her broad shoulders and motherly moon face, but she's in a blue raspberry bathrobe so fuzzy it looks like she killed some imaginary beast and now wears its pelt for warmth. She sits on the edge of a loveseat and the cancer is all through her. It's like the roots of a tree piercing dark earth and those roots drink and drink and drink, and they come from a gnarled tumor nestled tight against her pancreas. In her hand is a tall thin glass of iced tea with a crooked lemon wedge sticking up over the rim, and she goes to hand the glass to a large jowly man with a warm smile and she says to him, "It's not sweet enough, Steve. Nothing's really sweet enough anymore. Please take – " But then the electrical current that goes through her, that keeps her moving, that keeps us all moving, is gone – bzzt, power down, plug pulled, darkness waits – and the glass drops and shatters against a coffee table and–

–and Miss Wiz gives her a quick shove and Miriam topples backward, her head thudding dully against the earth.

The grass catches most of the lost twenties. Some of the bills ride a quick breeze and tumble end-over-end toward the river. Then they're gone.

Miriam sits up with a groan. Begins collecting the money.

Katey just stands there. Hands kneading hands. Eyes wet.

"I'm... sorry," the teacher says.

"Without standing, Miriam reaches over and grunts

as she grabs the fallen bottle of Scotch. "Alcohol abuse," she muses, then turns the bottle over and lets the last few drops plop onto her tongue.

"What did you see?" the woman asks.

"Do you really want to know?"

"I do. I want to know. I *need* this."

And then Miriam tells her, but what she tells her is a lie. She doesn't say that Katey has pancreatic cancer. She doesn't say that the cancer is present now, *right now*, and that the woman has nine months almost to the day to live. That's the truth.

Instead she says, "Heart attack in twenty years. You're eating an egg-white omelet at your breakfast nook and your heart seizes and that's that." She preserves one detail. "You drop a glass of iced tea. With lemon. The glass breaks."

Katey's face falls. Shoulders sag as she expels a long breath and as disappointment settles across her back like the yoke of a plow.

"Well. Thank you for that." Her voice quiet, nasal, the words clipped short as though cut at the ends by a razor. "I'm... sorry again about pushing you. That's not like me. Not like me at all."

And then the teacher walks away. Toward the school. Head low.

THIRTEEN
LIES, DAMNED LIES, & CANCER DIAGNOSES

The lie. There it waits. Like a sword over her head. Like a pubic hair in rum punch. A mystery. A sharpened question mark like a sickle ready to slit her throat.

She doesn't get it. It makes no sense. Why the lie?

She stands there, looking out over the river. Pitching pretzels into its mud-churned milk-waters. Picking at the lie. Teasing apart the motivation behind it.

Part of her thinks she's doing this woman a favor. Katey's got less than a year left. Pancreatic cancer – Miriam, that crow on death's shoulder, has seen it before. It's like an oil-fire. Once it starts, it won't go out. Spreads fast, too. Tell the woman about her diagnosis and it's – what? Just a series of debilitating therapies, each worse than the last. All futile. The door to despair thrown wide, the impossible and impending dark beyond.

Maybe, though, it's punishment. Maybe she wanted to punish this woman. Say, fuck you, you don't want my help? You spill my Scotch, cause a hundred dollars of my money to get swallowed by the river? Like a passive-aggressive child pushing a plant off the sill to make Mommy mad: She lied. A lie borne of small and secret vengeance. A momentary reprisal.

Even that doesn't add up. It isn't the whole picture. A part of the puzzle, maybe – the edge of it, the margins, painting by negative space – but it's not the whole of the image.

She does all she can do for the moment. She smokes.

What to do, what to do.

She's got a pocket full of money. She could do anything. Catch a cab. Find a greasy spoon. Hit a strip club. Ditch her cell phone, buy a burner. Grab a bus to somewhere she's never been. To nowhere. To Maine, California, New Orleans, Montreal, Tijuana. Lobster, avocados, beignets, donkey shows.

None of it sounds appealing. That surprises her. Those things should all be pretty great. But the very notion of escaping again doesn't do anything for her. Like a flat soda, the bubbles have all gone.

Miriam takes the tequila, breaks the cap.

Drink up.

Smooth and sour going down. It sits in her stomach like a gym sock soaked in cider vinegar and scorpion venom.

She belches. Nearby, scared birds take flight.

Right now, her thoughts are like hangnails. She wants to pick at them even if that means pulling them so far it unzips her arm into a bloody bisected mess.

Easy solution to soothe the soul: Hair dye. A balm for bad thoughts.

Goodbye, ugly chestnut mop. Goodbye, old original. Goodbye, good girl.

Hello, fuchsia motherfucking flamingo.

FOURTEEN
THE BAD GIRLS' CLUB

Well. That didn't work out.

Miriam sits outside the principal's office with a handful of flimsy brown paper towels wadded up around her collar. All of them, sodden. In her pocket, an as-yet-unopened package of pink hair dye.

Her scalp burns. Especially around the bullet-dug skin-ditch.

She figured, fuck it, I can dye my hair in one of the girls' restrooms. Who cares, right? She went in, wandered around for a while, found a bathroom. Started killing the old chestnut color with a bleach wash, and while she was in there she shared a couple smokes with some of the older girls who came in. One of them was a nice black girl named Sharise, the other her gawky white friend Bella.

They smoked. Talked about the hell of high school. Good times.

But then – po-po came rolling in. Five-oh. Someone must have seen her wandering the halls and called the front desk and before she knew what was happening she was being escorted here by a pair of security guards. One guy who looked like a hyper-roided authority machine with a shorn scalp and muscles ill-contained by his guard uniform. The other guy looking like the Italian plumber from that video game. But shorter. And a little fatter.

And now the principal's office. Or just outside it. Facing a wall with wooden wainscoting. Brass sconces. Dullsville. Boredopolis. Yawnworld.

Next to her is some red-haired little twat with a smear of freckles across the bridge of her nose, sitting there with her smug arms folded over a bunched-up navy blazer hugged tight against her chest. The girl smells faintly of cigarettes. Different brand from what Miriam smokes.

Wait.

Miriam gets another look at her.

"You're that girl."

The girl scowls. Sneers. Eyebrow arched. "What?"

"The girl. With the sketchbook. And the–" Miriam mimics the slap-down move. "Blammo."

"Oh. Yeah. She said my leaf looked like dog butt."

"Did it?"

"Mostly. But that's no reason to be rude. A lot of the world looks like dog butt. Doesn't mean you should go around saying so."

Miriam shrugs. "I dunno. That's how I treat life."

"Your breath is rank."

"And that's obviously how you treat life, too. Yeah, I know my breath is rank. I just drank tequila."

"Out of a Port-a-Potty toilet?"

"Cute. That'd be the bleach you're smelling."

"This isn't a hair salon, you know."

"My god," Miriam, "you are such a little See-You-Next-Tuesday."

"I don't get it."

"Spell it out."

The girl does. "Oh. I get it. Cunt." The girl rolls her eyes. "Whatever."

"Don't you roll your eyes at me, missy. And you shouldn't say that word."

"Okay, *Mom.*"

"I'm not your mom."

"I know that. I'm not a moron. Did you think that for a moment I actually believed you were my mother?" She thrusts her tongue into the pocket of her cheek with a bulge, looks Miriam up and down. "You're old enough to be my mom, though."

"I am not, you little fucking jerk. I'm only in my mid-twenties."

She shrugs. "So is my mom."

"You're what, thirteen?"

"Twelve." She sees Miriam looking at her. "Yeah, my mom was fifteen when I was born. And since I'm not a total tardcart, I can do the math, and that means she's twenty-seven. See? Mid-twenties."

"*Late*-twenties," Miriam corrects. "And even then, it's not like she's some old-ass *hausfrau*. Respect your elders. Or something."

"I would but she's gone."

"Gone. Like, poof, evaporated into nothing? Gone like dead? What?"

"Like, left me alone in her studio apartment a year ago to go off and see the world. Or shoot heroin. Because she really likes heroin."

"So she kind of sucks, then."

"Kind of."

"My mother was the opposite," Miriam says. She tries to picture her mother's face. It's hard. The face swims in a cloud of features – noses and eyes and cheeks and skin palettes. Some drift into place before floating away again, rejected. "Prim and proper. Had me locked me down pretty good. That woman probably could've *used* a little heroin. Loosen her up a bit."

"My mom could've used more prim and proper."

"We could trade moms."

"Deal."

The girl offers her hand.

Miriam stares at it like it's covered in spiders.

The door to the office opens – and Miriam notes that it says Headmaster, not Principal. A small man with slicked-back black hair, two dark cherry-pit eyes, and a navy blazer pokes his head out.

"Miss Lauren Martin," the Headmaster says, his voice long and drawn out and creaky like an old door. "Nice to see you again. We will attend to you shortly. First I must meet with Miss…"

He looks at Miriam, expectant.

"Black," she says. She thought about lying, but fuck it.

"Good. Miss Black, if you care to…" He steps back from his door.

The girl – Lauren – looks up at her. Hand still out.

"Do we have a deal?" she asks Miriam. "To trade moms."

Miriam knows she shouldn't touch the hand. What's the point? Just as she's starting to like this girl she's going to fast-forward to the girl's demise, however it goes. Drunk-driving accident at age eighteen or a head-cracking slip in the shower at age eighty-one?

And yet there's that urge, that familiar urge, the tingle in the tips of her fingers and the damp creases of her palm, and she reaches in and hesitates suddenly the way an airplane hovers above the landing strip before setting down on the tarmac and then–

She takes her hand and sees how the girl is going to die.

FIFTEEN
THE MOCKINGBIRD'S SONG

Early morning light shines gray through shattered window, capturing in its beam whorls of dust and flakes of rot, and the beam ends on the face of Lauren Martin, age eighteen, strapped to an old doctor's table. The leather padding beneath her is cracked and bites into her naked back, thighs, buttocks. Smells braid together: sweat, urine, steel, and through all of it the thread of a sharp chemical stink.

Lauren is gagged with barbed wire, wound all the way around her head, front to back – the rusty barbs tearing into the corners of the girl's mouth.

The wire binds her head to the table.

Her tongue and lips are dried. She's been here a while.

The walls around her are blackened and charred. Wallpaper bubbled like blistered skin. The ceiling is pulled down in places. Knob and tube wiring dangle, caught in saggy bundles of ruined insulation, bundles that look like gray clouds dragged down by hard rains.

Moths dance. Crickets chirp.

A man emerges out of shadow. He's singing a song.

"Young people, hark while I relate
The story of poor old Polly's fate
She was a lady, young and fair
And died a-groaning in despair."

The song is folksy, old, measured. His voice is gravelly, yet behind it the voice warbles and wavers from low-pitch to high-pitch, as pleasant as the tines of a fork dragged across a piece of slate. Sometimes the voice is a man's. Other times, a woman's.

"She'd to go frolic, dance and play
In spite of all her friends would say
'I'll turn to God when I get old
And then I'm sure he'll take my soul.'"

Lauren whimpers against the gag. Scabs at the corners of her mouth crack, and fresh blood flows over dry. Her palms are marked with Xs. Shallow cuts, but cuts just the same. Her feet bear the same marks.

"One Friday morn, Polly took ill
Her stubborn heart began to fail
She cried 'Oh no, my days are spent,
And now it's too late to repent'."

A new odor, a pungent odor, fills the air. Smoke. Strong of dry flowers, funeral flowers, rose and lavender and carnations, an oily tincture of bitter orange.

"She called her mother to her bed
Her eyes were rolling in her head
A ghastly look, she did assume
And then she cried, 'This is my doom'."

The man's face is that of a bird, a featherless beast

with flesh of leather and a beak as long as a child's arm. Wisps of greasy wet smoke drift up from holes in the beak. Human eyes blink from behind filmy goggle lenses bolted to the flesh. This is not his head but rather a hood, a hood that covers down to his shoulders and leads to a bare and sallow chest. Across that chest is a tattoo, blue as a vein, dark as a bruise: the boomerang wing of a barn swallow, twin tails sharp as a barbecue fork.

He reaches into the dark corner of the room, past a scorched mattress. From the shadows he draws a fire axe.

"She called her father to her bed
Her eyes were rolling in her head
'Oh early father, fare you well,
Your wicked daughter screams in Hell.'"

Lauren struggles upon seeing the axe. She rubs her head back and forth, trying to escape, trying to free some part of herself – her scream a hollow and harrowing call as the barbed wire saws into her cheeks.

Blood in her throat. Almost choking her.

The man in the beaked hood leans in, caresses the girl's face. His fingers return wet with red. He steps back, axe held against the tattoo's ink.

"'Your counsels I have slighted all
My carnal appetite shall fall
When I am dead, remember well
Your wicked Polly groans in Hell.'"

The man's eyes close. Rapturous. Ecstatic. The axe raises aloft. A pair of insects suddenly move to circumnavigate the blade: moths in orbit like tiny satellites.

As the man sings, the girl writhes and screams and cries.

"She wrung her hands and groaned and cried
And gnawed her tongue before she died.
Her nails turned black, her voice did fail
She died and left this lower vale."

The axe-blade falls heavy against the table. It falls into a groove that's not new. Lauren's head, silenced, tumbles behind the table. The man kicks it into a ratty wicker basket lined with a black plastic garbage bag.

The killer drops the axe to the ground with a clatter.

He picks up the head, still singing as he holds it aloft. Blood pitter-patters against the ruined floor. His voice changes now: gritty, growly, throaty. His own voice? The words now are barely sung. They're not even spoken so much as they're coughed out of his throat and spat to the earth. A crass expectoration.

"May this a warning be to those
That love the ways that Polly chose
Turn from your sins, lest you despair
The Devil take you without care."

The man pulls a pair of wire cutters from the pocket of his ragged jeans, then cuts out Lauren's tongue. He has to work to get a grip, and it takes a while for the cutters to bite through.

Her eyes, still wide, go still as placid pools.

The killer laughs, a throaty, happy trill.

SIXTEEN
PURGE

Every part of her jolts awake with a full synaptic shock, like a lightning storm is throttling every nerve ending in her body. Her limbs splay out. Her fingers tighten and curl inward. One of her nails breaks on the wooden floor. *Snap*. A face, blurry now but swiftly coming into focus, floats above her.

Mother?

An old woman, her silver hair pulled back in a long braid, shines a penlight in Miriam's eyes.

"Here she comes," the woman says, and the face resolves, a total stranger. "The strange woman awakens."

She offers Miriam a hand.

Not again.

Miriam can't handle that right now. Another touch. Another vision. More death, a ceaseless parade of skulls and bones and hungry birds. Instead she sits up and scoots backward against a cherrywood desk. Gasping. Mouth tasting of vomit.

The woman – mid-sixties, in a cozy blue shawl over

a white blouse – reaches for Miriam again. "Take my hand. I'll help you up."

"Touch me and I bite it off." Miriam clacks her teeth together to ensure that the literality of her statement is keenly felt.

"I'm not your enemy," the woman says, her voice crisp, prim. " I'm Miss Caldecott. The school nurse."

Miriam bares her teeth again. "Wait. Caldecott." Miriam squints. "Like the school."

Another shape moves in behind her. The Headmaster. Half his hands rest in his blazer pockets, delicate, the way a library card sits tucked in the back of a book.

"Yes," he says. "Eleanor Caldecott. I'm Edwin Caldecott, Headmaster. This woman is my mother. And, not coincidentally, the founder of this school."

"Great. Good. Fine. Whatever. What happened?" Miriam asks. But she doesn't need them to answer before it all comes spiraling into view. *Bleach hair, young girl, handshake, old-timey doctor's table, bird mask, fire axe, death sung to sing-song.* "Oh."

Her flailing limbs grab for a nearby metal trashcan, and she pukes into it. A hot tide of pretzels, peppers, tequila.

"Lovely," the Headmaster says. Nasal intonation. As though he's bored by these proceedings. He sucks air through the gap in his two front teeth.

Miriam rests her head against the side of the desk. Wipes a smear of drooly barf from her lip. "The girl. Lauren. I need to talk to her."

"We sent her away," the nurse says. Mouth a severe line.

"Who are you?" the Headmaster asks. "A relative to one of the girls? A sister? Mother? Are you on drugs?"

"I need to talk to that girl."

"We can't allow that, Miss Black. And if you continue to make such strange requests, I will be forced to call the police. I'm already regretting not doing so from the moment you tore one of our sconces from the wall, stumbled into my office, and had a seizure here on the floor."

"I'll go," Miriam says. "I'm sorry. I'll... go."

"Good. I've brought some friends to ensure that to be the case." He untucks one of his hands from its pocket and waves someone in. The nurse studies her the way a cat studies a mouse before the pouncing.

The two guards from before – Roidhead and Mario – enter, and reach to help her up. She fends them both off with the trashcan. Pukey vapors rise from within, and she hisses like a cornered puma. "Fuck off. I'm going. You lay one hand on me and I'll sue you so hard you'll be shitting legal papers till the stars burn out."

Clumsily, drunkenly, Miriam manages to stand by grabbing the edge of the Headmaster's desk. It's only now she gets a good look at the room, and it's almost ludicrously typical: old globe, dark shelves stuffed with books, everything in wood, everything oiled and dusted, no computer. An academic's nocturnal emission: Egyptian artifacts and books of poetry and a glass case featuring some old illuminated manuscript.

Nurse Caldecott reaches for Miriam, but she dances away.

"Miss Black. You should see a doctor."

Miriam says nothing. Just pushes her way out, flanked by the two guards.

She winds her way through the school and all its Victorian trappings: flower-pattern rugs and tea tables and school desks that seat two children each. It smells of dust and books and the faintest hint of strawberry lip gloss.

She passes by classroom after classroom, all filled with girls, some bright-eyed and ready to escape the sucking mud of their own pasts, others glowering and glaring as though to say, *This will do nothing for me*.

As they walk, Roidhead keeps coming up behind her and bumping her. Then laughing. Like it's an accident but it's not. He's fucking with her.

All she can do is point to him, give him a scathing I-will-stuff-your-balls-up-your-ass look. Anything past that right now would require energy she doesn't have. That vision didn't just take the wind out of her sails: It tore the sail to ragged ribbons so that the wind whistles through the tattered vents.

He doesn't care. Mario, on the other hand, watches. Cagey. Like she's a snake who might bite. *Good boy*.

And then, just like that, she's out. The day is bright. Noon-time sun at the tippy-top of its totem pole. The day is warm. But it doesn't matter. She still feels cold. A chill, down into her marrow.

Mask. Song. Axe.

They stuff her into a security guard car – a crappy four-door Ford sedan from the early Oughts, painted to look like an almost-cop-car. On the way, despite the heat, she catches early whiffs of autumn's approach: Somewhere, someone is burning leaves.

Rose. Carnation. Orange oil.

Chemical stink, piss, fear.

The guards ditch her at the gate. Homer's still there and he tries some more witty banter, but it doesn't take.

She can't even hear it.

The gate opens. She takes her chance and escapes this awful place.

SEVENTEEN
CRAPPLEBEE'S

"Todd," Miriam says, tap-tap-tapping on the edge of her glass. "You're going to need to put another Long Island Iced Tea in this motherfucker, and this time, you're going to need to crank it up a notch. Don't gyp me on this. Did you know that 'gyp' is a racist term? It's totally a racist term. Short for 'gypsy', because apparently the gypsies were always dicking people over. Stealing babies and shit. Whatever. What was I saying? Long Island. Iced tea. In my glass. Pretty please, Todd."

Todd's the bartender here at Applebee's. He's got a black polo on, and he's about as well put-together as a bundle of dry branches. He's probably twenty-one but he looks eighteen. His face has such a crass topography of zits it made Miriam set aside her mozzarella sticks.

"Sure thing," he says, his voice an uneven pubescent croak. He sets to making her a new drink.

It's dead in here. Might as well set up headstones at each booth and table, cover the whole place in cobwebs and grave moss.

She's not sure if it's the only bar in town. But it was the one she found first when walking away from that God-fucked girls' school. And at the time she figured booze was booze, greasy food was greasy food, and that was that.

Since that time, she's revised her opinion. All the bullshit tacked up on the walls is getting to her. Kitschy nonsense, street signs, faux-retro stylings, a fucking boat oar. *A boat oar.* What a boar oar has to do with anything, she doesn't know. Maybe it's to bludgeon unpleasant customers.

She wonders how long it'll be before Todd bludgeons her.

He seems too sweet to do that. Or dumb.

Maybe he'll take an axe and chop off your head, Wicked Polly.

No. No! She wasn't going to think about that. That's not why she came here. She's not here to stew. She's here to drink. And eat. And forget.

And talk to her new friend, Pizzaface Todd.

"Lemme ask you something," she says, slurring a bit. She damn well better be slurring. She's had – five? – five Long Island Iced Teas. Each of them individually weak but together they form a cauldron of foaming booze in her gut. "Todd. *Todd.* Lemme ask you something."

He places her next drink in front of her. "Huh?"

"You ever think that, okay, my life is meant for one thing, and that sucks, and you hate it, and... fuck. Right? But then you find out your life is meant for this whole *other thing* and in many ways that sucks *so much worse* than the thing you thought you had to do? You follow me, Hot Toddy?"

"Maybe. I dunno." He looks at her like she's got two noses and a vagina for a mouth. He's been this way all night. But that's okay. Todd's a perfect sounding board – and, her liquor-sodden brain tells her, *a good good friend*.

She pounds back the "iced tea." Still doesn't have enough booze in it. Then again, it could be a tall frosted glass of rubbing alcohol and it might not have enough.

From her right, she hears it: the clickity-click of claws on the bar-top.

At the end of the bar, where no one is sitting, a fat-bellied crow stands, drinking the last few drops of something from the bottom of a shot glass. Its beak *clinks* against the bottom of the glass.

Smoke slowly drifts from its beak-holes.

She blinks, and the crow is gone.

"I don't know either," she says, voice quiet.

A hot rocket surge of acid refluxes up into her throat. With it, a crass reminder: The girl with the red hair and the strawberry freckles is going to die.

Poor little Lauren Martin.

Not now, says the voice inside her head.

But dead just the same, says another.

Fuck it, not your problem.

Then whose problem is it?

SEP. Somebody. Else's. Problem. Who cares? Who appointed you Queen Fuck of Fatetown?

She's a poor young girl, and she's not just going to die, she's going to die spectacularly at the hands of some fucked-up monster in a freaky leather bird mask who gets high on smoking burned funeral flowers and… what? We're just going to let it go?

Who's we? We're just one person. Besides, you can't save anybody. And it's not like this is happening tomorrow. This is six years down the line.

Before she knows it, the drink is gone and her cell phone is ringing.

It's Louis.

Shit.

"Excuse me, Todd, I have to take this."

Todd isn't even standing there right now. She answers the call.

"Hey," she says, trying to sound nonchalant.

"Miriam," he says. "Listen–"

"No, you listen."

"Wait. Can I talk?"

"Fine. Sure. Whatever."

"I just wanted to say that I'm sorry. About earlier, about being pissy. It's just… hard sometimes. I know you don't want to be with me and sometimes we work and other times we're like fire and water and… you live at a much higher speed than me, Miriam. I'm just a lonely old bullfrog, and you're like, you're like a dragonfly flitting from reed to reed and–"

She interrupts. "Have you been drinking?"

"A little bit. It's been a bad day."

"Me too," she says. "Me too."

"My truck broke down."

"Oh. Oh, shit. That sucks."

"I still haven't delivered. I'm going to be a few days

getting back. I thought I'd be back by tomorrow but – I'm really sorry. Do you need me? I can catch a bus if you need me there."

"I don't," she lies. "Everything is… good here."

"How's Katey?"

"She's got pancreatic cancer."

"Jesus."

"Yeah."

"I should call her."

"Don't! Don't." *Because she doesn't know.* "She just wants to spend the night… assilim… assimilating the news."

He sighs. "Yeah. You're probably right."

"I am always right."

Deep breath. Like this is tough for him. "Everything else is okay?"

"It's all… peach fuzz and popcorn. I don't even know what that means."

"I'll call you again."

"Okay."

"I miss you."

"Okay," she says.

Silence.

Say it back? Don't say it back? Does she miss him? Does she hate him? Love him? Want to fuck him? Want to punch him? All question, no answer.

"I'll talk to you, Miriam." His voice is brusque now. Gruff.

"Goodnight, Louis."

He ends the call.

She holds the phone there for a while, clucking her

tongue. She says, "Miss you too."

Whatever. Fuck it. Fuck it all to hell.

"*Uno mas,*" she tells Todd, nudging the empty glass toward him. It feels like she's got a storm brewing deep inside her, a mean typhoon with an endless hunger. She might as well feed the beast.

EIGHTEEN
BROKE/N

Bam bam bam bam.

Her head feels like a water-logged cantaloupe.

Bam bam bam bam.

A muffled voice from the other side of the motel door: "Hey. You in there."

BAM BAM BAM BAM.

Now she knows why you're not supposed to tap on the aquarium glass. She feels like a goldfish undergoing a glacially slow aneurysm.

"Open the door or I'm coming in."

She crawls out of bed like a clumsy drunken baby, wearing nothing but a pair of panties. On hands and knees, head throbbing like it's bouncing around the inside of a kick drum, she creeps toward the door.

Door open. The light from outside is a curtain of white fire.

"Ow," she murmurs. "Wuzza?"

"You owe for tonight or you gotta go."

The fire recedes as her vision adjusts. Standing there is the motel manager. Not the lumpy pedo-bear who mans the front booth but rather a beefy Guido with hair so slick it looks like LEGO hair, like you could snap it on and snap it off. *Pop, pop.*

Miriam winces. Squints. Feels brain-squirrels – each famished, weaned on a week's worth of cheap delivery pizza and gallons of alcohol across the entire booze taxonomy – chew at the wiring inside her head.

"I'll bring you the money soon," she lies. She's out of cash. She's been hunkering down here for days. The room fee plus the food plus the booze plus the awful porn she's been buying non-stop (that and a few weepy boo hoo chick-flicks, whatever, shut up) has left her pretty much broke.

Louis hasn't come back, either. He got his truck fixed but said he had some "emergency work."

She figures he doesn't want to see her.

She doesn't blame him. She doesn't want to see herself, either.

"You gotta pay or you gotta go."

"I said, soon. Gimme a few minutes."

"You don't got a few minutes. You're already hours past the deadline. Pay up or pack up." He looks her up and down. A dismissive sniff. But hungry, too. Like his eyes are mouths and they're enjoying the meal. "You don't have the money?"

"Fine. No. I do not have the money."

"Then you gotta go."

"Whatever. Just give me fifteen minutes and I'll be out."

"You don't have fifteen minutes. You have one minute."

"What? No fucking way. Nobody can do anything in one minute. You can't even microwave a cup of coffee in a minute. Don't be an asshole."

Her skull pulses, like her heart has taken the elevator to the penthouse and now throbs dully behind her eyeballs.

"Well," he says, and she knows what's coming before he says it, "you know, we could work something out."

And his gaze drifts over her thighs, her hips, her tits.

His licentious stare finally reaches her face just as she punches him–

Curled up, fetal ball, neon lights from a bar or a strip club or a schmaltzy motel bathe him in alternating pink and blue. He's forty-eight and drunk and he's been drunk for a long time. His liver looks and feels like a football packed with beef fat, bound up tight with a crusty leather belt, and it's then that the alcohol poisoning punches him hard – he lays down, passes out, pukes in his own mouth. A sharp hitch of breath brings the regurgitate into his lungs – aspirating his last meal, which was basically a shitload of vodka and bar peanuts. Death by lungbarf.

–in the nose. The bridge of the nose in particular.

Right now, he's probably seeing stars.

Twin trails of blood crawl from his nostrils like mealworms.

Miriam slams the door, throws closed the night latch, and then hurries through the room, yanking on clothes and pitching her stuff into her bag. It's hell on her hangover, and it feels like she's in a nightmare running through wet concrete but what's done is done. That asshole's either going to call the cops or–

BAM BAM BAM

KICK KICK KICK

"You fucking bitch!"

–he's going to come in here and beat her into a gelatinous pulp.

Miriam goes to the bathroom, pushes out the back window. Gets one last look at herself in the mirror – the pink streaks she dyed in her hair a few days ago please her, the rest bleached white like fingers of bone – before squirming through the open hole and dropping onto the back parking lot.

She runs. Far as she can without wheezing and needing a cigarette.

She finds herself back at the river. The water today – winding along a weed-choked abandoned lot – is gray and foamy. The sky above the color of slate. Water and sky, merging together. An unappealing liver-mush.

Cigarette. Lighter. *Ahhh.*

To her right: a twig-snap. The Guido. She wheels.

No. Not him.

The Trespasser.

"Your gash is healing nicely." It's the girl. Lauren. Not the young girl but her eighteen-year-old future self. The skin around her neck is a vented flap crusted with blood.

Breath whistles through the slit.

Miriam moves and feels the place where the gunman's bullet dug a gully in her head. It's healing up. Still, she could peel the scab if she wanted to. She thinks about it. Doesn't, for now.

"Yours isn't." She looks at the girl walking with her by the river. Overhead a plane drifts. "Maybe try a little Neosporin on that neck."

"Oh, Miriam. Deflect, deflect, deflect. Trying to forget."

"I prefer when you visit me in dreams. The hallucinations freak me out a little."

"I prefer the term 'visions'."

"Like, vision quest? Maybe I'm doped up on some kind of trippy jungle tea and soon it'll be time to fight the Jaguar Queen, cut out her heart, eat it."

"Maybe cut off her head."

To this, Miriam says nothing.

The Trespasser begins to sing: "*Signs, signs, everywhere a sign. Blocking up the scenery, breaking my mind.*" The girl cranes her neck. Exposes the bloodless hole of her esophagus. "Did you see the killer's tat?"

"The bird."

"The swallow."

"The swallow, right."

The Trespasser nods. "In Egyptian myth, the swallow used to sit at the front of any boat going into the Underworld. But it went beyond that. Some cultures see the swallow as a malignant, malevolent creature. A real *dirty-birdy*. A curse. The swallow is all over mythology."

"I don't know that. So how do you know that?"

A happy trill. The killer's laugh."The *swallow,*" the Trespasser continues, "is a symbol cast far and wide. You should look into it."

"Sounds like school stuff."

"Maybe it is. If only you knew where a school happened to be."

"If only," Miriam says, seeing ahead the driveway leading to the iron gates of the Caldecott School. "If only."

"You have work to do," the Trespasser says.

"I know. I know."

She knows.

But the Trespasser is gone.

NINETEEN
THE WAY IS SHUT

"Uh-uh," Homer says. "Nope. No way. Go on. Get out of here."

Miriam stands at the iron bars, hands wrapped around them, face pressed between them. "I'm not going to be long. Seriously. Let me in."

"Hell no. You messed up. You're on the list." He leans out of his booth and lowers his voice. "And between you and me, *it ain't a good list.*"

"But I'm a friend of Louis."

"I don't owe that dude anything! He's just a nice one-eyed white man who comes up here and does a little charity work for the school. We ain't war buddies or anything. He didn't save me from a shark attack. Shit."

"I'll give you money."

Homer's eyes narrow. "How much money?"

"How much will it take?"

He thinks. "Fifty bucks."

"Forty."

"*Fifty.*"

"Fine."

"So why don't you hand it up through the gate now."

She winces. "Yeah. I don't actually have fifty dollars."

"Ain't that a shame."

"I'll owe it to you."

"I don't take IOUs from crazy bitches."

"That's not nice."

"But it's true."

Yeah.

"What if I just… climbed over the fence?"

"Then I'd call the cops on your ass."

"But oh, the paperwork. I'm sure you'd have to do paperwork. And paperwork sucks. Am I right? Damn the man. And his… paperwork."

He laughs. "What, you think I got something better to do? I sit here in a booth watching a gate that generally ain't worth watching. I'd do some paperwork just for a change of pace. Might even doodle some smiley faces or boobies up in the corners for fun."

"Okay. Fine. What if I snuck in elsewhere? You wouldn't know."

"Electric fence would probably zap your ass."

She furrows her brow. "Electric fence? You're shitting me."

"Nope. Bzzt."

"That's a bit extreme."

"Sometimes the girls try to run away. Since some of them are court-mandated to be here and others actually end up in the school's custody, they ain't necessarily allowed to leave."

"So this place is like a prison."

"For some. A real nice-looking prison, but a prison all the same."

She rubs her face. She's tired. The hangover behind her eye sockets paces in its cage, clawing the ground.

"So. I'm not getting back in here, am I?"

"Guess not, lady."

She snorts. "Lady. That's a good one." Miriam thrusts out her hand. Option of last resort. "It's been real, Homer."

He shrugs like *whatever*, takes her hand–

Hospital room. All gray but for the few flowers that brighten the place and a TV flickering in the corner. Homer lies in bed, staring up at the ceiling, eyes like blank chalkboards because nobody's home. He's dead but he's not dead – body still ticking, brain mostly gone, mind a dead garden of rotting vegetables. And then it's like whatever last bit of him is standing on the lip just… slips off into darkness, and suddenly the monitors are going off and a resident comes in with a crash cart. A woman and a young girl rush in, the woman crying out for her father, the young girl shell-shocked because she's never seen anything like this before, and then Homer's gone, really gone, gone-gone.

"You've got a granddaughter," she blurts, pulling her hand away.

"So?" he says, suddenly suspicious.

"She's not a student…" Miriam tosses a thumb at the Caldecott School.

"No. Hell no. She's a good girl. Got a mother who takes care of her. And me."

Miriam isn't really in the mood to be genuine, but here goes. "You know why I'm here, Homer?"

"I bet you're gonna tell me."

"I am. I see things, Homer. Wanna know what I spy with my psychic eye? That you have a daughter." Miriam closes her eyes. Remembers the vision. "She's about five-five. Smells like lavender. Hair short. Got a birthmark on her neck. Like a little pinky print. Her daughter, your granddaughter, well, right now I'm guessing she's around eleven or twelve. Pigtails. Braces."

Homer tightens up. "Doesn't have braces." He looks down. "But they're saying she needs 'em. And I gave Wanda the money already so that she can go ahead with it. How you know all this? How I know you're not just messing with me? Some kind of con-job."

"You don't. But here's what I'm gonna tell you, Homer-old-pal. I'm going to tell you that there's a girl in there, a young girl about the same age your granddaughter is now, and this girl is going to die. Someone is going to kill her. I know this because I can see this, and I'm going to stop it. But I can't do that if you don't let me back in there."

"You're crazy," he says.

"Maybe. Probably. Yeah. But I'm also right."

"I'll let you in," he says, finally.

"Thanks. You want to know how you die?"

He chews on it. Shakes his head. "Naw."

And with that, he opens the gate.

TWENTY
TRUE CONFESSIONS OF A LIVING DEAD GIRL

The girls stare. They watch her sneak in through a side entrance. A few look worried. Others giggle and smirk and turn away. Some give Miriam a little head-nod, as though in recognition from one bad girl to another.

It's between classes. The girls don't have lockers: They have cubby-holes, all open, no doors. No way to hide a pack of smokes or a bottle of Jack or any other contraband. Or so Miriam thinks until she walks up to one set of cubbyholes, interrupting a huddle of girls there. Teen girls. Around fourteen or fifteen years old.

They turn toward her with a gasp, their faces covered in crumbs.

One girl, a Latina with fake eyelashes that look like tarantula legs, turns away. Another, a white girl with chubby cheeks but a body as thin and featureless as a leafless sapling, wipes a smear of chocolate from her lips.

A wrapper crackles as they try to hide it.

Another girl quickly slams shut a textbook, the pages hollowed out as though to conceal a gun or–

"You're hiding *food*," Miriam says, flabbergasted.

"What?" Chubby Cheeks says, a red algae bloom rising to her cheeks. "No! No. Uh. No?"

Latina just clicks her tongue. "Yeah, whatever. We were eating Tastykakes."

"And that's a bad thing?" Miriam asks.

"HFCS."

"I don't know what that is."

"Corn syrup."

"I still don't get it."

"We're not supposed to eat unhealthy food," Chubby Cheeks blurts out, seemingly embarrassed at having done so. "Sorry."

"Right," Miriam muses. "Sure. So, here's the deal. You give me some information and I won't tell the Headmaster that you're hiding naughty sugary boogity-boogity foods in your textbooks. I also won't tell him you're smoking crack and carving shivs out of your Trapper Keepers."

"We're not smoking crack!" Chubby Cheeks bleats.

"What the fuck's a Trapper Keeper?" Latina asks.

You're old, Miriam, an old-ass twentysomething broad with a memory of Trapper Keepers and Tastykakes. "Never mind. Just tell me where I can find Katey's – uh, Miss Wiz's classroom, will you?"

Chubby Cheeks describes, in excruciating detail, how to get there.

Miriam finds herself outside a classroom that screams *English Teacher!* so loud its voice must be hoarse. Books everywhere. Posters of Shakespeare and James Joyce and Mark Twain. There's Stephen King and Kermit the Frog, telling everybody to READ. On the blackboard is a pyramid labeled "Freytag's Triangle."

Behind a desk – on which sits a wooden apple with a faux-bite taken out of it – sits Katey Wiznewski.

As soon as she sees Miriam, she's up on her feet, shaking her head.

"You should go," Katey says. "I heard about yesterday. You in the Headmaster's office. I never should've had you come here, like inviting a snake into a parakeet cage–"

"You're dying."

Those two words. A falling axe.

The teacher stops. Like the breath has been kicked out of her by a mule.

She smiles then. A little laugh. Nods. "Go on."

Miriam swallows. "You've got nine months. You die on May 3rd, a few minutes shy of noon. It's pancreatic cancer. I'm so sorry."

She tells the teacher everything.

How the cancer has already spread.

How the iced tea isn't sweet enough.

How she drops the glass.

How she does not die so much as just… stop.

How that's a good death – as good, at least, as a death can be.

It's then that Katey ushers Miriam back into the classroom. She gently shuts the door and goes and sits behind her desk.

She opens a drawer with a small key while Miriam pulls over one of the two-seater Victorian desks and plops her butt onto it.

The teacher withdraws a bottle of wine and a red plastic cup. One cup becomes two as she separates them.

She plunks them on the desk, fills them both up, and holds out one to Miriam.

Miriam takes it and drinks. It's a lush, bitey red. She's not a wine fan. Everyone always says they can taste something in wine (chocolate, pipe smoke, figs, grass clippings, the sweat off a nine-year-old Cuban boy who's been floating around the ocean for two weeks on a raft made of banana crates), but Miriam can only ever taste "angry grape."

All the same, it's good going down. Toothy, acidic, just right.

"I knew it," Katey says, nodding after taking a long pull of the *vino*. "I *knew* I was dying."

"Sorry," Miriam says. She's not sure what else there is to say.

"Don't be. Well. You should be sorry, but only for lying to me." Katey chuckles, shakes her head. "I *knew* you were lying, too."

"You seem almost happy."

"I'm relieved, really. Everybody thinks I'm crazy. But maybe I had a little psychic something going on upstairs in my own head, you know? Because I... I just felt like it was true. And you're the only one who confirmed it."

Katey finishes her wine. Pours another.

"So, what's your plan now?"

"Gosh. I dunno. What do you do when you learn you're going to die?"

"Beats me." *This isn't usually how it works,* she thinks.

A flash of sadness crosses Katey Wiz's face, like the

shadow from a cloud passing in front of the sun. Or the shadow from a buzzard above. Or a red balloon.

But then it's gone.

"So be it," she says, tapping her plastic cup against Miriam's. It makes an unsatisfying *thunk*. Then she tips it back, finishes it. "It reminds me of the old song: London Bridge is falling down, falling down, falling down. Everything falls apart and entropy wins in the end."

"Cheery."

"It gets cheerier. You know the London Bridge story?"

"Not so much."

"The story is they used to sacrifice children to bridges – a dead child hidden in the brickwork would keep the bridge up, or so the legend went. But it didn't matter. Because in the end, all bridges collapse." It's then that Katey holds her cup aloft and affects a haughty, academic, almost-British accent. "Shall I at least set my lands in order? London Bridge is falling down, falling down, falling down. *Poi s'ascose nel foco che gli affina. Quando fiam uti chelidon* – O swallow, o swallow, *Le Prince d'Aquitane*–"

Miriam snaps her fingers. "What the hell is that?"

"It's from a poem."

"A poem."

"Mm-hmm. T.S. Eliot. *The Wasteland.*"

"A swallow. Why a swallow?"

Katey has snapped fully into English-teacher mode, a mine cart locking onto its tracks. "The phrase *quando fiam uti chelidon* is Latin. It means, 'When will I be like the swallow?' Though the whole phrase is *quando fiam uti chelidon, ut tacere desinam*, or, 'When will I be like the swallow so that I may stop being silent?' It's a reference to the myth of Philomela, who has her tongue cut out–"

Crunch. Miriam doesn't realize it, but her hand has tightened around the cup and now it sits crushed in her grip. A dribble of red wine escapes the shattered plastic and crawls down her forearm, dangling at the elbow.

Miriam swoons. *Swallows and severed tongues and dead children trapped in bridges.* A barrel fire of fear and uncertainty lights up bright and hot in the deepest dark of her gut.

"We need to talk about this. But not now. I need you to help me with something and I know you're not going to be inclined to help me but I need your help just the same. I need to know about a student."

"Oh. I don't know. I shouldn't–"

"Lauren Martin. I need to know where she is. Right now."

"I can't give you information on a student."

"If you don't," Miriam says, "she might get hurt. I don't need personal information. I just need to know where she is. So I can go talk to her. C'mon. Katey – you gotta help me."

Finally, the teacher concedes. She pulls a Macbook laptop out of her desk drawer, and then pulls up a schedule.

"Lauren Martin, Lauren Martin. I don't have her as a student but I know her a little bit… ah, here we go." She traces a finger down the screen. "Right now she's in Self-Defense class. With Beck Daniels. Downstairs, not far from the cafeteria. What's going on?"

Miriam sucks on her lower lip. "I don't know yet."

As she moves to head out the door, Katey calls to her. "You want to get a drink tonight? Maybe a meal?"

Miriam hesitates, but sees opportunity. "All right. I'm in."

"Applebee's? Say, six o'clock? I don't know if you know where it is–"

Miriam forces a smile, crosses her fingers. "Me and Applebee's, we're like *this.*"

TWENTY-ONE
FIGHTING DIRTY

At the doors to the gymnasium, Miriam pops her head up just in time to see through the porthole windows Lauren Martin, twelve-year-old ginger pixie, knee another girl in the crotch, flat-punch her in the throat, and flip her over onto a blue gym mat.

The ground shakes a little.

The other girl, a pale porcelain thing with a black mane bound up in a scrunchie, gets right up, though, and the two girls bow.

Time, then, for her entrance.

Miriam opens the double doors quietly, sliding in through the crack like a slip of paper through a sewer grate. The girls are already moving back into formation: a dozen of them in a line, all in the same Caldecott School gym uniforms.

The man at the fore of the class is long, lean, and ropy. His chest is a point-side-down triangle trapped behind a too-tight white tee. Dark eyes. A swoop of sweat-slick hair. A jawline like a bent rebar.

He claps his hands. "All right. Remind me again of

the six primary strike zones."

The girls, in unison, speak the mantra: "Eyes, nose, throat, groin, knees, and feet."

"Again. Faster."

"Eyes nose throat groin knees and feet."

"Again! Louder!"

"Eyes nose throat groin knees and feet."

He claps his hands together and bows.

As he does, Miriam sees a whiteboard behind him. Those six words, the strike zones, are all listed.

Above it: HOW TO FIGHT LIKE A GIRL.

Miriam approves.

As the girls bow to their teacher, he spies her out of the corner of his eye.

He doesn't approach. He addresses her with, "Yes?"

The girls all turn and stare.

"Oh. Uh." That was unexpected. "I'm looking for my sister."

"Your sister. Well, did you find her?" He's grinning.

"Yep. That's her." Miriam points to Lauren. "Lauren."

He waves Lauren over. She eyes Miriam up and down. "May I go, sensei?"

"And this is your sister?"

The girl doesn't miss a beat. "Yeah, that's Megan."

"Then you may go, Wren."

Wren? Lauren. Lau-ren. Ah.

Great. Another fucking bird.

The girl trots over, giving Miriam a wary look. She pushes open the door and empties out into the hall, backing away. "You're not going to touch me and freak out again, are you?"

Miriam thinks about it. "No promises."

"You really spazzed out."

"Yeah. Well." Miriam can almost smell the burning flowers. Can almost feel the way the ground shakes when the axe falls. *Don't think about it.* "So. You have a sister named Megan?"

"Nah. Just felt right at the time."

"Nice move."

The girl is dubious. "Uh-huh. What do you want? You know we're not actually trading moms. That was just a joke."

"Yes, little girl, I understand the concept of a joke."

"So what, then?"

"I just… wanted to see you again." She doesn't know how this helps her solve a murder years before it happens, but what else can she do?

Wren's face scrunches up. One eyebrow raises so high it looks like the St. Louis arch. "You're some kind of creeper."

"No, I'm just protective."

"Like I said, creeper. What are you, some kind of gash-lapper?"

"I'm trying to *help you.* You know what? You're a pain in the ass."

"Nice. Real nice."

Miriam thinks, *Fuck it, the truth shall set you free*. She's only been hamstrung by lies lately. Better to puke up the truth than stand sick with a belly full of bullshit.

"Here's the poop, little bird. I have this power. Like, a psychic power? Except, not your everyday average psychic hoodoo. I can't levitate shit, I wouldn't know palm reading from a pile of donkey guts, and Tarot cards weird me out a little. But what I can do is touch a person and see how they're going to die. I saw how you're going to die. And I don't want that to happen."

Blink, blink.

Wren takes one ginger step back. "Yeah, I gotta go."

"Wait. Hold up. You don't want to hear more?"

The girl backs toward the gymnasium door. "I'm good, thanks."

"You're going to be murdered."

Wren gives a thumbs-up, fake smiles, nods exuberantly. "Uh-huh! Sure, no problem, let's talk again!" Then the façade falls and she mutters, "*Psy*-cho."

"Wait!"

The girl's butt bone thumps the door open, and she ducks back into the gym. Leaving Miriam alone.

Shit.

Well that didn't work.

She's about to go outside, maybe have a smoke, when the gymnasium door opens again. It's the teacher. The "sensei." Mister Firm-Jaw, Mr Strong-Chin

"Miss," he says. "Hold up."

The dude radiates confidence. Chin up, back straight. Self-assured smile. He seems healthy. Together.

It's a total turn-off.

"What's up, Caine-From-*Kung-Fu*?"

Broad white teeth. Run your thumb over them, they'd probably squeak.

"You're not Wren's sister."

"Really? I'm not? You heard her. I'm Melissa."

"Megan."

"Right. Megan. Melissa for short. Nice to meet you. Beck, was it?"

"Short for Beckett."

"It's a good name. You get a pass."

"You're the woman from the Headmaster's office."

Miriam narrows her eyes, pretends to think about it. "Hmm, no, no, doesn't sound familiar. Sounds like a porno I might've watched, but those aren't real. They're just fiction, silly. Do you think girls *bend* like that? We do not. And most guys don't have giant wangle-rods the size of a fat baby's arm, either. You ever wonder how much Viagra those dudes have to pop to keep that shit going? Those porno dicks are pretty freaky looking, actually. That's the problem with porno these days. Too many close-ups. You can see every vein, every ingrown hair, every mole, crab, zit, cigarette burn–"

"I want to know what it is you think you're doing." His façade doesn't crack. Smile so placid it drives her batty.

"Standing here, soliloquizing – is that a word? – about pornography with some kind of girls' school karate-master. I bet those girls like having you for a coach. Don't they? Uh-huh. Real eye-candy."

Blunter this time: "What do you want with Wren?"

"To help her."

"She has all the help she needs here."

"Yeah. I don't believe institutions are all that helpful, honestly. Besides, this is not the kind of thing they can help with. This is something of an *edge*-case. Requires a *specialist*."

"And you're that specialist."

She winks, fake-kisses the air.

His gaze flicks to the right, down the hall at the T-bone intersection, and Miriam follows his eyes–

Coming out of a stairwell are Roidhead and Mario, security guards extraordinaire.

"You called the cops on me," she says. "How sweet."

"I'm very protective of my girls."

She shakes her head. "*Now* who's the creeper?"

Heavy footsteps – running now, not dawdling – come from the direction of the guards. She doesn't have to look. They're bolting toward her.

Which means it's time for her to bolt, too.

She breaks away down the hall, giving him the middle finger as she flees.

The guards are hot on her tail.

Up ahead, the cafeteria doors.

The murmur of lunching students getting louder and louder.

Perfect.

Miriam gets to the doors and cuts a hard right, shouldering them open and darting into a cafeteria full of girls.

TWENTY-TWO

FIGHTING DIRTY II: FOOD FIGHT BOOGALOO

This isn't your typical grade-school cafeteria.

Girls sit at round wooden tables, not long ones of steel and laminate. Beneath their feet is a dusty old red carpet. Above their heads are not buzzing fluorescents but rather chandeliers with a warm golden glow.

At the far end are the food stations. Drink machine. Buffet. A guy in a froofy white chef hat slicing prime rib like he's serving guests at the White House.

The smells hit her: gravy and pizza and something sweet, something with apples and cinnamon. Hunger pangs tweak her gut.

I wish I had school food like this, she thinks.

No time to take it all in.

Because her pursuers are upon her.

As everybody stares, Miriam darts between tables.

A younger 'tween in pigtails crosses in front of her with a tray. Stops, stares, a deer in headlights.

Miriam moves right, ducking away from Roidhead's swiping hand as she hops up onto one of the tables and runs straight across it. Her foot lands on someone's plate and she almost loses her balance and busts her head but her arms pinwheel and her legs catch up with her body and somehow she recovers.

She jumps to the ground. Flits past one girl just standing there like a dummy, past another loading books into her bag.

The guards don't cross the tables. Mario (or is it Ron Jeremy?) is falling behind.

Oh, what a week's worth of porn will do for your POV.

Roidhead, though, this guy's a bull in a China shop. His elbows are knocking past girls left and right. Tables bump. Drinks spill. Girls shriek. He's got a vein sticking out on his bald head that looks big enough to grab onto with both hands – like the handlebars on a Huffy bike.

Miriam grabs food off a plate, hurls it at his head. A chicken leg thuds dully between his eyes, then plops to the floor.

She turns, slaps her chest. "What? *What*? You want a piece?"

As he closes in, she kicks a chair in front of him.

Need an out, she thinks.

The exit is behind her. Red glowing sign. Emergency door.

There.

She turns again, bolts for the door, pulls a rack of trays – all with old food spackled to them – behind her, and it collapses with a clatter.

He leaps over it like a beefy, grunting gazelle.

She turns to run toward the door.

Just as a young girl is coming out of the cafeteria restroom–

A black girl. Hole in her nose where a nose-ring once went. Her hair frizzy and wild, like she dipped her toe in a cup of water and then stuck it in a light socket.

Her face pulses. The image of a skull, ochreous and watery as though bobbing in a jar of formaldehyde, floats over her face.

As though projected there from afar.

Miriam tries to avoid her, but the girl zigs when Miriam zigs, and she holds up her hands and Miriam holds up hers and–

Burning flowers. Orange oil. This time in a rusted husk of a burned-out school bus. The girl lies on the doctor's table. Same girl. Older by two years.

"She wrung her hands and groaned and cried
And gnawed her tongue before she died.
Her nails turned black, her voice did fail
She died and left this lower vale."

The song, sung. The man in the bird mask, the man with the swallow tattoo, here he is, axe in hand. He thrusts his foot down and locks the table brake to stop the table from rolling because the bus sits on a slight lean.

Barbed wire gag. Slashed Xs in the palms and the feet. All her hair's been cut off, clipped off into ragged puffs as though by an eyeless barber.

She screams as the man steps up onto the ruined bus seats to get into position.

He stands over her. Singing. Voice up and down. A man's voice. A woman's. A child's. Back again, warbling between them

"May this a warning be to those
That love the ways that Polly chose

Turn from your sins, lest you despair
The Devil take you without care."

The axe falls heavy.

Her head hits the aisle between the bus seats, tumbles under the legs of the table toward the front of the vehicle. The man chases after it like a bird after a worm, giggling as though it's a game. The axe is no longer in hand but now a hooked blade. For cutting out tongues.

–the two bodies come together and pull apart and Miriam feels like she's just been on an out-of-control carousel ride that's been going around and around and now she's dizzy and sick and doesn't know what way is up, down, left, right.

She turns, woozy, and sees the EXIT door.

Roidhead is on her like stink on spoiled meat.

Bam. They crash through the exit. The door swings wide. Pigeons take flight as both bodies tumble out onto a concrete platform. They'd keep going and fall to the parking lot ten feet below if it wasn't for the green metal railing.

It catches them like a net.

Which gives Miriam all the opportunity she needs.

She grabs for his head–

He's gone fat. His gut isn't just a spare tire, it's a tractor tire packed in forgotten mushy muscle and lumpy lipomas. He's forty-five now – it's over a decade since he worked at the school – and he pops the collar of his shirt and waddles down into the basement and there he sees his old friend: the weight bench. He regards it for a time like he's not sure, scratching his neck under the collar, but then he gives a what-the-hell shrug. With a grunt he shimmies himself under the bar, but it's no easy fit – like shoving a tomato under a closed door. Still, he manages. Gets those slick mitts under the bar. Lifts. The bar rattles, doesn't move. More sweat pops out on his brow like so many Whack-a-moles. He starts making a sound like he's trying to squeeze a baby out of his ass, and suddenly his eyes go wide, bulging like googly cartoon eyes, and the heart attack rips through him the way a grizzly bear would rip through a screen door–

–and *whong* slams his skull hard into the metal railing.

Roidhead makes a moosey sound, a bugling cry of inchoate rage, and wraps his big arms around her in a crushing grip. Her head pulses like a balloon filled with blood and getting bigger and bigger.

She's got no wiggle room. It won't be long before Ron Jeremy, Italian Plumber, joins the fray. Probably with pepper spray or a stun gun. And then it's over.

Roidhead's face leers into her own. He shows his teeth like an animal.

Miriam cranks her head backward and smashes her forehead into his nose. It elicits a gurgling cry from her grappler – but, even better, earns her enough slack to wiggle free.

As she clambers up over him, she leaps over the railing and breaks for the woods, churning on a heady rocket-fueled broth of adrenalin and nausea.

Roidhead still back there, bent over, holding his face.

Nobody behind her.

Nobody but two dead girls. Headless. Tongueless. Feels like their ghosts are harrying her forward – the ghosts of two girls who aren't even dead yet.

But she feels like she's being chased by a ghost. The

ghost of not one girl, but two. Each headless. Each carrying their own tongueless heads.

By the time she makes it to the guard gate, she's panting and hacking and wheezing – she tells herself it's all this awful clean air and not lungs shellacked with hardened tar and nicotine. She lights a cigarette. The smoke fills her lungs. Clears her head.

Homer looks out of the booth, watching her like she's some kind of funny squirrel or monkey escaped from the zoo.

"You don't look so good," he says.

"I feel great. Top of the pops. Total tits." She looks down beyond the gate, finally sees Roidhead galloping down the drive. She coughs again, blows a two-pronged swallow's tail of smoke from her nose. "Can I, uhh–"

She gesticulates toward the gate. He nods, hits the button.

They start to swing open.

"Good seeing you again, Homer."

"You too, Miss Black. Will I see you again?"

A voice inside tells her: *You don't ever want to come back here again*. But then the faces of two living dead girls swim in the dark wet hollows of her mind.

"Yeah. You probably will."

He gives her a wave.

And like that, Miriam is gone.

TWENTY-THREE

DRINKS WITH A DEAD WOMAN

Miriam's in a mood. Were she a cartoon character, above her head would float an angry scribble of dark lines. Inked by a black pen that pushed too hard and left dents in the paper.

She's in a booth at America's Most Mediocre Restaurant, nursing a glass of vodka. Todd – on duty again tonight, the innocent pizza-faced lamb that he is – went through their catalog of whiskies, and none of them were worth a shit.

So, vodka. Clean. Nearly flavorless. Kicks like an ostrich.

A shadow falls across the table.

Miriam closes her eyes. Expects the waitress to appear except she'll probably have a bird head and from the bird's nose will drift curls of velvet smoke and the birdface will squawk something about dead girls and work to do.

But it's Katey instead.

The teacher sits.

She's beaming. There's an energy about her. A flush to her cheeks.

Miriam scowls over her vodka. "You look..." She blinks. "Pregnant. Like, they always say pregnant women get a glow. You look pregnant."

Katey waves her off. "I'm not pregnant."

"Yeah. I *know*. I'm just saying, that's how you look."

"Well. You're in a bit of a mood."

Miriam shows her teeth, bites the rim of her glass. Stares over the vodka like a feral dog guarding his bone.

"Listen," Katey says, "if I have my math right, I've got 268 days of life left in me and I don't want to spend them unpleasantly."

"Nngh. Fair enough. So, Teach, tell me. How *do* you plan to spend them?"

Katey smiles. Not a fake smile. Maybe tinged with sadness but a smile just the same. "I don't really know yet."

"Well, don't think on it too long." Miriam polishes off the vodka. Slides the empty glass to the edge of the table. "You're buying my vodka tonight. I don't actually have any money."

Katey shrugs. "Okay. I'll buy you a meal too, if you want it."

Miriam's stomach gurgles. She still feels unsettled, her gut a shallow pool of acid. Food might help. Or she might throw it up, but hell with it, it's not her money. She mumbles thanks.

"Answer me something," Katey says. "You say I'm sitting there talking to someone when I die?"

"Mm-hm. Big fella. Name of Steve."

"I don't know any Steves. Well. There's my cousin Stevie, but he's a few years younger than me and not much bigger than a cricket."

"I dunno. It's a future vision, and at some point in the future you meet some dude named Steve. And he's there when you... you know, take the great big cosmic dirt-nap."

"Huh." Katey nests on that for a while. "Do I get chemo?"

"What?"

"You know. Chemo. Does it look like I get chemo?"

Miriam scrunches up her nose, the skin between her brows forming a crumpled V. "No, I don't think so. No hair loss. Not too much weight loss, either."

"Aw, heck. I could've used the weight loss. Still. I think you're right. I don't think I will get chemo. Quality of life and all that. I want to keep things the way they are for as long as I can."

"You going to keep teaching?"

"I am."

"Why? Why not... quit, escape, fuck off to an island somewhere, go get rub-downs and happy endings by some cabana boy named Manuel?"

"I'll do some of that. I have some time off. But I can't leave my girls."

"You're just a teacher."

"*Just* a teacher? You know how to make a girl feel real good about her life choices." Katey laughs. "I see the look in your eye. You never had one of *those* teachers, did you? A teacher who inspired you to learn more, to be better?"

"I never had a teacher get up on a table and read me poetry, if that's what you're asking. None of them ever took a bullet for me or sent me roses or tried to fuck me." She drums her fingers and closes them suddenly into a fist, wishing she could smoke in here. "Okay. I did have one teacher. English teacher. Introduced me to Poe and Plath and Dickinson."

She thinks, *And Keats and Donne and Yeats and all those lovelorn assholes who made me want to go out and get goofy on Crème de Menthe in the woods with Ben Hodge, Ben whose brains were blown out of his head, Ben whose baby ended up dead.*

"I hope I'm the kind of teacher my girls remember. Maybe that's why I'm here. To leave something behind." The waitress comes, and Katey orders some tropical drink for her, another vodka for Miriam, telling the woman to cut it with a little cranberry juice (to Miriam's sour-faced chagrin). "These girls need help. Some of them are just a little lost in the fog, but others are deep in the dark. Girls who were abused by parents. Or molested. Some of them were substance abusers or are bipolar or they cut themselves. Their families – heck, the whole world – have in many cases left them behind. Abandoned them to the wolves and lions of the plains and jungles. They need our help. Because we're the only ones giving it to them and not asking for anything in return. Which means I've still got work to do."

You've got work to do, Miriam.

The waitress shows. No bird-head. No scar marks on her neck. A banner night.

She gives Miriam a vodka-cranberry. Then she drops a drink in front of Katey that looks like a fishbowl full of Windex that's been garnished with orange slices and cherries and not one but *two* little paper umbrellas.

It's a drink so girly Miriam can feel her uterus twinge.

"I gotta tell you," Miriam says, "that school doesn't feel like a school for damaged goods. It feels like a rich girls' school. Hoity-fucking-toity. Like these are all chicks who fought tooth-and-claw to be there, whose parents pay out the bunghole to ensure their kids a spot. These are girls with a guaranteed shot at a big school with Greek columns and a heraldry crest and ivy crawling up the walls."

"That's the idea. We're not trying to give these girls the bare minimum. We're trying to give them everything. A full-access pass to a real life." Katey sips her drink from a little red straw so narrow it looks like a petrified human capillary. Her eyelids flutter with delight. "Mm. Mm! Mm. So good. You want a little taste?"

"I don't drink hull cleaner."

Katey waves her off. "Your loss. Anyway. Some parents *do* pay out the wazoo. Rich girls can be troubled, too. Sometimes rich girls have the worst problems, believe you me. Anorexia. Oxycontin."

"Shopping addictions!" Miriam exclaims in faux-horror.

"Be nice."

"It's not my strong suit."

"They have problems same as the rest of us. And their parents help – perhaps unknowingly – to fund the tuitions and room and board of the girls who cannot afford it. We also get donations and state subsidies.

All to help these poor girls not just get through, not just survive, but excel."

"But not boys."

"Girls are targets. They're assumed to be weak. The world treats them as though they're inferior, a second-class citizen to men. We've had to fight longer and harder–"

Miriam's cell rings.

Louis.

She holds up a finger to Katey, and then she holds the phone between thumb and forefinger like she's picking up a jizzy tissue.

Plunk. She drops her phone in a glass of water.

"See?" Miriam says. "I refuse to be a second-class citizen to men. Totally on board with what you're saying. Um. What were you saying again?"

"Uh. Well." Katey can't help but look at the phone sunken inside the water glass. "I'm just saying we need to fight to keep our place at the table. A man gets killed, nobody asks whether he deserved it. A woman gets raped, they ask, well, what was she wearing? Did she come onto him, lead him on? Did she say *no* loudly and clearly enough? As though those loopholes make rape okay. Young women have it even worse. They don't have a voice. They don't have advocates. That's what we do. We give them a voice. We give them power."

To this, Miriam says nothing. Her inclination is to call bullshit, but she knows it's true. She's been out there for almost ten years now, floating and drifting, and few have ever treated her like a beautiful leaf on a stream. Most acted like she was a piece of trash bobbling on a tide of sewer run-off. Like she's nothing but an empty McDonald's bag filled with dirty syringes.

Louis was one of the rare few who treated her like something special.

Louis.

Shit, shit, shit.

The two of them order food and Miriam tries for a hamburger and it's about the most mediocre hamburger she's ever had, but it's not *bad*, not exactly, and she figures that since they burned it to a hockey-puck consistency it certainly won't make her sick with e.coli – "e.coli" just being code for "somebody's poop germs" – and the vodka will help ensure that any such germs are bathed in a scathing wash of antiseptic alcohol.

Katey talks while Miriam eats.

At the end of the meal, Miriam's picking pieces off her leftover bun and sopping them in leftover ketchup before popping them in her mouth.

This meeting has a reason, so it's time to get to it.

"There's a serial killer," she says.

Katey almost laughs. "What?"

"I told you that Lauren Martin might get hurt. What I meant is she might die. Worse, I just found out that she's not the only victim."

Miriam tells her the story.

She doesn't withhold anything: the barbed wire, the carved Xs in the palms and feet, the doctor's table, the bird mask, the axe, the funeral flowers, everything. Heads rolling. Tongues extracted. By the end of it, the teacher looks harrowed out.

"You see things like that," Katey says, matter-of-factly.

"Yeah."

"That's horrible."

"Pretty much."

"This is who you are."

Miriam just nods

"Oh." Katey blinked.

"These visions I get, I see things in them, and sometimes those things don't add up. Details lead to questions that don't have answers. To that end," Miriam pauses, takes a drink, "I want to talk about swallows. The bird."

"Why swallows?"

"The killer has a tattoo. Earlier you said something about Philomena."

"Philo*mela*. A... Princess of Athens."

"What does she have to do with swallows?"

Katey tells Miriam the story.

She tells her how Philomela was daughter to King Pandion and sister to Procne. Both girls were beautiful. Procne married Tereus, King of Thrace, and went to live with him. Five years passed and the sisters had not seen each other and Procne missed Philomela.

She sent her husband to fetch Philomela so that the sisters could again be together. But upon seeing Philomela, Tereus found her more beautiful than his own wife. So beautiful that he could not control himself, and he raped her.

To silence Philomela, Tereus grasped her tongue with pincers and cut out her tongue with his sword. Then he hid her away, telling Procne that her sister had died.

"Men," Miriam says. "Always such charmers. What happened after that? Where do the swallows come in?"

"Philomela was hidden away, but she began to weave the most wondrous tapestries – tapestries that secretly explained what happened to her. She packed the tapestries up and sent them to Procne as an anonymous gift. Procne saw the truth of what had happened. She went and found her sister, and together they planned their revenge."

"And did they get it?"

"They did. Procne invited her husband to dinner. He sat down and enjoyed plate after plate of succulent meats. As he finished, licking his fingers, rubbing his belly, Philomela emerged from the kitchen and dropped onto the table the severed head of Tereus' first son, Itys. Procne had had the boy killed and his body butchered into the meal that Tereus ate and enjoyed."

Cut tongues.

Severed heads.

"Those Greeks knew how to party." Miriam takes a long sip from her too-sweet too-tart cran-vodka. "Still not clear on the swallow thing."

"Well." Katey takes another long sip of her radioactive cocktail. "Tereus was, of course, none too happy about having just consumed his first and best son. Men, you might say, are sore losers, and Tereus was no different. And so he chased the women down with a sword. He had them cornered, and he was just about to slay them when…" Another sip.

Miriam makes the *I'm-over-here-impatiently-waiting* face.

"The gods took pity and turned them all into birds."

Ah. There it is.

"Right. I can guess what Philomela became."

"A swallow. The swallow was at the time thought to be a silent bird with no song and no call – not true, of course." Katey stares off into the restaurant, no doubt trying to imagine how this all relates to a dead girl named Lauren Martin. "Procne became a nightingale, while the King turned into a hoopoe."

"A hoopwhat? Now you're just making shit up."

"Hoopoe. I thought it sounded fake, too, and some myths have him as a hawk. The hoopoe's an… ostentatious bird, black and white but for the crown of bright orange feathers on his head. A crown like a king's crown."

Miriam sniffs. "Even in the end the guy gets to be the prettiest bird. Stupid gods. If I had the powers of the divine, I would've turned him into a – well, I don't know my birds. A little one-winged parakeet flopping around at the bottom of his cage in piles of his own bird shit."

"I don't know what to say about all this." Katey finally plucks the straw from the cocktail and pitches it onto a napkin. Blue Curacao bleeds. Katey cups the fishbowl with both hands and finishes it off. Then gets the shivers. "I think I needed that."

"Yeah," Miriam intones, dry, tired. A gutted husk. In her head a storm of birds takes flight. Some carry severed tongues. Others together share the burden of carrying severed heads aloft. "*Yeah*. It's time I hit the bricks with my getaway sticks."

"We should do this again."

"Mmn." A non-committal grunt if ever there was one.

"Where are you staying?"

Miriam stands. Hikes her bag up over her shoulder.

"No idea. Got kicked out of my motel this morning for non-payment. I'll find something."

"Something."

"Underneath an overpass. Maybe I'll get lucky and find an abandoned car."

"You're homeless." The teacher says the words in the same way you might say, *You have pancreatic cancer and you've got nine months to live.*

"It would not be the first time. In fact, at this point in my life, a third of my existence has been on the road. No home of which to speak." She shrugs as though to echo her mother's old refrain, *It is what it is.*

"Come stay with me."

Miriam snorts hard enough she thinks she might puke up her vodka. "You're joking."

"No. What do you have to lose?"

"Better question is, what do *you* have to lose? To which I answer, your safety, sanity, a general sense of togetherness and well-being. Health. Happiness. Hope."

Katey shakes her head and offers a sad smile. "You have this dark cloud about you, Miriam. It's like you want it there. A cloud of flies, or a storm passing overhead."

"I'm a poison pill. I'm a Mister Yuck sticker. I'm not good for people. You want to know how I see the world? How I see people? Bunch of rubes. Just waiting to be taken for a ride. And if I'm not careful, that's how I'll start seeing you. And I'll take you for a ride, and a ride with me is a log flume splash through blood and tears that drops clean through the Devil's open mouth and out his ass. I don't want that for you, Katey. You're just too nice a lady."

The teacher gets quiet. She takes out her debit card and slides it next to the check. When she looks up, her eyes are wet. Glassy and shimmering like an old snow globe.

"I'm dead in nine months. Nothing you can do to me changes that."

"I can turn those remaining precious days to shit."

"Let me do this for you. It'll kill me 267 days early if I have to think of you out there somewhere laying your head on a dirty pallet of cardboard boxes. Stay with me."

Miriam hesitates. But in the end, what else can she say? It's a bad idea but she's the queen of bad ideas.

And this one wasn't even hers.

"Let's go, roomie. I get the top bunk."

TWENTY-FOUR
LOUIS RETURNS

Katey's got a townhouse a half-hour from the school in Sunbury. Still not far from the river – look out the bathroom window upstairs, you can see moonlight pooling on the distant water. Glittering like broken glass.

The décor makes Miriam want to dry heave – it's all down-home country fun with a curious fixation on roosters. Katey hangs her keys on a wooden rooster whose feet are little hooks. She takes a cookie out of a ceramic jar shaped like a rooster. Embroidered rooster pillows. A rooster rug by the door.

Miriam tries to bite back the words but they're like butterflies that duck the swooping net. "You sure do love cock," she says.

Katey blanches, shocked. Blood draining from her face.

"Sorry," Miriam says. "Couldn't help myself. It's like a sickness."

But then the teacher quivers and shakes and erupts like Vesuvius, her sudden and uncontrolled laughter swiftly drowning out worry.

"I guess I do love..." she says, tears streaming from her eyes. "Cock!"

The way she squawks that word makes Miriam laugh, too, and for a good half-a-minute the two of them are caught in the throes of a cackling jag. Eventually it fades, and Katey says, "Oh, that felt suprisingly cathartic." She rubs her eyes. "I think that means it's time for this old lady to get to bed."

The teacher sets up Miriam on the couch with a fuzzy brown blanket heavy and soft.

But Miriam's not tired.

The vodka should be dousing her torch by now. But it isn't.

Her head keeps spinning. A carousel of awful images.

Two girls. Not one, but two. Wren and another girl. Only connection she has so far is the school. Do the girls know each other? Are they friends?

Philomela and Procne.

Silence the swallow. Cut out the tongue. Take the head of the children.

London Bridge is falling down...

No. No, no, no. Not now. Nothing to be done tonight. Put it away. Shove it in a desk drawer. Lock it. Burn it. Walk away from the fire.

Miriam gets up. Roots around the kitchen. (Rooster fridge magnets). Opens the freezer. Finds a pint of Haagen-Dazs chocolate ice cream. Plops on the couch, screws the pint between her thighs, digs in. Turns on the television.

Cooking show.

Flip.

Something about volcanoes in Hawaii.

Flip.

Infomercial. Blah blah blah, Super-Mop.

Flip.

American Werewolf in London. The climax. The titular wolf rampages through London's Piccadilly Circus. Mayhem. Foolishness. Cars honking. Screaming. The beast rips off a bystander's head, flings it into traffic.

Click.

TV, off.

Miriam feels dizzy. Overwhelmed by the task at hand. Sitting here, nursing a pint of fudgy ice cream, thinking what a shitty savior she makes. *Well, girls, I'm the only savior you got right now. You get what you paid for.*

Of course, the thing she tries not to think about but thinks about anyway:

Solving their murder isn't all you have to do.

You gotta kill the killer.

It's then she hears something.

A footfall. Outside Katey's door.

Through the window next to the front door, Miriam can see a shadow stirring beyond the curtains. Out there in the dark.

The doorknob rattles.

She reaches in her bag, finds a cheap Chinese-made spring-loaded knife she bought at a Jersey flea market about eight months back.

She wishes suddenly that Katey had one of those little peepholes.

Miriam hits the button, pops the knife-blade, and then throws the door open.

And almost stabs Louis, his big meaty hamhock fist poised to knock.

"Miriam," he says. The look on his face is raw, pained, desperate. A look like that stokes her engines. Water on hot coals. Steam.

"One-eyed Frankenstein," she says back. Smiling. Beaming. Electric.

She flings the knife backward over her shoulder, doesn't care where it lands. The way she leaps on him is like two magnets snapping together. A perfect and irresistible fit.

Strong hands lift her high.

Her legs wrap around him. His cock is hard like rebar.

Mouths are open. They smash together sans grace, driven by hunger.

"I missed you," she hisses in his ear. Bites it.

He drops her ass on the coffee table. Palms the space between her legs like it's a basketball. A thermal lance of heat drives straight from her crotch to her brain and she wants him inside her, all the way to the hilt, to the heart, to the brain.

"Take off my shirt," he says, his voice dry, croaking, hungry. "Hurry."

Her fingers, usually nimble, fumble with the buttons on his corduroy L.L. Beam special. Hell with it. She grabs the first button with her teeth. Bites it off, spits it against the wall. It clatters onto and into a heating vent.

Her fingers search out the spaces between buttons. Like a rib spreader ripping open a chest to get at the viscera, she tears the shirt open. A rain of buttons like bullet casings fling to the four corners of the room.

And everything stops.

His chest, his bare chest, lays exposed.

His chest hair is gone. Shorn from the flesh.

A swallow tattoo – red and puffy, as though freshly drilled – rises from the skin.

She looks up in Louis's face.

"No," she says, her voice a whimper. "Not you."

He brings back his fist and hammers her hard in the nose. She feels it burst, break, a blood squib that pops and squirts two jets of red down to her chin.

Miriam tumbles back onto the table as Louis sheds his shirt.

"You like the ink?" he says.

"Fuck you," is her answer.

He piston-punches her in the gut. She doubles up and rolls off the table into the space between it and the television. Blood wets the carpet. Inside her it feels like something is collapsing in on itself.

A tiny crying baby.

Louis grabs both ankles, drags her out. The carpet burns her back as her shirt pulls up behind her.

He's got the knife, *her* knife, in his hand. It almost looks like a toy, it's so small in his cement-block grip. Louis smiles but it's not his smile. It's Not-Louis. Ghost-Louis. The Other.

"You," she hisses and spits.

"Give me your hand," Louis says.

"Trespasser. *Trespasser.*"

Not-Louis just laughs.

He takes her hand. Slams it palm-down on the carpet.

Then he gets to carving.

She can't see what he's doing, but she can feel it. The bite of the knife tip as it parts the skin. The pain draws a line. The misery makes a shape.

Two-pronged tail, swoop-back wings, head and beak thrust upward.

The swallow.

Like the tattoo on his chest.

"You're the Swallow," Not-Louis says. "I'm the Mockingbird."

"I don't know what that means."

"You will find out. I will *make you* find out. Think you can just walk away from this? Let this serve as a reminder, Miriam Black, Fate's Foe. Let this remind you that–"

He pulls the knife away, his fingers greasy with red.

"–you have a job to do and we won't let you walk away until it's done."

Miriam screams. But it isn't her voice coming out of her mouth.

It's the scream of Lauren Martin as she is beheaded.

PART THREE
A TRAIL OF INK AND BLOOD

Philomela:

"Now that I have no shame, I will proclaim it.
Given the chance, I will go where the people are,
Tell everybody; if you shut me here,
I will move the very woods and rocks to pity.
The air of Heaven will hear, and any god,
If there is any god in Heaven, will hear me."

Metamorphoses, *Ovid*

TWENTY-FIVE
BROKEN CRAYON

Drive too long and too late and the road starts to run like paint, like something out of a Salvador Dali picture. Louis uncaps another mini-bottle of 5-Hour-Energy and slams it back. It tastes like someone strained cough syrup and vinegar through a gym sock.

Tonight, a haul of cable spools on a flat bed. From New York state to Charlotte, NC.

He's taken the scenic route. It's slower, adds time to the trip – which is a mistake – but Louis doesn't care. I-77's a nicer drive. Longer, leaner, fewer cars.

Right now, it's just him and the road. The occasional pair of headlights coming and going. Strobe. White flash. Gone again.

The clock on the dash – LCD blue – silently flicks over to 12:00AM.

He's been pushing it of late. Pushing it in a way he hasn't done in years. Long hauls. Late nights. More hours, more money.

But that's not what this is about. Louis doesn't need the money. He's not rich, not exactly, but he's a man with few bills, save the loan payments on a trailer just outside Long Beach Island in Jersey. Most Americans rack up debt. Louis is the opposite: He collects money the way other folks gather dust bunnies under the bed.

His father used to do that, too. Always saving for retirement. Always *talking* about retirement. How glorious it would be. Shangri-La. The Seventh Heaven. The day they open the cage door, let the animal run free.

The man died a year before retirement. Forklift accident.

Louis ended up with the old man's savings, what with his mother having died from emphysema only a few years before that.

With that money Louis paid for CDL class. Bought his first truck.

And now here he is, doing the same thing. Saving, saving. Waiting for something.

Or maybe, just maybe, running away from something.

Miriam.

Even now he's running from her but he can't avoid her. She's like a ghost that haunts the person, not the house. No matter how far you run, there she is.

He's not sure that he loves her. Not sure you can love a person like that. But he knows he cares about her. Deeply. Completely. Whether he likes it or not (and right now, he most certainly does not).

The itch. He lifts the eyepatch, scratches at the margins of an eye he no longer has. Whenever he thinks about Miriam, the ruined socket itches.

It's her fault that he lost his eye, and it's also because of her that he's not dead.

That's the *real* twist of the knife, right there.

He doesn't blame her. At least, that's what he tells himself. Some nights like tonight, when it's just him and the white reflective margins of the big slab of highway and the dotted yellow line that looks like the stitching of an autopsy incision, he's not so sure.

Still. He can't stop thinking about her.

It makes him feel like an addict. This trip was to help him get clean.

It's not working.

He turns on the radio. Sets it to scan for something, anything. The stations warble between static and country music and religious broadcasts until he finally settles on a night flight of Art Bell and his Coast-to-Coast AM, on which the commentator talks about conspiracies and UFOs and all manner of American weirdness. Art Bell: a trucker's best friend.

Driving like this feels like being on a boat in the fog. Drifting aimless.

It's then that his high beams catch something. A shape.

A shape that slowly resolves into a car. A wreck. In trucker lingo, a "broken crayon."

The cars sits in the middle of the lane.

He has time enough to react, apply brakes, slow the Mack. He could probably drive around it – the car is turned perpendicular to the highway's edge, but there might be enough room on the other side. But he should call this in. It's dangerous. And somebody might need his help.

The lights are on inside the car.

Steam or smoke rises in coils from under the hood.

He stops the truck. Leaves the lights on. Peers out the windshield.

Honda Accord. Five, six years old. Maybe it's not a wreck. He can't see any structural damage. Both tires on this side are flat.

He leaves the truck idling. Beams on bright.

Louis gets out of the cab.

The smell hits him: that acrid tang of anti-freeze, like bitter green blood running on the asphalt, pooling around the front flat.

Louis orbits the car. The tires on the other side are flat, too.

Nobody's inside the car. But the interior lights remain on.

Louis hears something behind him.

A shuffle. A scritch, a scratch.

He wheels on it–

And his breath catches in his chest.

It's like something out of that Hitchcock movie. The whole road, blanketed with birds. Blackbirds. Starlings. Grackles. Crows. Shifting uneasily. Claws clicking on asphalt. *Click click. Click click.*

Beaks pointed away from him.

Eyes pointed *toward* him.

Some of them murmur. Or caw. Or make a low chirrup in the backs of their throats. He thinks, any minute, any one of these birds could come at him. Or hell, all of them at once – wings and beaks and talons. A fear runs through him, a fear in which the birds swarm and come for his face and he loses his last remaining eye, leaving him blind and in the dark forever.

Get away from them. Get away from them now.

His truck, though – it's too far away. Twenty feet isn't much, but having to cross that space covered in creepy birds is twenty feet too many.

The car. Get in the car.

He eases toward the vehicle. Pops the door as slow and quiet as he can. Slides his large frame into the Honda.

The steering wheel presses tight against his chest. The seat's up too far.

He feels around, looks at the side of the seat and then beneath it for the lever that lets him pop the seat back–

And when he looks up again, a fat crow stands on the dashboard. Inside the car. With him. Louis resists the urge to freak out – his first thought is *grab grab grab it, twist its head off like a bottlecap* – but he takes a deep breath and waits.

Little curls of smoke rise from the crow's beakholes.

Smoke that smells like a smoldering Marlboro.

What's up, Lou?" the crow says, speaking with Miriam's voice

Louis about pisses his pants.

Outside, the birds are hopping up onto the car hood. Worse, he hears the scratching of talons above him on the roof and behind him on the trunk.

"Hey," the crow says again, still perfectly mimicking Miriam's caustic tongue. "*One-eye.* Captain Darling of the S.S. Cyclops. You listening?"

"This isn't happening," Louis asserts.

"Oh, it jolly well *is* happening, cupcake. Like it or not. I have a message for you. Open your big dopey ears and listen. Are you listening?"

"I'm... listening."

"Miriam's in trouble. Hip-deep in it and sinking fast. She's not just up Shit Creek. She's up Shit River. No paddle. No boat. Not even a pair of those little inflatable arm-floaties. The forces of darkness are aligning against her, Lou. They don't like that she's been stirring the soup. She's a fate-changer, and fate has a funny way of pushing back hard. *Real fucking hard.*"

"What are you telling me?" he asks. Then he squeezes his eye shut and mutters, "I can't believe I'm talking to a bird."

"I'm telling you she's dead meat on a stick unless you go to her. Now. Put away all the bullshit and the bad feelings and go. She isn't invincible. If you don't pull her up out of Shit River, I can promise that she's going to drown." The bird's beak clacks. "The river is rising, pal."

"Who..." He can't bear asking the question.

The bird can. "Who am I? I'm a friend, Lou. A friend."

And then the bird takes flight.

In the car.

At his head.

He swipes his arms in front of his face and grabs for the bird before it claws his eye out–

And when he lowers his arms he sees.

He's not in a Honda Accord.

He's in his own truck. Still sitting there. Engine idling with a low thrumming growl. The "broken crayon" – the Honda with the flat tires – is sitting there in the beams of his headlights.

Just a dream. You fell asleep. Long haul. Long night. Low fog. Hypnotic. You zoned out and drifted to sleep and that's bad, that's real bad, but damn, it's better than the alternative. What you saw wasn't real. Wasn't real at all.

But then he sees the crow walking atop the car. A gawky, Charlie Chaplin walk. It looks up into the truck and flies away into the night.

Louis pulls the truck back onto the road and drives. Hell with the abandoned car.

It's then he feels it: an itching sensation.

Behind the eyepatch. Normal itching, he thinks. Like whenever he thinks about Miriam. He lifts the patch. Scratches beneath it.

But the itching gets worse. It burns.

Five miles later he pulls off at an exit, finds a gas station, and parks the truck.

He flips the patch like a mailbox lid and starts going to town on the fleshy eyeless pucker – *scratch scratch scratch* – until suddenly his index finger brushes against something sharp. Something sticking out of the hole.

A sick feeling shoots through him.

He pinches his fingers. Feels for whatever it is.

Begins pulling it out.

He feels something wet brush against the sides of his sockets, and then he feels a horrible feeling like a thing moving through him, out of him–

It's a feather. A wet, blood-slick feather.

But he's not done. He keeps pulling because there's more, more, more.

Hair. Wet hair. Wound around the far end of the feather. It smells strong, fetid, like–

Like river water.

Louis opens the door. He throws up in the parking lot. Nobody's around to see.

When he's finished and composed, he goes and unhooks the flat bed.

He's got to get to Miriam. There's no time to mess around. No time to deliver the trailer, and taking it with him is tantamount to stealing.

Leave it here, then. He calls into dispatch, tells them it's an emergency, lets them know where they can grab the load. They won't hire him again after this. This is a black mark. One he hopes won't get around to other companies.

But he has to do it.

He can't shake what the bird told him.

He tries Miriam's phone number. It goes right to voicemail.

The forces of darkness are aligning against her, Lou.

"I'm coming, Miriam."

TWENTY-SIX
A BIRD ~~IN~~ ON THE HAND

Blood on the carpet. That's what Katey wakes to in the morning. That, a cracked coffee table, an overturned pint of chocolate ice cream, a spoon stuck to the couch, and Miriam hunkered down in the middle of the floor like a gargoyle. Perched over an old-school phonebook.

Katey blinks. She looks like nine kinds of Hell stuffed into a ratty pink robe. "There's... blood," she says, throat froggy.

Miriam doesn't look up. Instead she holds up the back of her hand: carved upon it is a swallow.

Nearby sits the knife that did it. The tip, rusty red.

Miriam's finger traces another phone number. Scribbles it down on a pad of paper next to the open phonebook.

Katey's voice gets quiet. "Oh, Lord. You're a cutter."

"What?" Miriam leans her head almost backward, seeing Katey upside-down. "*I* didn't do this."

Well, that's not entirely confirmed. While her nose isn't busted, the coffee table is, and the swallow on her hand sure is there. The lines of the bird are already crusting over with a fine crumbly ridge of scab. She's not sure how it happened. This isn't the first time one of her visions has gotten grabby, but it's the first time one's left this kind of mark.

That should be freaking her out.

Right now, though, she just doesn't have the time.

"I'll clean up," she lies. "I just – I have these visions and sometimes they get out of control."

"If you didn't do this, then who did?"

"Like I said, the visions."

"That's… that's crazy."

"Yeah. *Duh*. I know." She flips the page. Begins writing down more numbers. And addresses.

Katey stands next to her. Staring down. Shell-shocked. "I don't know that…." Her words trail."

Miriam can hear the apprehension in Katey's voice. Like the unsettling hum of a television in a distant room. Time to get ahead of this.

"Listen. You don't like this, say the word. I'll get out of your hair. But I'm the vampire and you invited me in. And I warned you. This isn't going to be fun. You drop a tempest in your teacup, you better expect a little blood on your carpet and some crazy-ass conversations at five o'clock in the morning. You want me out, no harm, no foul. I'm gone. I'll pack my bag and you will never see me again." Now she stands, and she holds Katey's face so that the teacher's gaze meets her own. "This might be your last chance to get off the ride. The Miriam Black Experience is about to depart the gate, and you're either strapped in or left behind. Time to commit, Miss Wiz. The lady or the tiger."

"I... need coffee."

The teacher stumbles away, zombie-like.

Miriam calls after her. "Make me a cup too. A big cup. Black as the Devil's seed. Thanks!"

Eventually, Katey returns with a bowl full of black coffee and sets it down in front of her. "Biggest thing I could find."

Slurp. "Nice. I feel very... Asian."

Back to the phonebook.

Katey says, "Did you sleep?"

"I did not."

"Oh."

The teacher goes around the room, picking up the mess. The ice cream pint, the spoon, the knife. "What're you doing with my phonebook?"

"I was going to use your laptop, but I don't have your password. And it took me awhile even to find the phonebook – I mean, do people even use these anymore? Guess it's good you do. I'm looking up tattoo artists."

"About the swallow."

"Mm-hmm." Miriam wraps both hands around the bowl, takes a long pull. She gives in to coffee's warm embrace, the black comforting oblivion of bean juice. "Ah. I like my coffee like I like my men. Hot, black, and coming down my throat."

"I'm just gonna ignore that and ask, is there anything I can do to help you?" Katey asks. "With the... girls."

"Got the phonebook. Now I need the phone."

"It's in the kitchen. Cordless on the charger."

"Yeah, I kinda need your *cell* phone."

Katey pauses, then nods. Again unsure. "I'll go get it for you. I don't much like having it anyway. Always felt like a bit of a leash."

"Thanks, Katey."

"You're going to stop the killer, aren't you?"

"I am," she says. Whether she believes it or not.

TWENTY-SEVEN
VALENTINE'S DAY

Fuck fuck fuck *fuck*, rent is due and it's not paid and this shitty closet Annie Valentine calls an apartment isn't going to even be *hers* anymore if she can't put up the money somehow. Already this morning they came to her door and the sun's just coming up. Pounded on it. Left a red slip – not pink like the last one or yellow like the one before it – under her door. Eviction. *Eviction*. Fuck fuck fuck *fuck*.

In her head, her mother's voice, a chiding invisible presence: *You never want to work for anything, Annie. Even as a baby you never wanted to hold your own bottle.*

That's Mom's favorite thing to say.

When you were a baby…

You didn't hold the bottle.

You didn't talk early, not like your brother.

You didn't learn how to use the potty until after all the other girls learned.

You couldn't fix the car or grout the bathroom tile or do Mommy and Daddy's taxes like a good little girl.

They never called her stupid. Never said a mean

word. But the insults were always there. Hiding beneath other words like monsters under the bed.

She's eighteen. Just eighteen years old, and she's supposed to have her life figured out. They invited her to move back home but she's not going to do that, oh hell no, she'd much rather snap her tits in a bear-trap than go back to that hell.

Which means she's got to keep this apartment.

But she doesn't have a job. She got fired from the Wendy's. Got fired from the U.S. Gas – the Yemeni guy accused her of embezzling from him, which sounds like a fancy way of saying she was stealing. Which she was. Not that he could have known that. That cow Marjorie – the old cranky bitch with the frizzy wig – must have told him even though she was dipping into the till, too.

Now what? *Now what now what now what* fuck fuck fuck.

Calm down.

They're not kicking you out until the end of the week.

It's all cool. You just need to find your focus.

She opens up a WalMart bag near the rat-trap pull-out couch and snatches from within its plastic depths a pair of pliers, a screwdriver, and a burned-out light bulb whose frosted glass is smeared with carbon-black soot.

The first time she did this she broke the light bulb. Little pieces of glass stuck in her palm. She had to pull each piece out with tweezers. With shaking hands. Some of them she accidentally left in there until her body pushed them out.

Now she's getting pretty good.

With the pliers, she carefully removes the bottom of the bulb. Not all of the metal fixture – just the very bottom.

With the screwdriver, she pokes out the rest of the bulb-guts. The center coil and all its little connecty bits.

Annie reaches into the bag again. Grabs a can of air duster, a box of drinking straws, and a roll of black electrical tape.

Phase two.

A blast of air from the air duster cleans out the inside of the bulb.

From underneath her couch cushion she rescues a small wooden box. It used to hold her Tarot cards, but those things were bullshit. They never told the future, and you always had to use the stupid little book to figure out what the fuck was going on in the first place.

In there now is a small plastic baggy of glittery white powder. Up close, it looks like sea salt, or maybe like the glass dust she just blew out of the bulb.

Into the bulb goes the crystal meth.

Then she thrusts the tip of a drinking straw into it, and winds the tape around it so it's all sealed up nice and tight. Like a sippy cup.

She fishes around the floor for her lighter. It's under the couch.

Annie misses her glass pipe, but Jeffy stole it, that fucking dickwipe. Jeffy's always taking her shit. And yet she lets him. She doesn't know why. He's a parasite and somebody should remove him from this earth and yet she does whatever he wants (*wherever* he wants) because she really loves him and hopes that one day he'll finally be nice to her. Instead of hitting her. Instead of holding her down and pinning her arms and doing her from behind because "he likes her ass, not her face

Whatever.

A hit from this will calm her down.

Flame under the bulb. Drug bubbles. White turns to muddy black. Vapor rises. She sucks it in.

Clarity tolls like a bell inside her mind. *Gong.* Everything snaps into focus. She's both calm and wired at the same time. She knows why they call it what they call it because she feels, well…

Crystal.

It's like looking into a mirror that reflects other mirrors. Smoking this stuff shows her all the possibilities. All the things she can do.

Her cell phone rings.

Tiny Tempah ringtone. "Miami 2 Ibiza."

She should check who it is before she answers but she doesn't think about it and by the time she hears her mother's voice it's too late to do anything about it.

"Annie," her mother says. "Annie, it's your mother."

It sounds like she has a cold.

"What?" Annie barks. "What do you want?"

"Annie, I know about the eviction notice."

How the hell does she know that?

She's been spying. That's what it is. Mom's been spying again.

"Goddamnit, leave me alone. I don't–" *Focus up, breathe deep*. "I don't need you to ride my ass anymore. I got this."

"I just want to help. I don't want to see my baby girl out on the street."

"You put me there. It's all your fault." That adds up. That tracks. It *is* all her mother's fault. And Dad's fault, too, for sitting there night in and night out like a lump, like a fatty tumor, grotesque but not even so powerful as to be malignant.

"I'll give you money."

That phrase, like a bomb. A flash grenade meant to blind and stun.

"Seriously?" Annie asks, teeth clacking together. Then grinding together. Then biting so hard her jaw cramps.

"I don't have much. Enough for rent."

Enough for rent? That'd be a life-saver. Except. Maybe she'll buy crystal instead. Crystal helps her think. It'll help her think her way into more rent money. Twice as much. Three times as much.

Smart girl.

"Okay, but I need the money now," she says.

"I can meet you."

"Where? When?"

"The bus stop by your apartment. The one by the river."

"On Archer."

"That one. Meet me there in an hour."

She finally asks, not because she cares but because she feels she should feign compassion what with her mother giving her cash and all: "Are you sick? You sound like you're stuffed up."

"Just allergies. Autumn's coming. Pollen and mold are high."

"I'll see you in an hour."

"I love you, Annie."

Annie can't go that far. She wants to, but...

She quickly thumbs the button that ends the call.

The hour feels like it stretches and shrinks and collapses upon itself a hundred times. Annie cleans the apartment. Searches high and low for her keys until she realizes she doesn't need them because the bus stop is only a five-minute walk downhill. She tries to eat but isn't hungry. Smokes the rest of her crystal.

Everything bright, clean, clear. All of life in high-def.

Finally, it's time. Past time, actually. Already ten after the hour. Already late.

Fuck fuck fuck fuck *fuck*.

Mom's going to be irritated. Anything she can do to be pissed, she'll do it. It's like she wants it. Like she's a dog rolling around in roadkill – she loves the stink. A real martyr.

Annie hurries down the hill from her apartment. It's raining. She didn't realize. Not heavy. Just a spritz. Like God spitting in her hair.

A few kids in hoodies hang out by the defunct tennis courts, leaning up against the chain-link fence. She gives one of them, a kid in big shoes sucking a lollipop, a nod. He nods back.

His name's Chase. He goes by Chizzy.

He's only thirteen, but he sells mad ice. She'll see him soon enough.

Soon she hears the river. The hushed rush of turbid water.

By the road, a line of oaks. A few leaves turning

yellow. Some are already on the ground. A few of them helicopter down to the pavement.

She tries not to slip. Wet asphalt and shitty sneakers make for such a hazard. That's what crystal does for her – makes her hyper-aware. Careful. Smart.

The bus stop at the corner isn't much to look at. Not a fancy Plexiglas one like those in the city but an always-moist moss-slick wooden box with ads on each side (plumber on one, funeral home on the other). It's splintering and fraying at the edges, the wood looking like the bristles of a broom.

No mother to be seen.

She hurries into the bus stop. Someone's there waiting for the bus. Some reedy stranger in a heavy coat. It's not yet cold enough for a heavy coat, but hey, it's a free country and people can wear whatever they want. He's just standing there, a floppy hat pulled low.

At her feet are torn pages soaked and sodden. Mailer inserts, a Penny Power, the yellow pages of... the Yellow Pages.

She asks the dude, "Did you see a... a woman here?"

"Mm? Hm-mmn. No."

"Short woman. Hair cut short. She would've pulled up in a..." What the hell is her mother driving these days? "Ford, I think. Blue Ford Focus." It's a nice car. Annie wishes she could have a car like that.

"I said *no*."

Okay. Whatever. Thanks for the help, asshole.

She steps out into the spitting, pissing rain again and looks left and right down the road. Nothing. No parked cars. No mother. She was either here and bailed or she's late.

Mom's never late.

She hears a scuff behind her – the man moving, his shoe on the ruined pages of forgotten publications.

But then she hears something else: her mother's voice, whispering behind her.

"Wicked Annie."

She's about to turn around, but–

Something heavy clubs the back of her head, and the world goes pitching forward into a dark hole. For a moment Annie blinks and finds herself on her hands and knees on the ground, a yellowing leaf crawling in front of her like a crab, swept that way on a brief and sudden wind.

Another blow strikes the back of her head.

It's lights out for Annie Valentine.

TWENTY-EIGHT
TROJAN HORSE

Rain – more a steady mist than an actual rain – collects on a windshield already streaked with pollen. The wiper blades do a fine job smearing it all.

Miriam asks Katey about the two girls. Katey knows the black girl with the frizzy electrostatic hair. Tavena White is her name. Her mother's a drunk and on welfare. Daddy is long gone to jail for running a chop shop out of Scranton.

"I think it's funny when black people have the last name White," Miriam says. Katey gives her a look. "What, that's not racist. That's just *appreciative of irony*. And see, it's doubly ironic because..."

Wait for it. *Wait* for it.

"Miriam Black," Katey says.

"Bingo, bango, bongos-in-the-Congo."

I'm sure when Tavena gets her head chopped off she'll think this is funny, too.

A chill crawls up Miriam's spine. A parade of baby spiders.

Ahead, the school.

The iron gates are open. Homer stands vigil over them. A car pulls in front of them, and Miriam sees whoever the staff member is flash an ID and go inside.

Katey pulls up next. Goes to flash her ID. Miriam gives Homer a flip little wave and then Katey's already pulling ahead.

Katey pulls the car into the teacher's lot. The first several rows are already full. Miriam figures some people have been here all night – this *is* a boarding school. A whole wing of girls is just waking up. The school must have persistent staff. Cleaning, overnight guards, that nurse lady.

"I told you," Katey says, easing the car into a spot. "I can take the note to the girls."

"Uh-huh. And if you get caught, you get fired, and you get fired, then that's on me. Nah. It's early. I can sneak around here pretty good, I figure."

Katey turns to her. "It's good you want to help these girls. Once we let them leave, they're on their own. We have college placement and job placement and some of them do really well. Most of them, probably. But not all of them. Some fall back into bad habits. Or go back to their terrible families. Drugs. Prostitution. Petty crime. Nothing we can do about it. Especially once they turn eighteen, because we can't keep them here after that. You'd be amazed at how many just … disappear."

"Disappear."

"Sure. Hightail it to the cities, I guess. Harrisburg. Pittsburgh. Maybe Allentown or Philly. You hear a lot of girls talking about New York."

Girls disappearing at age eighteen, Miriam thinks. *Or are they taken?*

An oily black feather tickles the back of her brain. Are there more than two? Are Tavena and Wren just the start? Or part of a far longer and fucked-up pattern?

More chills. More baby spiders.

Nothing to be done about that now.

"I need money," she tells Katey.

"What? Oh."

"Cab fare. Or bus fare."

The teacher hands her two twenties. "That good?"

"That'll do me." She pauses. "You know, once upon a time, I would find someone like you and I'd just… wait. Till the cancer takes you. And then I'd rob you. Credit cards, cash on hand. Maybe pawn your laptop."

"How do I know you're not doing that now? How do I know that everything you say isn't an outright lie?"

Miriam knows Katey asks the question but doesn't believe it – she's a fish with a hook in her mouth. It's just this time, the hook happens to be real.

But just the same, no good answer is forthcoming. All she can do is shrug.

INTERLUDE
ECSTASY

Rich boy. Club kid. Dead man.

He coughs. Blood bubbles onto his lip. His right hand finds Miriam's knee. His left idly paws at a slush puddle in which a dirty Chinese food container floats.

His name is Nick. He lies there in the alley, staring up at her.

"Where were you?" he asks. Each word punctuated by the wet smack of bloody lips.

"I decided to be somewhere else," she says. Petting his hair.

"They came out of nowhere."

"I know."

"They robbed me."

"I know."

He's got the eyes of a car-struck rabbit. Wet and scared. "They took my phone. They took my, my, my watch. They took my *money*, and I didn't even get the E. They didn't even have any pills." He pops the P in pills. Flecks of blood dot Miriam's cheek.

She doesn't wipe it away. Seems rude.

"They didn't take your shoess" she says.

"You gotta call the hospital."

Miriam gnaws on the inside of her cheek while stroking his. "It's not going to help, Nick. You're not going to make it." He reaches for her but she pulls away and hunkers down by his feet, lifting his right leg up at the calf.

"Whaddya mean? I– I– I'm not even in pain. I'm just cold."

"That's because you're lying in a slush puddle. Take it as a blessing. It's numbing the wound." She pops the shoe – an expensive Nike sneaker – off his foot. She's surprised the thugs didn't jack his shoes. Surprised without being surprised She knew this was how it happened when she first met Nick and made out with him to shitty dubstep music two weeks back at that club.

"I'm okay. I'll get up and show up. I'll get up. You'll see."

He tries but can barely lift his head.

"The knife hit your kidney. Which is pretty bad but fixable. The real problem is the artery. You're going to bleed out."

"What? How do you know that?"

"Because I know, Nick. I just know. I've known this whole time." She says it and wishes suddenly that she didn't because now he sees who she really is.

"Why didn't y-y-you do something? I needn't need to score E tonight. You coulda told me. You coulda stopped me."

Inside his shoe she finds the two credit cards. They may have stolen his cash but the real wealth is here.

Daddy's credit cards. Nick has no leash, and Daddy has deep pockets.

"I couldn't have stopped you," she says, crawling back over to him. "That's the thing, Nick. I've tried. And it always sucks because I just make it worse. I could have told you what I knew and you wouldn't have believed me. I could have handcuffed you to a radiator and you would have gotten away. I could have bashed you over the head with a toaster and I would have missed and you would have run fast as you could and you would have run right here into this alley and those dealers would have still shanked you in the back."

"You're a monster," he says. Like a petulant little boy, he adds, "I hate you."

"I know you hate me. I would too. But I'm not a monster, Nick. I'm just the monster's cleanup crew. Sorry it went like this. Thanks for the good times. You were sweet."

She kisses his cheek as his body starts to shake like a haunted séance table, blood pooling beneath him into the slushy pothole.

TWENTY-NINE
DEAR DEAD GIRLS

The school at morning is quiet. The building settles here and there – a pop, a squeak, a banging pipe behind the walls. And the wood beneath Miriam's feet creaks and groans even when she's walking on the dusty old rugs that line the floors.

Filmy gray light, fractured by rain, comes in through the windows, dim and watery. For some reason it calls to Miriam's mind a feeling of drowning.

Hair dyed with river water. Capillaries burst in yellow eyes.

Motes of dust drift in the pillars of wan light.

The girls' cubbyholes are labeled: not with swatches of tape but rather with little plaques screwed to the wood, a name engraved on each.

The school has only five hundred girls across seven grades (sixth through twelfth), but that's still five hundred cubbyholes – culminating in what looks like a big version of a wine rack, the holes turned on their sides like empty diamonds.

She would have to look through them all. That is, if

Katey didn't tell her where to look. *Good having an ally on the inside.*

First, drop off the note to Wren. Then, Tavena White.

Miriam floats along the cubbyholes like a nervous hummingbird.

"Elizabeth Hope. Gwen Shawcatch. Trisha Barnes." No, no, no. "Molly Deerfield, Carla Rodriguez, Becky, Nellie, Lakeesha, Cristina–"

And then she sees it. Lauren Martin.

She squats down, slides the note into the hole.

Behind her, someone clears his throat.

Oh, goddamnit.

Miriam turns.

She sees Beck Daniels standing there. Jeans and a black V-neck T-shirt. His lips forming a firm line across that prodigious jaw.

I could swing on that jaw like it was a jungle gym.

"I know you," he says.

"'Sup, Ninja Warrior?"

"Find anything interesting in the girls' cubbyholes?"

"That's an awfully dirty question."

Beck remains unflustered. "You should probably get away from those."

"I'm just leaving a note. For my sister."

"Uh-huh. That train has left the station, Miss Black."

She stands up. Crosses her arms. "Oh. Right."

"Mind telling me what you're doing here?"

"The sister part was a lie, but the note part is on the nose. I want to talk to Wren Martin. Just one more time." *And Tavena White,* but no need to give that away. "Hey, give me a heads up: Did you call five-oh on me again?"

"You mean the guards."

"I mean Doctor Steroids and his Italian plumber porn-star buddy."

"Sims and Horvath. Respectively."

"No respect here, chief."

Is that a smile? "No, I didn't call them. Seems the other day you did a pretty good number on Sims – I watched the security footage. Pretty impressive."

"It was." She winks. "Still. I'm kinda busted here, aren't I? You gonna haul me off to the hoosegow yourself?"

"Hoosegow?"

"It's a word. Means prison."

"I know what it means."

"What? Don't you like words? I like words."

"Good for you. No, I'm not going to haul you in."

"You could call the real police. I'm a little surprised nobody called them the other day. Especially if there's video footage of my little cafeteria romp."

He shrugs. Gets closer to her. Just one step but the threat is there just the same. An exciting threat. A threat Miriam likes.

"We don't bring the cops around here if we can avoid it. Some of these girls have seen far too many cops. We don't want to disrupt the progress we're making with the more troubled ones. So no, I won't call the police. Not as long as you tell me why you're leaving a note. Why do you want to talk to her? What's your deal? Why you're so fascinated with her to begin with."

Slowly, Miriam begins to pace to the right. He moves to the left. They're circling some unseen point, some maypole to which they're both invisibly tethered.

"I'm trying to protect her."

"Protect her? From what?"

"You wouldn't believe me if I told you."

"Try me."

"Not in a million years, Kung Pao chicken."

Circling, circling. Moths around a light. Blood down a drain.

"I like to think I'm her protector," he says. "Not you. Me. And the other teachers here. We're the ones who watch over these girls."

"You're doing a shit job."

That stings him. He folds in a little bit. Like an invisible hand just popped him in the gut. Surprising. And strange. Is he really so committed?

"Tell you what," he says. "I saw the footage. You got some moves. Let's go to the gymnasium. We'll spar a little. You beat me, I'll let you go, won't ask any questions."

"And if *you* beat *me*? Which, by the way, won't happen."

"Then I call the police."

"Deal." She thinks, *No deal, dummy. What are we, two gentlemen about to duel?* Honor doesn't mean a sack of slippery dicks to Miriam Black. It's just a nonsense idea people made up. Honor. It calls to mind an old drinking toast–

Here's to honor–

clink

–get on her, and stay on her.

And then wrap her mouth in barbed wire and cut out her wagging tongue.

Her hands coil to fists.

"You okay?" he says. "You look like you saw a ghost."

"Quit your jawing," she says. "Let's do this."

THIRTY
F-BOMBS

The gymnasium is one big echo. Every footfall on the blue mat. Every shift in stance. Every sniff, knuckle-pop, and lip-smack.

Beck goes to bow – steeples his hands into little Buddhist temples and then bends slowly at his waist. But Miriam doesn't have time to fuck around.

As he bows, she kicks him in the head.

Her black boot connects with the side of his skull, and he staggers left.

But he doesn't go down, and he doesn't lose his focus on her. He just shakes himself off. Begins roving left and right, like a boxer – or like a cobra rearing up to strike.

Screw you, sensei – go ahead and be the cobra.

I'll be the motherfucking mongoose.

"Gonna be like that, huh?" he asks, licking his teeth.

"Gonna be like that."

"Let's see your next move, then."

No time like the present. She steps in and fires off a straight punch. But he's already ducking it, and grabbing her wrist–

Twenty years from now. Beck Daniels. Hair shorn to the scalp, salt-and-pepper. He's lost weight. Leaner. Meaner. Tougher and tighter like corded, braided leather. He looks around his office. Plaques and pictures, medals and cups, all signs of championships won – his girls, out there, fighting the good fight. One picture – him twenty years back, cheering on one of his girls at the moment she pops a kick into the dead center of an opponent's chest. Next to the picture, the wall is dented, as though by an elbow.

–and kicking his knee up into her gut, hard but not so hard she loses air or barfs up her coffee-and-cigarettes breakfast. As she's bent over his knee, he shoves her forward and downward until she's flipping over onto her back–

He pulls up a rolling desk chair, sits. Opens his lower desk drawer, pulls out a stack of yearbooks from the last dozen years. The yearbooks are slim and leather-bound, with the Caldecott crest on the front. He opens them, begins to look upon the girls there. A knot in his throat. A heartbeat drumming faster.

–and he moves in for the kill. He strides above her like the Colossus. But he's still got honor flashing in his eyes. So she punches up. Straight into his balls–

He sets the yearbook down. Rubs his eyes. Tilts his head back and takes a long cleansing breath through his nose.

–but he turns just so and takes the punch to the outside of his thigh. Again he grabs her wrist, and this time turns it and sees the swallow carved into her hand, the scabs broken, trickling blood, and–

Beck Daniels now opens the middle drawer of his desk and withdraws from within a .45 M1911 pistol with the serial numbers filed off. The pistol is tarnished and dotted with canker sores of red rust. He pops the clip. Checks it for bullets – a new .45 slug rests comfortably at the top, gleaming brass catching the light. He pops it back in.

–he hauls her to her feet the way a child tosses a sock monkey. She twists free, swings for his head. He ducks. Normally she'd fight dirty, real dirty, *double* dirty, throwing sand and feeling around for a golf club in the weeds. But here those options do not exist and so she goes for a four-finger jab against his throat with her now-bloody hand. But his chin tilts down to block the thrust, and before she knows it, he's got his leg behind hers like a gaff hook and he's dropping her to the mat once more and–

The gun tastes like pennies; the sight scratches the roof of his mouth. Footsteps sound outside his office door, someone knocks, and BANG. Brains like black pudding splattering out of an open blender hit a plaque behind him hard enough that the plaque shakes as his body falls off the chair.

–he's got her on the ground. She bows her leg and smashes the bottom of her boot into his cheek, turning him over so now *she's* the one on top. But that doesn't last, oh no, he traps her with his legs and rolls hard to the right until she's again beneath him, and he pins her there.

And before she knows what's happening, his lips find hers, and her tongue is crawling around inside his mouth like a mouse looking for cheese. His hands are under her shirt. Her hands are tucking into his pants, hiking them down.

Everything is hunger and fire and the distant echo of gunshots and the warm and wonderful (and more than a little sickening) collision of kindred spirits, damaged and weak, finding each other for a brief time.

They tumble into his office. Above their heads, the fluorescent lights buzz like three bees trapped in a jar.

It's different, but the same.

Fewer plaques, pictures, awards. That collection is just getting started.

The desk is neater.

The room is cleaner.

He picks her up by her hips and drops her down on the desk. Her knee goes between his legs, but this time it's not a kick – it's just pressure and heat and *intent.*

She lifts his shirt up over his chest. The muscles there are like the rungs in a ladder – it feels like she could climb them.

His hands press against the sides of her head. He pulls her close.

A hard shove and he staggers back. Smiling. Licking his teeth again.

"That's my job," she hisses, then licks his teeth for him. Her hand dips past the hem of his pants, deeper down until she gets a fist around his cock. He whirls her around and she slams into the wall, her elbow hitting the drywall, rattling a framed picture–

(Him twenty years back cheering on one of his girls at the moment she pops a kick into the dead center of an opponent's chest. Next to the picture, the wall is dented, as though by an elbow.)

Worlds collide. Alarms go off. Klaxons. *Awooga, awooga*.

The office isn't an office anymore. It's a tomb.

Phantom blood on the wall.

Brains, black and dead, on a plaque.

An echoing gunshot.

The smell of spent powder invisible yet present, like a ghost.

None of it real. Not today. Not for twenty years.

He's damaged goods. Death by suicide. She pictures herself splayed across his desk, face up, shirt pulled so that her tits are out, legs hanging over the side and a pair of panties dangling from her big toe.

Death has settled into this room like birds in the eaves and, once again, it only serves to get her hotter. It feels like a brushfire that wants to eat and eat and eat, fires seeking other fires.

Beck hoists her up, her legs wrap around his hips, and he starts to take her shirt off. But then she sees–

Behind him stand three ghosts.

Louis with his eyepatch flipped up, a greasy blackbird's head sticking out of the ruined socket.

Lauren Martin, her head tilted back too far, the wound in her throat tattered and fringed, air gurgling and blood bubbles popping.

And Beck Daniels himself. In twenty years. Age fifty. The back of his head a blooming flower with petals of shattered skull and oxidizing brains in the middle.

Miriam squirms out of Beck's – the *real* Beck's – grip.

No.

He thinks it's part of the game and he reaches for her again, but she pulls away. He catches her wrist. She resists. He still thinks she's playing, but she's not. She tries to pull away, but he's strong–

No! Miriam backs up against the desk. She uses it to stabilize herself and then kicks hard with both feet into his chest, knocking him backward. A few manila folders tumble off a black metal file cabinet, their contents sliding across the floor.

"I don't get it," he says.

"I can't."

I want to.

But Louis…

Wren.

Tavena.

"Why not?"

"I have work to do."

"You work around here?"

"Nnnn – yes." It's easier than explaining what she means. "I'm running late."

"Oh." He's crestfallen. "Oh. Of course. The first bell's soon, so… I should call you." He says it like he's not sure.

"You should." Not that she's going to give him her number.

"Is your… hand okay?" The blood is drying again.

"It's all good in the hood."

"It's a bird, isn't it."

"A swallow."

He goes pale. Like he suddenly realizes who she really is. "Of course."

Nothing more to be said. She pulls her shirt down, re-buttons her jeans, and quietly removes herself.

THIRTY-ONE
BLACK & WHITE

Miriam feels off-balance from what just happened with Beck Daniels. Like she's still fighting him, still getting thrown to the mat, still almost fucking him.

By the time she makes it upstairs to find Tavena White's cubbyhole, the girls have started to spill out of the dormitory wing to get ready for class.

There, by the water fountain, is Tavena White.

Hair still an inky scribble. Eyes big and expressive.

Talking to a group of friends.

Miriam doesn't know why she's nervous. Shades of her own school experience haunting her at an inopportune moment.

She walks up to Tavena.

"Hey," she says. Waving her little folded-up note like it's supposed to mean something.

"Uh, hey," Tavena says, and the other girls all give her the stink-eye. Realization blooms then in Tavena's eyes. "You're that woman from the cafeteria."

"Nah, must've been someone else." Miriam tries to hand her the note. "Here. I wanted to give this to you."

But Tavena doesn't take it. She and the other three girls pull away. Miriam sees that she's trying to give the girl a note with her bloody hand. Oops.

Tavena starts looking around like she needs someone to rescue her.

"Just take the note," Miriam says, forcing a smile and a chirpy laugh. "This isn't a stranger-danger moment. I'm just a friend passing along a message. That's not blood on my hand. That's paint. It's paint. Just paint."

Tavena's eyes flash like pennies. "My mom always told me, don't talk to strange white women."

"Your mother knows of what she speaks. Good think I'm one-sixteenth Cherokee," Miriam lies. "Here, I just need you to have this note–"

Tavena sees someone behind Miriam. "Miss Caldecott, Miss Caldecott–"

Miriam turns. Sees the school nurse approaching, hands clasped at her front.

"You little snitch," Miriam grumbles.

"Miss Black, isn't it?" the nurse asks. "Here I hoped we wouldn't have to meet again."

"What can I say? I'm like a cold sore. I just keep popping up."

"Run along, girls."

Tavena and the others high-tail it. With Miriam still holding the note. *Damn.*

"Can I go too?" Miriam asks.

"I'm beginning to grow concerned over your fascination with our girls."

"Nothing to worry about. I'm harmless."

"First I see you bothering Lauren Martin. And

now Tavena White. Is there something you'd like to talk about?"

Miriam says nothing.

"Your hand is bleeding. We could go down to the nurse's station. I could take a look at it for you."

"So you can call the cops on me while I wait? I don't think so." Miriam starts backing away, confident this old woman can't take her. "Nice school you have here. But I gotta run."

"There will be trouble if you come back," Caldecott says.

"I won't," Miriam lies. "Cross my heart, hope to die."

She even makes the motion – two swipes of the finger over her breastbone.

Besides, she has some work to do.

THIRTY-TWO
AS THE SWALLOW FLIES

In any town, in any city, the bus is like the filter in a filthy swimming pool: It catches the dregs, the rotten leaves, the dead toads, the used rubbers. This one's no different. The guy at the front smells like piss and Doritos. He's dressed in the latest *hobo chic*, though whether he's homeless or just a incontinent hipster is unclear.

Then there's the emo kid with more metal than face: He doesn't just look stoned, he looks like he stood under a drug bomb, a real bunker buster, and took the entire blast right to his slack-jawed, hazy-gazed face.

Behind him, the doofy dude in the side-cocked trucker hat who must have taken a bath in Drakkar Noir. He bobs his head to music nobody else can hear.

Across from him, a morbidly obese house-cow, her graying hair shoved under a shower cap like a tabby cat trapped in a plastic bag, talking on her cell phone *super-loud* about her Valtrex prescription.

And then Miriam.

Sitting in the back.

Earlier, after the school, she waited at the bus stop. Just making phone calls. Tattoo parlors and artists all over the tri-county area. From Bloomsburg all the way down to Harrisburg.

Every call, the same question: *You ever give someone a swallow tattoo?*

Turns out, the answer was yes. Dozens. *Hundreds*. The swallow tattoo? Hugely popular. Totally common. Sailor Jerry, they say. Ed Hardy. Suddenly it's not a needle in a haystack: It's a needle in a basket of needles. Shit.

She tried to describe it.

She told them it was plain. Nothing fancy. Mostly just the shape of the bird – like a silhouette with the eye cut out. Inked on a man's chest. Not above some girl's tit. Not on some flabby bicep.

No, they said. Nothing like that.

But then she talked to Bryan. Guy who ran a joint called Ink Monkey. He said he'd done some like that. Real simple. He echoed her words: *nothing fancy*.

She hung up with him.

Then she got on the bus.

The thing is, this guy's tattoo studio is in a town called Ash Creek.

Miriam knows that town. Because it's where she grew up. Or, rather, just outside of it – but Ash Creek was their mailing address.

That's why everything's starting to look familiar.

The bus drives past an old farm stand, The Honey Hole! She knows that stand. She used to walk there sometimes – she'd bring a buck, drop it into the box, and take a few honey sticks.

The stand was once brick red, red like a freshly painted barn. Now it's got a rotten cock-eyed lean. Paint's peeling and most of the color is gone. The letters of the sign have faded. Now it just says, *he Honey Ho.*

Get your head in the game, Black.

The feeling inside is tight, like her internal organs have been cinched up in a series of binding knots. A breeding ball of snakes.

Someone tries to sit next to her. The bus hasn't even stopped but someone's jostling for a new seat. Skinny bitch. Probably forty, looks sixty. Crazy cat lady. Or maybe an art teacher. Or both. Big earrings. Tie-dye frock.

Miriam flicks open her spring-loaded blade, begins using it to pick at her fingernails – makes sure the woman sees what she's doing before planting roots. Miriam adds, "If any part of you touches me, I'll cut it off."

Skinny Bitch hovers but doesn't sit. She flees to find another empty space.

Outside, everything's coming together. She knows these trees. These mailboxes. Close now.

"No, no, no," she tells herself. "Don't you even think about it."

But she's thinking about it.

Not just thinking about it. *Doing* it.

In the battle of fate versus free will, she's not sure who's doing what or whose side she's even on; all she knows is she's standing up.

Reaching up.

Grabbing the emergency brake cord.

And giving it a hard yank.

The bus brakes. Everyone lurches forward.

Don't do this, don't do this, don't do this.

She walks to the front. The bus driver is looking at her like she's got a third eye, one arm, a pair of tits on her chin: freak, mutant, disruptor.

Just sit back down, you stupid twat.

"I need to get off," she says.

"What?" the bus driver, a big black dude with liver spots on his shorn head, says.

"Open the fucking door!" the hipster-hobo with the piss-and-nachos scent shout-mumbles.

Miriam scowls. "You heard the... whatever that guy is."

The door hisses open.

And Miriam steps out into the rain.

THIRTY-THREE
DARK HOLLOW

Dark Hollow Road.

A long, single-lane road. Halfway down, it turns to gravel.

Miriam stands at its mouth. Staring down its length she sees a long asphalt tongue pitted with holes and plastered with leaves, the trees bending over it like they're trying to smother it, rip it apart, erase it from the world. From here she can't see any homes – this never was a road with many people on it – but she'll see them soon enough, old farmhouses like hard white teeth, windows like eyes, all ready to swallow her up and spit her out.

The rain has upgraded itself – no longer a curtain of mist, it's leveled up into a deluge. Wouldn't be the first time she's looked like a soggy dog.

As she walks, she hears footsteps to one side or the other.

Leaves, usually. Falling. Scraping across the ground in the wind before finally being pinned to the road by rain.

Another time it's just a squirrel: a gray flash of fur across open ground and up a tree. Shaking his tail at her as though to threaten her, or warn other squirrels away.

Then she looks and there he walks. Hands stuffed in his pockets.

Ben Hodges. The back of his head blown out, a red gummy crater. Skull bone like a broken cereal bowl.

"No bird picking at your brains this time," she says, speaking over the shushing rain. A small act of defiance.

"I don't know what you're talking about," he says, but then he smiles. And it's Ben's smile through-and-through. It's like an arrow through her chest, the shaft broken off at the breastbone so the pointed tip stays forever lodged. "Oh, don't look so sad. It's not your fault I killed myself. Not *all* your fault, anyway."

Her jaw locks. "Don't fucking pretend you're really him. You're not."

Another smile. "No, I suppose I'm not."

"So. What now? Why are you here on this perfectly lovely not-yet-autumnal day?" As though to answer her compliment, the sky grumbles with distant thunder – like the sound of a tractor trailer bounding over a bump in the interstate. "You here to kick my ass again? Break a coffee table? Carve another bird into my other hand?"

"Nah, I just thought you looked lonely. You're so close now. But this going home thing, it's just a distraction. Why bother?"

"Fuck you. I want to."

"Do you?"

She doesn't answer. She doesn't know.

"You know, you could just tell me what to do." She hurries in front of him, walks backward as he walks forward. She offers him an open palm. "Put a name in my hand. On a slip of paper. Give me the address, since you're Mister All-Knowing Trespasser. Point me towards the killer and I'll go give him a stern talking-to."

"Talking won't do it. And I don't have a pen. Or paper."

He smiles. Now she sees the worms winding between his teeth.

In her head, the cries of a whimpering infant.

Another arrow in her heart.

"So *manifest* one," she snarls. "You're not real anyway. Reach into your gooey brain pocket and pull one out. Or have a bird bring it to you."

"Doesn't work like that. I don't know any more than you do."

"You lie."

He shrugs. "Do I?"

Fuck it. She takes a swing for him – but her fist finds open air. She hears the rustling and flapping of wings, as though a whole flight of birds just took off – and the sound grows louder and louder until it's a deafening roar – and yet she sees no birds, no birds at all. She spins, looks up, looks around, but all that's here is the rain and the leaves and yet that noise won't stop, and her ears are ringing and–

It stops. Gone. The sound doesn't fade away – it just hits a wall.

And when she turns around, she sees where she is.

She's home.

Jesus, the house looks like hell.

It's an old farmhouse – a narrow two-story stone home, the outside with four corners but the inside with countless more, all tight channels and odd turns and what Miriam used to call little gnome doors.

Once upon a time her mother kept the place impeccable – come autumn she'd have pumpkins and gourds on the front stone steps; she'd have mums in all colors potted in baskets. Birds would play at the feeder. The shutters might get a fresh coat of paint. Everything in its place. A speck of rogue pollen would hit the ground and there would come Mother with a pair of tweezers, ready to pluck the invading tree-sperm from her immaculately groomed property.

It's an exaggeration. But only barely.

Now, though…

No flowers, no feeder, no mums. No pumpkins, no gourds, no nothing. The shutters don't look like they've seen a coat of paint in years. A couple of them hang from their moorings below the windows to which they belong.

The stone steps are crumbling around the edges. A few pots sit off to the side, all broken and cracked.

Weeds have claimed this place for their kingdom. Agents of entropy, these plants – committing a tireless assault on this old house, breaking the stone walkway, creeping up through cracks in the steps and slowly but inevitably widening the fissures. Fingers of ivy threaten to pull the place down. Not now, not soon, but one day.

Gutters, rusted. Stuffed with leaves and nests.

One window, cracked.

The mailbox, a downward-facing dog. Sad Snoopy nose pointed toward the earth.

In fact, the whole building seems to have a slight lean to it. As though it's creeping toward collapse, toward what passes for a house and home's demise.

Miriam thinks, *Just walk away. Now you've seen. Now you know.*

But there's more to know isn't there?

Just another ten feet to get onto the porch. A simple knock would suffice.

You can see your mother again.

And that's the problem.

Does she want to? Is she ready? Will it be worht it?

The phone rings. Katey's cell.

A blocked number.

Fuck it. She answers.

"Hey, Mom," says the voice on the other line.

"Wren?" she asks.

"I got your note."

"Did the note say to call me Mom? Because that's fucking creepy, little girl."

"No, but I told them I was calling my mom and that's how I got phone privileges. It's fine, they're not listening anymore. I won't call you Mom again. Jesus."

"Good."

"So what do you want, psycho?"

Miriam stares at the house. Did she just see the curtains move? No. Maybe. Not sure. "I want to save your life."

"This again. Where are you?"

"What? Uh. Standing outside my old house. My mother's house, ironically."

"I thought you didn't like your mommy."

"I don't. I didn't. I dunno. I haven't seen her in years."

The girl pauses. "That's sad."

"Maybe. Maybe it's a good thing, though. I'm not good for her. She's not good for me. Why go through life with that kind of stored-up conflict?"

"Just the same, I'd love to see my mom. I kinda hate her. But I want to see her."

"Good luck with that."

"Thanks." A long inhale. "So are you really psychic?"

"You bet."

"Prove it. What am I wearing?"

"What are you, a phone sex operator?" Miriam says. "Besides, that one's a slow-pitch softball. You're wearing your school uniform."

"Oh. Yeah. Duh. Okay, then. What am I holding?"

"I dunno. Teddy bear? Dead squirrel? Soup can full of human teeth? It doesn't work like that. My voodoo is about one thing and one thing only. Death. I see how people are going to die and that's it. Game over."

Wren *hrms*. "That sounds like a sad life."

"Well, it is, thanks for bringing it up. Guess I'll just go and find some toxic mushrooms in the woods and eat enough to kill me. And then my corpse will be raped and eaten by bears."

"That's a real nice thing to say to a young girl. Filling

my impressionable head with images of non-consensual ursine love-making."

"Ursine. Good word."

"Thanks. So cut to the chase, psycho."

"Psy*chic*."

"Uh-huh, whatevs. Why did you want to talk to me?"

"I just want to tell you to keep your eyes out. The killer – he's not coming for you now, but I think he kills other girls before you. And who knows: Maybe he's out there watching you already. Maybe it's someone you know. Just... let me know if you see anything weird."

"This whole place is weird."

"Yeah, I know."

"Did you know the school nurse actually owns the place?"

"I did know that."

"Also, there's a catfish in the river. Big enough to eat a person. Or at least a child. Some people say it's just a rogue manatee from Florida, though."

"I'm pretty sure none of this is what I'm talking about, nor do I believe it to be true. Just do as I ask and keep your eyes peeled. Okay? Call me if you see anything."

"Fine. Whatever, *psycho*."

"I hate you so bad, little girl."

"Sure you do. That's why you keep crawling up my butt. Say hi to your mommy."

Miriam starts in with, "You can't tell me what to do–"

But the girl hangs up.

What a little bitch.

Again, Miriam's left alone with the house. The rotten house. The ruined house. Has her mother gone rotten? Is she ruined, too?

Say hi to your mommy!

You can't tell me what to do.

And with that, she turns and walks away. Walks back to the road.

Turns right.

And keeps going.

Not today, she thinks, *not today.*

But behind her, she hears a click and a squeak as the front door opens.

A voice calls after her.

"Hey! Who's that?"

A male voice.

Huh.

She turns, squints, holding up an impromptu visor made of her flattened hand to keep the rain out. A man stands in the doorway of her childhood home, wearing a ratty white T-shirt and a pair of pin-striped boxers. He's got a bowl of cereal in his hand. A scraggly goatee collects milk. He's older. Mid-fifties, maybe.

Miriam creeps back toward the house.

The dude holds the spoon like it's a shiv.

It's then that she recognizes him.

"Do I know you?" he says, scrunching up his face and pointing with the utensil. More milk drips from his beard, and he drags the back of his wrist across it. "You look familiar."

"Hey, Uncle Jack," Miriam says. Gives a little wave.

"Oh." Blink, blink. "Miriam. Look at you"

"Yeah. Look at me."

"You, uh, here for your mom?"

I don't know. "Sure."

He frowns then. Shrugs. "Well, come on in, I guess."

THIRTY-FOUR

WHAT HAPPENED TO MOTHER

It almost breaks Miriam's heart.

She's not a neat freak. But her mother was. And here the house sits, rundown. Filthy. A place pigs wouldn't be comfortable calling home.

Right off the front door, the kitchen is a holy terror. Bowls and plates stacked up. Food dried onto Formica countertops. A dirty microwave – the same microwave Miriam grew up with – with the clock blinking 12:00. Empty cans, *dog food* cans, and she thinks, *Oh, god, Uncle Jack is eating Alpo.*

But just then a little dust-mop dog scurries up, claws clicking and sliding on the wooden floor – pink tongue obsessively licking Miriam's boot.

Uncle Jack nudges the dog with his callused big toe. "Go on, Pookie, get out, leave her alone. I said, go on!"

The dog paws scrabble on the floor, get traction, and the beast shimmies away.

"Come on, then." Jack waves Miriam in.

The smell of the place matches the look. Mold, must, dust, dog, and an underlying layer of–

Oh, god, Mother.

Death.

It's that faint piss and shit smell. And the deodorizer spray used to cover it up. The smell of hospitals and nursing homes. Miriam's smelled that hundreds of times in visions. She knows the odor intimately and it's here, now, not in a vision but right in front of her. She feels woozy.

Jack plods into the living room, collapses into a puffy blue second-hand recliner that wasn't there ten years ago, and begins finishing his cereal – Fruity Pebbles or some cheap facsimile – in earnest.

Water stains on the ceiling. Paintings hanging askew.

Their old TV in the corner, and atop it, a smaller flat screen using the dead box as a base.

"Just tell me," she says. "How did Mother... go?"

He narrows his eyes. Studies her while slurping milk. "How'd you know?"

"I can smell it."

"Yeah? Oh. Well. Uh. One day she just up and left us. You of all people know how that is."

You of all people.

"But how did it happen?"

He snorts, and she hears a snot gurgle in his sinuses. "Jeez, well, I don't know the mechanics of it. I just know that one day she made a decision and that was that."

A decision.

Suicide? A do-not-resuscitate?

"Was she sick?"

"I'd say so." He seems angry. "I still don't understand it."

"Christ, Jack, stop dancing around it. How did she go?"

"I don't know!" he says, suddenly flustered. "Bus, I guess? And then, damn, I guess a plane? I think it was a plane. Not my business how she travels."

"Bus. Plane. Travels?" Miriam pictures the Grim Reaper flying the friendly skies, jauntily tipping his captain's hat and adjusting his shiny bat-wings pin. "Jumping fucking Jesus, what are you talking about?"

"Your mother. How she got to Florida."

"Flor... fucking Florida?"

"Man, you ended up with a pretty sour mouth, young lady."

"Shut the fuck up, Uncle Jack. You're saying she's in Florida. Not dead."

He looks at her like she's got some kind of brain disorder. "Yeah, that's what I'm saying." He laughs. "You thought she was dead? That's funny. Nah, she just high-tailed it down south."

"Why didn't you just *say* that?"

"I thought you knew! You said you knew. That you could... smell it." He wrinkles his brow, noisily sips the dregs of colored sugar milk from the bowl. "Come to think of it, that was a pretty strange thing to say."

"Yeah, you think?" Miriam feels her internal organs slowly untwisting and realigning to their cardinal positions. "So what's with the smell in here?"

"What smell?"

That smell is him, isn't it? Him or the dog.

"Never mind. When did Mother go to Florida?"

"About... two years ago, I guess. Went down to help

build some new church and decided she wanted to stay."

Florida. Ugh. There goes the Grim Reaper again, except this time he's riding a jet ski along the coast. Swooping up old folks left and right with his reaper's blade. Fun and sun and skin cancer and colostomy bags.

It's hard to picture her mother there. That little walnut of a woman. Severe, like a kidney stone. Pale, too. Doesn't tan so much as blister.

Miriam tells herself she's happy that the reunion didn't happen. Not today, maybe not ever. But that curdled feeling – what's that about? Is that the stirred mud of disappointment clouding these waters? Disappointment over… what? She's not going to get to see Mommy Dearest? Mommy, who treated her like a second-class citizen every day up until she revealed she was pregnant?

"So," Jack says, setting the bowl down on a stack of hunting and fishing magazines. "How you been?"

"Delightful," Miriam growls, plucking a cigarette from a pack. "Can I?"

"Long as you give me one."

She flips a cigarette into his lap. He rescues it, and by the time he's got it between his hangdog lips, there she is with the lighter.

"Where you been?" he asks.

"Around."

"Been a long time since we've seen you."

"We? Come on. I saw you maybe once every couple years." *Whenever you needed money. Or a place to crash. Or to hide out from the cops.* Her pious mother, harboring a lawbreaker. The woman's excuses were always different. *God forgives.* Or, *that's what family does for one another, Miriam. We take care of each other even when it hurts us to do so, and you'd know that if you weren't so selfish.*

"Doesn't mean an uncle can't miss his niece."

"Quit it. You didn't miss me. Please."

"Well. Maybe not. Your mother did."

She shrugs. "I'm sure."

"Don't get the wrong idea about me. I've changed."

"People don't change, Uncle Jack. They just put a new face on old problems."

"That's awfully cynical for a young woman like you."

"And I'm usually so *rosy*."

He pulls out a crumpled tissue from his pocket, gives his nose a good blow. "I get it. What happened to you was some rough stuff. With that boy and the..." His voice trails off. "I'm just saying, I get why you took off. But you should've come back. Or called. Your poor mother got left holding the bag. You sucker-punched her and ran."

"Well!" Miriam chirps. "This has been super-fun. I'm going to go now."

She blows smoke, turns tail to leave.

Jack doesn't get up. "Uh-huh. Go on, run away again."

"I'm sorry. Did you just say what I think you said?" She wheels on him. "You got a lot of nerve, Guy-Who-Used-To-Steal-Cars-And-Hide-Them-In-Our-Garage. Oh! Remember that time we didn't see you for two years and then one day you drove drunk into that old oak tree *right across the street*? The power was out for days but did you hang around? If I recall, you stumbled out of the car and just… wandered off, like Moses out into the fucking desert. You were a bum then and, by the look of this fucking *midden heap* you live in, you're a bum now. I'll see you later, Jack. Tell Mother I said… well, tell her whatever you want."

Now she's really leaving. Stepping over that squirrely little froo-froo dog, striding through the doorway to the health hazard that passes for a kitchen.

Jack comes up out of his chair and follows hot on her heels.

"Oh, I'm bum, but what are you?" he's saying as he dogs her escape. "You don't look like you have a pot to piss in. Sure. Okay. I'm just a bum. I get that. I don't have shit. But that's not all my fault. I'm learning disabled. And I got depression issues. Give your damn uncle a break."

She stops in the doorway, turns to face him. Sees now just how haggard he looks: the hollow pits below his cheekbones, his sunken eyes, those teeth the color of tobacco spit. But she doesn't find pity stirring there. Only anger. Maybe it's for him. Maybe it's for someone else.

"Sorry you're both sad *and* stupid," she says. "But that's not my fault. I've got my shit under control, Jack. You know I used to think you were pretty cool? God knows why. Why don't you just tuck your little pity party between your legs and fuck-off back to your flea-bitten Barcalounger, yeah?"

"You got mean," he says.

"I got *honest*," she hisses. "All the bullshit was beaten out of me on a high school bathroom floor."

He reaches for her, but she pulls away.

She doesn't want to see how he dies. It's going to be a pathetic, meaningless demise. He'll probably leave a lit cigarette in his lap lying there in that chair, and he'll combust like a dried-out Christmas tree. Or maybe he'll hit his head on something and that dog will eat his face.

Miriam marches off.

"Why'd you come here anyway?" he calls after her, standing there barefoot on the front steps.

She doesn't bother answering him.

"Don't you at least want your mother's number? Or address?"

She keeps walking.

Because she has work to do.

THIRTY-FIVE
THINK INK

She walks the rest of the way. Down Dark Hollow. Back to the main road. The rain soaks her to the bone and beyond. It's another half-hour into Ash Creek, which even now isn't much more than a quadrant of streets with a stoplight at each of the four intersections. Not much else going on here. Plenty of cars. All of them passing through, passing by, leaving this town in the rearview.

As she did, years ago.

Some things look the same. The sausage-and-onions joint is still there. The ice cream parlor next to it is boarded up, the pink plywood cone hanging loose from the sign, the paint scraped away by the tireless assault of time. On the corner is the five-and-dime, and it's still called that, too. Benner's Five-And-Dime. Not that you can buy jack shit for fifteen cents anymore. Even a crusty gumball from the machine outside costs a quarter.

Other things have changed, though.

Pappy's Gas is now an Exxon.

The little park in the center of town is gone. Now it's a block of boxy little condos and townhomes.

Luberto's Brick Oven is now a Rite-Aid.

And where the Pepper Pot café once sat is now Ink Monkey Studios.

Miriam has to smile. Her mother would have pissed her pantaloons over that. A tattoo parlor? *My word.* Might as well construct the Tower of Babel and dare God to knock it over like a big ole Jenga game. A bazaar of sin and depravity. Get your umbrellas and your dinghies and a pair of lions because surely the next Deluge is fresh on its way!

She still can't believe her mother is in Florida. *Florida.* Land of the Mouse. Of the gator. Of Cubans and old people and cockroaches so big you could ride them to work.

Whatever.

She goes inside the tattoo joint. A charming little bell rings.

Ding-a-ling.

She expects dingy, grungy, industrial – low-lit, the smell of cigarettes and incense, maybe the stink of spilled beer. Something growly on a CD player.

But it's clean and bright. Polished Pergo floor. Shiny display case with T-shirts and bumper stickers and lighters all branded with the studio's logo.

Ugh.

Behind the counter, tat designs are on display: sugar skulls and dragons and American flags and faux-mystical Asian bullshit.

In the corner, a little box TV hangs bolted to the wall. playing local news.

A customer leans over the counter. A girl with Miriam's build. Powder-blue jeans pulling away from her pink blouse, showing off a whale tail that's the same pink as the streaks in Miriam's hair.

She's chatting with the dude on the other side, a young guy. His spiky hair is meant to look like he doesn't care, but it probably took him two hours to sculpt it with some kind of putty product. His earlobes hang low, shot through with a pair of fat-ass lug-nuts.

Between the two of them is an open book. Tattoo designs.

"I just don't know," the girl says. "This is my first tattoo. I want it to *matter*. I want it to *mean* something."

She flips the page as the guy nods knowingly.

Miriam rolls her eyes.

She scooches right up next to the girl, giving her a little hip-bump.

Miriam faux-giggles, then says, "Gee, sorry. *Ex-cuse-ay moi!* Oh, hey. Did you ever think about getting a butterfly? Or a unicorn? Or, *oh-my-god*, an Asian symbol that means 'butterfly landing on a unicorn's horn'?"

The girl blinks. She's not sure if this is a joke. Her gaze darts to the guy behind the counter, and she asks, "Do you do that?"

"Eh," he says, stymied. "Maybe?"

Miriam flicks the girl's nose–

She's a hundred years old. It's her birthday. Big cake. One candle, not a hundred, because Lord knows she won't have the wind to put out a hundred candles. Kids and the children of kids and others have gathered to celebrate and she leans back to build up a gusting breath in those old cheesecloth lungs and she moves to exhale and – a blood clot fires into her brain like a .22 bullet and the stroke kills her dead. And as she topples backward, her feet sticking up in the air like the witch who got crushed by Dorothy's house, a little blue butterfly – now stretched like an image spread across Silly Putty – decorates her ankle.

–and the girl recoils.

"Ow! Hey!"

"No, dummy, they don't have that. If you want your tattoo to mean something, you don't just come along and pick it out of a stupid book. You come in here knowing what you want. You slap down a design on the counter and you say, 'I want this fucking tiger sketched permanently on my ass-cheek because by golly, you know what? I *am* the eye of the tiger! I'm *ready* for the cream of the fight. And I'm rising up to the challenge of my rival'."

"Maybe I'm not ready."

The tattoo artist watches this unfold. Blasé and largely unaffected.

"You're *not* ready, dingbat. A tattoo is an expression of your inner self inked on your outer self. It's some deeply spiritual shit."

"Oh god, you're right. What tattoo did you get?"

"A pair of handlebars right over my booty-crack. So when a guy is plowing me from behind, he has something to fake-grab onto. Am I right?"

The girl looks horrified.

Miriam snaps her fingers. "If you're not going to get inked today, why don't you go get a fro-yo across the street."

"But they're all boarded up."

"Maybe you didn't hear me. I said, *fuck off.*"

The girl pales and hurries out of the store.

The dude behind the counter blinks. "That was interesting. You do realize she was a customer?"

"She'll be back. She gets a butterfly. Trust me. Oh, and you don't seriously have an Asian symbol that combines both butterflies *and* unicorns, right?"

"No. I don't think so."

"Good. Then we can continue. You Bryan?"

"I'm him. Why?"

Miriam wants to shake his hand but – she holds back. *Contain yourself, girl.*

"I called. About the swallow tat."

"Oh. Right. Here we go." He bends down, and with a grunt pulls out another book – this one a real mamma-jamma, stuffed to the gills with pages and pictures. "I take photos of all the ink I lay."

He starts flipping pages. Skeletons on motorcycles, names of wives and girlfriends, ivy around a bicep, the Devil's face on the inside of some chick's thigh.

He flips one page, and on it is a coil of barbed wire around some girl's wrist.

Miriam ill-suppresses a shudder.

Next several pages: swallow tattoos. Dozens of them. In pinks and blues, feathers like clouds, sweet eyes, many with banners in their beaks showing off names of loved ones. Bryan gets to the last page, taps a photo taped there. "Here."

The Champagne cork does not so much much *pop* off the bottle so much as it *thuds* dully against the floor.

"That's not it," she says. Shit.

This one's on some guy's bicep, for one. And while the forked tail and swooped wings are there, it's got way more going on: lots of detail in the feathers, in the eye. "This isn't right. The one I'm looking for is on a dude's chest. It's got roughly the same shape as this one, but less detail. Dude, it's like I said on the phone. Just a shape. The only detail's the eye, and even then, it's just a little round hole where the artist didn't ink."

"Nah. Sorry. This is the only one in the–"

The last word he says is "book," but the sound goes all distorted and wobbly, like someone's playing with knobs and levers in the sound booth that is Miriam's own head. She feels hot, and her vision tries to fold in on itself.

She takes a step backward, and it's then that she sees.

On the television in the upper corner of the room.

A girl's face. On the news.

A skull hovers over it. Mouth open. Streaks of blood from the sockets.

Everything snaps back to normal.

Bryan asks, "Is everything o–"

But she silences him with an index finger.

She listens. And watches.

"The girl, eighteen-year-old Annie Valentine, was seen being dragged into the back of a Type A school bus by a man in a hooded sweatshirt. The witness reported seeing blood on the girl's head."

"A school bus," she mumbles.

They show the picture again. It looks like a snapshot pulled off Facebook. Long, straight dark hair. Unexceptional face. The kind of girl you marry, not the kind of girl a guy dreams about. She looks drunk in the picture. She's holding up a plastic cup of something piss-colored. Bud or Coors or some other watery light beer.

The skull hovers, fading in and out.

Just like what she saw over Tavena White's face.

A sign. Like a road sign, pointing her toward her destination. But here her destination is bad mojo, a bridge out, a storm-swept river that's oh-so-hungry.

"No, no, no," Miriam says. It's happening. It's happening *now*. Not in two years. Now. Maybe it's been happening all along.

"What? You know that girl?"

"I… don't." But how can she say what she's thinking? The truth won't help her. (She hears Wren's voice in her mind: *Psy*-cho.) All she knows is, now she's on the clock. Maybe she was *always* on the clock, but two years is a pretty good stretch of time. But now a girl's been taken. She might already be dead.

Miriam can hear the ticking in her ear. And the rustle of wings.

"You seem awfully shaken over some girl you don't know."

Her skin itches. It feels like her teeth are vibrating inside her mouth. All the stresses of the day – her mother in Florida, Uncle Jack's bullshit, whatever-the-hell-happened with Beck, and now this – feel like a stiletto at the base of her neck, pressing harder and harder.

"You got like a… a computer around here?"

"What? Yeah."

"I need to use it."

"I'm sorry, it's private use only."

"I'll say it again, I need to use it."

"This isn't a library."

She reaches in her pocket, pulls out a crumpled twenty-dollar bill. Drops the little money boulder onto the counter. "That's my first offer. My second offer is going to be a lot less lucrative and a lot more of me flipping the fuck out. My advice is, twenty dollars in pocket is better than whatever you'll spend on me going apeshit here in your very nice, well-kept, well-lit store. What's a broken display case cost, anyway?"

He studies her. She wears her crazy, and he must be able to see it glowing there like a giant electric bug zapper. Snapping and crackling.

"Come on back," he says, warily scooping the twenty into his hand.

THIRTY-SIX

LORDS OF GOOGLE, HEAR MY PLAINTIVE CRIES

The computer is a laptop, and it sits on a little side-table next to a reclining hydraulic chair the color of oxblood. It has all the accoutrements next to it: the ink gun, swabs and swaddles, bottle of alcohol.

Bryan kicks over a small wheeled office chair and Miriam stares.

"Go ahead," he says.

"You sit. I want to pace."

"Seriously?"

"Serious as a pulmonary embolism. Which is, by the way, very serious. Now make the Google happen."

She stands, lets him sit. He clicks an icon, a browser-window pops up.

Google across it in colorful letters.

"What am I searching for?"

"School bus."

He shrugs, starts to type it in.

"No, wait. A... *type-A* school bus. I wanna know what that means."

He pulls up images of school buses. Then she gets it.

"It's a short bus," she says. "A tardcart."

"That's offensive."

"Oh, *sorry*, buttercup, I didn't mean to tap-dance on your sensitive demeanor. You want a balm or perhaps an unguent for your rashy vagina?"

"I'm trying to help you here. You're being very rude."

"*You're* being very rude," she retorts.

He turns toward her and stares. "My niece is mentally handicapped. She didn't ask to be. And she didn't ask to have bullies like you call her names she doesn't deserve. You could stand to be nicer."

"Oh. Fine. Yes. Sorry." She sees he doesn't believe her. "*Sorry*. I know. I'm abrasive. I'm a jerk. I am genuinely sorry. Can we just get back to the Googling, please?"

"What next?"

She thinks. The school bus in the vision – the vision in which Tavena is killed – could have been a Type-A. But that bus was burned out. "Look up 'bird mask'."

He does. Again, he pulls up a page of images.

Tweety Bird, Angry Birds, Mardi Gras masks–

"There!" She taps the screen.

Her finger pokes an image – a drawing – of a man in a long leather robe and a bird mask like the one in her visions.

Click.

"Plague doctor," Bryan reads. "Also called... let's see. Beak doctors."

"Because of that scary fucking mask."

"Looks like. The eyes of the mask were generally

glass. The beak has holes in it and was meant to serve as a kind of... medieval respirator."

She doesn't have to see the screen to know. "They put aromatics in there, didn't they? Dry flowers and whatever."

"Camphor. Bergamot oil. And yeah, roses and carnations."

Plague. Beak. Bird.

School bus.

Swallow tattoo.

"The swallow. Google that. Not just that – the tattoo. Google the tat."

"I don't need to Google the tat. I know the tat."

"What, do I need to buy you dinner? Didn't your mother ever teach you to share? Tell me what you know, Human Google"

"Okay. Uh. Used to be a sailor tat. Seamen used to get them–"

"I'm going to pretend you didn't say 'semen'."

"–and one of them was the swallow. Reason sailors got swallow tats was to show how many nautical miles they traveled. Like, for every swallow, you'd know the sailor traveled a few thousand few thousand miles. Sometimes it indicated crossing the equator? I dunno. When they die at sea, they say a swallow carries them to heaven."

A psychopomp.

Miriam feels an invisible beak picking at her brainmeats.

He continues. "Eventually guys like Sailor Jerry popularized his version of the design, but it sounds like what you're talking about is older than that."

Miriam groans. "Okay. Well. Thanks for your help." She says it but she's aware that it sounds like she doesn't mean it. Because she doesn't.

"No, no, wait, hold on." He stands up, snatches a phone off its charger. Punches in a number.

"What?" she asks.

His turn to hold up a silencing finger.

"Yeah," he says into the phone. "Dad. It's Bry."

Pause.

"Hey, I got a question–"

Pause.

"Yeah, of course we're still going fishing."

Miriam is having a hard time imagining this kid with a fly rod.

"No, I know, dinner after, tell Mom I'll be there – listen, Dad, hold up. Listen. You know how you used to do ink for the officers down at NAVSUP?"

Pause.

"I need to know, you ever do any swallow tattoos? The bird. Right, right, with the forked tail."

Bryan cups the phone, says to Miriam, "He's done a handful."

"Ask him if any of the guys were… I dunno. Skinny. Ropy. Ooh! Ask him if any of them were a little… cuckoo upstairs, you know?"

Bryan relays the request.

Pause.

Bryan looks to Miriam. Offers a slight nod. "Okay. Yeah. He says there was a guy, everybody thought he was a little off his rocker. This was like, forty-some years ago, though."

Really? Did the killer look that old?

Maybe. The darkness in her vision, the uncertainty. And that mask…

Could be, rabbit, could be.

Besides, it's all she has.

"I need a name," she says. "An address. Something. Anything."

Bryan says into the phone: "Hold on." Then to her: "Why?"

"What?"

"Why do you need this?"

She licks her lips. Feels the blood pressure tightens in her neck. "I just do."

"That's not good enough."

"Fine. For real? I'm a psychic. I think this guy's out there killing girls and will continue to kill them – by chopping off their heads before cutting out their tongues – unless I do something about it. There. Truth bomb." She mimics an explosion with her hands, puffs her cheeks out. "Boom."

Bryan's eyes are as wide as the headlights on a big-rig truck. He doesn't look astonished. He looks horrified. Like he just opened the door into a padded room and was dumbstruck by her madness in all its fecal-hand-print-screaming-gibbering-fingernails-digging-sores-into-pale-flesh glory.

And he says into the phone, "I'll talk to you later, Dad."

And he hangs up.

Her heart kicks like a cranky mule.

"Why did you do that?"

"You need to go," he says. "I helped you. Now go."

"I'm not crazy."

"Whatever." He holds his hands up. "Leave. Please. C'mon."

"Call your goddamn father back. I need this. *I need this.*"

He says the final word on the matter. "No."

Before she even knows what she's doing, she's got her knife in her hand – the thumb finds the button and the blade springs out like a biting snake. She's got the point against his Adam's apple. A bead of blood dribbles down the hollow of his neck and disappears beneath the V-neck of his tee.

All the while, she doesn't touch him – not with her skin. She doesn't want to see. She's *afraid* to see. Afraid that if she learns how he's going to die it'll be by her hand, right now – a slip of the knife as it sinks into his throat, giving him a second smile, a human blowhole.

"I like you," she says through gritted teeth, "but I'm dangling by a delicate cunt hair, you feel me? I will perforate your trachea in the blink of an eye unless you get on the phone with your father and get me some information."

He nods, slowly. Eyes wet with fear.

Bryan takes the phone. Hits redial.

"Dad. Sorry." Voice shaky. His eyes watch her arm in such a focused way she's afraid he might burn a hole in her skin. "Had a... customer. Do you have any information on that – oh. Okay. Gr-great. Yeah. Great."

He whispers to Miriam, "Carl Keener. Says he moved off of NAVSUP years ago and moved up around here somewhere. Northumberland, Dad says."

"NAVSUP. I don't know what that is."

"Naval Supply. They handle..." He's frazzled. "I don't know. *Supplies.*" He pulls the phone closer to his ear. "Dad says, uh, food service, postal service, some ordinance and munitions... Says Keener worked there in one of the warehouses."

"Fine." That'll have to do. She steps back. Doesn't lower the knife, but makes sure it's not against his neck.

The tip of the knife is red as a match-tip. Bryan's blood glistens.

"Thanks," she says. Calmer now. It does little to soothe him, though. He still looks rattled like a cup full of loose teeth. "Sorry. For whatever that's worth."

"Is this what you do to people who help you?"

She can't answer that.

Or maybe she doesn't want to.

THIRTY-SEVEN
THE RIVER BREAKER

Hi, I'm looking for Carl Keener? He was a Naval buddy of my Dad's. They worked at NAVSUP together and Daddy hasn't seen Carl in maybe twenty years, and now Dad's got prostate cancer and they say it's curable but just the same he's trying to... well, he wouldn't put it this way, but he's trying to reconnect with old friends. Just in case.

That's the story she spins.

She caught a cab to Northumberland and now she's wandering down the streets of the wasteland suburbia – duplexes and split-levels and single-ranchers and little green lawns all stuffed together on the grid-pattern streets of this nowheresburg – and the sky keeps pissing rain and she's drenched and so are her hopes of having this impromptu plan yield any fruit.

Nobody knows this guy.

Not so far, at least. The town's a lot fucking bigger than Ash Creek, that's for sure. And by now the day is crawling into the afternoon, and with every hour – hell, every *minute* – that passes, Miriam knows that the girl, Annie Valentine, is one moment closer to death. And may already be dead.

She's wet. Tired. More or less lost. And she hasn't eaten a thing all day.

Hopeless.

This is barrel-scraping time.

Northumberland rests at the crux of the Susquehanna, ten miles north of where the Caldecott School has planted roots. It's like the town of Northumberland is an old god standing in the waters and there he holds out his hands and splits the water. Off to one side shoots the North Branch, and the West Branch to the other. Northumberland ever in the middle.

The river-breaker.

And so Miriam backtracks. Back to where she started. She had the cab drop her off at a little park called Pineknotter (with, she noted, no pine trees in sight). From there she walked north under a train trestle overpass and ended up along what must pass for Main Street around here – Water Street, running along the riverside.

That's where she goes. Back along the river's edge. Back to where the buildings are old Victorian. Back to where she saw a couple places to grab a bite to eat, because if she doesn't put some food into her body, she's going to fall over dead herself. She sees a place, the Blue Moon Deli.

She starts to go in and collides with someone coming out – a roly-poly accountant-looking dude with a squash-shaped head and a pair of big shop-teacher glasses. She's about to bite his head off, but for once she bites her tongue. (*Or he'll cut it out.*).

"Excuse me," she says, and she spills her story – blah blah blah, Daddy, cancer, reconnect, blah blah blah – just as the man's son is coming out. A mop-top teen in an orange vest and a pair of baggy cargo shorts.

"No," the man says, "I'm sorry, I don't–"

"You say Keener?" the teen asks.

Miriam says yes, that's what she said.

"I dunno if it's like, him, but a guy named Keener works part time at the tech school. Janitor. He's an older guy? Kind of maybe a little..." He suddenly shuts up.

"A little what?"

"Well, he's kind of a little weird. Says weird shi... stuff sometimes. And he stares at the girls."

Creepy janitor. Stares at young girls. Babbles at the students.

Yes. *Yes*. Yes! That has to be him.

"What's the school?" she asks.

"The tech school."

"Yeah, but what's the *name* of it."

"Sun-Tech," the kid says.

The father jumps in. "It's not in town here. It's just outside New Berlin. You'll have to go back south on Route 11, then take 15 north to 34 west, if you see the billboard for the hospital it means you've gone too far–"

"How long a drive?"

"Oh, twenty minutes or so."

Miriam feels in her pocket for the remnants of cash

lingering there. Six bucks and some change. Enough for a quick meal here at the Blue Moon, or enough to grab another cab and head to the tech school to see if she can – well, she doesn't know what, exactly. Find some employee records, maybe. Get an address.

Hunger's pretty irrational. Miriam gets cranky when she doesn't eat. Just the same, she doesn't feel like sinking her teeth into a pastrami sandwich and with every bite hearing the plaintive cries of a dying girl. Already in her head she can hear the killer's song, can hear the axe fall, can hear the sound of blade cutting through tongue.

And, there it is. Appetite gone. Decision made.

"Thanks," she says, and she lets the accountant and his son go.

THIRTY-EIGHT

FORGIVE US OUR TRESPASSES

The cab takes an hour to show. That's how it is in these parts. Not like in the city where you just hold your hand out or whack a passing cab with your bag to get the driver's attention. Here you call. Then you wait. And wait some more.

She calls from inside the Blue Moon.

She smells the smells from within. Deli mustard. Chicken soup. Bread baked fresh – bread, that yeasty bounty, that carbolicious belly-filler.

It's enough to put images of murderers and dead girls out of her mind.

For the moment.

Someone leaves a half-eaten sandwich on the table. Sitting on a tray. They didn't even bite it – they cut it in half and left the other half alone.

She sees a glimpse of ham. A tease. Like a girl flashing a little thigh.

She creeps up on it, a hunter stalking her prey.

A bell rings. The door opens. The cabbie asks loudly, too loudly, "Hey, who ordered the cab?"

She holds her hand up, says, "Yeah, just hold on." But by the time she turns back around the smiley happy girl from behind the deli counter is already swooping the tray's contents into a nearby trash can.

Miriam thinks of cutting *her* head off.

Fast forward ten minutes. Miriam sits in the back of a cab.

Rain batters the windshield.

The wipers rock back and forth, and since the driver's not turning on the radio, that's all she hears: the back and forth, the click and swipe, the shushing susurration of tires on rain-slick trees.

She opens the window. Lights a cigarette. Doesn't ask if it's okay.

Blows a jet of smoke out the window.

Wishes suddenly that Louis were here. Even to tell her not to smoke.

And especially to drive her ass around.

She flicks the butt – a spiraling shape, an ember in the gray rain – and is about to roll up the window when she smells something.

A chemical stink on the wind. Like a super-dose of cheap shampoo, like Garnier Fructis if it was first run through the bowels of a dead possum. It burns the eyes and Miriam suddenly feels overwhelmed, like the cab is pressing in on her, about to crush her like a bug in a soda can smashed by a human boot–

She can't breathe. She feels cold.

Her fingers curl inward. The nails bite into her palms.

It hits her: *I know that smell.*

She doesn't know it from personal experience.

She knows it from the vision. The first vision. With Wren as an eighteen-year-old girl getting her head chopped off in a burned-out house.

Sometimes her visions give her an olfactory sense. Other times, they don't. No consistency. Maybe she gets thirty seconds of the person's life. Maybe five minutes. It's whatever the vision gives her.

Whatever the crow-headed monsters and ghosts inside her head allow.

But now that olfactory memory is hitting her dead in the face.

She swallows reflux and steadies herself enough to ask a question.

"What…" *Do not throw up do not throw up*. "What is that smell?"

"Heh?" the cabbie asks, apparently lost to the hypnotism of the road.

"The smell. The goddamn… that chemical odor."

"Oh. That? Sheez, yeah, I don't usually smell that anymore. Sometimes it washes over the town and I catch a strong whiff, but most of the time I just tune it out, you know?"

She growls, "You don't *tune out* a smell, you tune out a – you know what, never mind, just what the fuck is it?"

"The Sus-Q Color Plant." Sus-Q for the Susquehanna. "They do pigments and paints and stuff."

He lives near that plant. Carl Keener lives somewhere near the Sus-Q color plant. He has to. She feels it scratching the base of her neck like a knife.

"Change of plans. Head toward the plant."

"But that's north, and you wanted to go west, to New Berlin."

"Yeah. I get that. That's why it's called a change of plans. Just do as I ask, will you? Christ on a cookie."

She feels close now.

All the cells in her body hum like flywings.

THIRTY-NINE
THE COMPOUND

"Here!" she yelps, swatting the cabbie. "Pull over here."

The cab tires grind on the broken earth of the road's shoulder.

Rain runs down the cab window, distorting her view.

Just the same, she knows what she's seeing.

This has to be it.

A dirt driveway empties off the road. A chain-link fence and gate block anybody from coming in. The top of the fence is ringed with clumsy coils of rusted barbed wire.

Stuck in the earth and wired to the fence are signs. Pieces of plywood or scrap metal, the messages spray-painted in drippy, inconsistent lettering – some letters big, others small. All crazy.

No Hunting!
Num. #One God is Watching!
LIAR GOD KNOW
Is There Life After Deth? Intruders findout
STOP OR SUFFER
Do Not Go B-Yond This Fence

And, of course:

NO TRESPASSERS

Trespasser. Miriam knows that word.

Finally, the deal-sealer, the clincher, the Hail-Mary-Praise-Jaysus: Seven ravens. Some perched on signs. Others atop the gate.

Watching her.

"Here," she says, throwing the rest of her money over the seat at the cabbie. Then she gets out. When the door opens, the birds stir, take flight into the surrounding trees and settle into the branches.

Thunder complains overhead as the cab does a U-turn in the road.

And then it's gone. Miriam is alone.

The chemical stink hangs in the air.

From here, she can't see much. Beyond the gate is just more dirt road. Dirt that's now churning into mud. Curving into the woods. In a strange way, it reminds her of the Caldecott School. Instead of a school crest, it's crazy person signs. Instead of iron gates topped with *fleur-di-lis*, it's a warped chain-link fence topped with razor wire.

The razor wire, she notes, tilts inward. Not outward.

It's not that he doesn't want people to come in. He doesn't want them to escape.

Caldecott is a place where girls come for second chances. To learn and to grow.

But here...

This is a place girls come to have those chances stolen.

To suffer and to die.

A girl might be in there now. Dead or dying.

No time like the present. Miriam throws her jacket over the coiled wire and begins clambering up the chain-link like a monkey. The jacket protects her from the bite of the barbs as she scoots over and lands on her hands and knees in the mud.

She tries to rescue her jacket, but it's stuck up there. Shit.

Can't worry about that now.

She hoofs it, adrenalin puppeting her legs. The pit of her stomach is sour from bile and hunger. The muddy road sucks at her boots.

The ravens follow her progress. Hopping from tree to tree. Silent black shapes behind the curtain of rain.

As soon as she rounds the bend, she sees where Keener lives.

It's a junkyard. Not a functional junkyard where people go. No, this is his dumping ground. Acres upon acres of worthless scrap and debris. A defunct Oldsmobile. A bunch of shipping containers and dumpsters. Plow blades, sheets of tin, machines and engines of unknown purpose.

A school bus. A long school bus – not a Type-A – sits rusted among the mess. Not far from it is a little white house with black mold growing up the stucco like a stain creeping up out of Hell itself.

As soon as she sees it, the ravens in the tree stir.

They begin cackling and cawing in alarm, all seven of them taking flight into the rain–

Miriam hears the sound of tires on mud.

Quickly she darts into the junkyard and ducks behind a shipping container with corroded and partly caved in sides.

A yellow short bus – a Type-A, like the kind you might see shuttling tourists or old people around – pulls up.

Headlights beaming. Light capturing knife slashes of falling rain.

For a while it just sits like that. She can't see who's in there. All Miriam can make out is a shape.

Eventually the headlights darken. The driver cuts the engine.

And finally she earns her first look at the killer without his mask.

He's tall. Arms like corded ropes. Like in the vision. Older, too – Keener's in his late fifties, early sixties. A tall body stooped over. Shoulders up, head and sharp chin pointed down. Even from here she can see he's got dark eyes and a nose that sits – once broken, never set straight – off to the left as though he's perpetually pressed up against a pane of glass.

Her breath catches suddenly.

Oh no oh no oh no.

He's got her jacket.

She hears another set of tires. A cop car – state police – pushes in behind the school bus.

A stark nightmare plays out in her mind: The cops arrest Keener, take him away, and then he's gone, out of her reach, locked away in courthouses and jails where she cannot touch him – and then he's released in time to kill again with nobody to stop him. Fate moving its pieces into place. To ensure that what must happen will happen.

The cop steps out of his car, and it's like Keener's expecting him. The cop stands under a black umbrella but Keener, well, the rain doesn't seem to bother him.

Keener hands him the jacket.

The cop's a bulldog type. Shorter, squatter, a dark horseshoe mustache highlighting, rather than concealing, the chin-thrust of his underbite.

She can't hear what they're saying. But they both turn toward the junkyard. As though they're looking for someone. Someone like her.

Miriam pulls her head back behind the container. Holds her breath and squeezes her eyes shut as though that'll do anything at all.

She listens to the rain. The murmur of voices. The low thrum of the cop car's idling engine and the thunder above moving across the sky.

Then: tires on mud.

Who is it now?

This is getting to be a regular party.

But when she looks, she sees it's not someone coming but rather, going. The cop turns around and drives back out to the road. Disappearing behind the trees. Miriam's not sure whether to feel sickened or relieved when he's gone.

After all, the cop was looking for her. Wasn't he?

Tipped off, perhaps by poor Bryan at the tattoo parlor. Why *wouldn't* he call the police? She had a knife-point at his neck and kept throwing Keener's name around like he was the target of a vendetta. Like she was going to hunt him down and kill him.

Aren't you?

The question pinballs around her head.

Keener heads toward the house, but then stops halfway there. Peers around with his head on a suspicious pivot. Turns. Marches instead toward the maze of junk. Feet slapping against greasy mud.

He's coming right for her.

Quickly, she scrambles away from her hiding spot and to another – this time behind a dumpster filled to the brim with scrap wood.

She stays her breath. Holds it. *Don't pant like a dog, you bitch, he'll hear you.* Keener found her old hiding spot. He's there. She can hear him and his footsteps. Can hear him grunt, kick the mud around. Splish splash.

Here he comes again.

She can't jump into the dumpster because it's full. Instead she presses her back against it and slowly works around the side. As Keener comes up the one side, she slides around the other, trying not to bang the metal and cause an echo.

"Someone out here?" he calls. His voice is like two asbestos shingles rubbing together, like stone grinding on stone. "This your jacket?"

Go away go away just go the fuck away.

He starts moving around the dumpster. Toward her.

She darts straight away, finds a rusted-out once-white Caddy and dives underneath it onto her belly. Her shirt pulls up as she does so, rainwater and oily mud sliding against her belly and into the waistband of her jeans. With anchoring fingers she digs into the earth and pulls herself all the way under.

She looks behind her just in time to see Keener looking her way.

Like he might have seen something.

Like he's not sure.

The monster wipes rain from his eyes.

And starts heading toward her.

Don't move. Grass, black with mud, hides her face, but just to be sure she presses herself deeper into the muck.

Keener walks slowly. Like he's waiting for her to erupt from her hiding place, a deer spooked from the brush. So he can pounce and tear her apart. His face is feral. He hungers for a taste.

He reaches the car.

He's right here. Right on top of her.

His work-boots, grimy steel-toes, are only inches from her head.

Don't look under here.

Her hand slides into her pocket. Pulls the spring-blade knife from her pocket. She hovers her thumb over the button.

Stab him now, she thinks. *Stick him like a pig.* Will the blade puncture the boot? Does she have the leverage? What if she slips? *Do it, this is your chance.*

But then he grunts again–

And starts to walk away.

Miriam lets out the breath she's been holding as he heads back toward the house, winding his way through the labyrinth of rubbish and refuse.

She lies there like that, on her belly, for a while. Blood pumping so hard in her ears she's afraid she's having an aneurysm.

But then, a new sound. Not footsteps, not a Keener grunt.

A voice.

A girl's voice.

She can't make it out, but it's not far.

Miriam crawls out from underneath the passenger side of the Caddy and hunkers down into a gargoyle stance – just in case Keener is looking. *Stay low,* she thinks.

For a time, she just listens. Ear cocked. Trying to pull other sounds out of the white noise of the rain.

Then she hears.

"Is someone there?"

A girl's voice. Close by.

Miriam hurries forward, bent at the hip in a scoliosis run, and flattens her back against a rogue oak tree – a twisted living thing growing up out of this artificial wasteland.

There. The voice, again: "Help me. Please."

Small. Echoing.

Across from Miriam is another shipping container: this one forest green, a company's logo long scoured away by Father Time and Mother Nature.

This container is longer than the other. Twenty feet deep. Maybe more.

The voice. It's coming from inside the container.

He's keeping the girls inside them.

It makes sense. In a sick fucking way. Hide them away from the world. Out of the house. But he sometimes brings them inside to do the dirty work, doesn't he? Or is that a change he makes? A change that arrives in the years to come?

No time to worry about that now.

Miriam dashes to the container. Puts her ear to the side. Taps on it with just her index finger – quiet enough not to draw any attention but loud enough that anybody inside would know it's more than the rain falling.

She presses her ear against the cold metal.

Hears: "Who's there? Hurry. *Before he comes back.*"

Miriam zips around to the front of the container – finds that it's open. The inside is dark, but she can make out the girl – barely, just barely, a shape shrunken in the back as though shackled there.

"I'm here," Miriam says. "I'm here to help."

One foot after the other, she creeps into the dark container.

"Please," the girl says, sniffling, whimpering.

"I'm coming."

"Save me," she whispers. "*Save me.*"

And then the girl is up. Moving fast at Miriam: a white shape in black shadow, footsteps reverberating *boom boom boom–*

It's then that Miriam sees.

It's not the girl. Not even *a* girl.

It's him.

Keener.

No time to run, no time for anything – she'll slip, fall, and he'll be on her. Instead she stands her ground. Flicks the button on her knife, the blade springing to life–

But Keener's fast.

He's got a weapon, too.

A 2x4. Splintery. From the dumpster full of scrap.

She screams, sticks the knife–

–feels it sink into flesh–

–he howls as the 2x4 connects with the side of her head.

She goes down. Face up. The knife is gone – still stuck in Keener. She sees stars and snowflakes. Turns over. Hands and knees. Scrabbling forward.

Hears him grunt.

Hears her knife clatter against the ground.

She crawls out into the rain. Gets her legs underneath her.

Goes to launch into a run–

But a hand with strong spidery fingers grabs her heel and yanks hard. Her leg goes straight and she falls, chest-down, into the mud.

"Help me," Keener says, mimicking a girl's voice with eerie precision, not a swallow but a mockingbird. But then he lets his own voice take over, a growling tongue emerging from the girlish pleas. "You're a trespasser."

Trespasser, she thinks. *Help me.*

The 2x4 connects with the back of her head.

And then it's mud and rain and nothing.

INTERLUDE
THE CANDY HOUSE

Wham.

Her mother drops a cardboard box on the ground in front of her. CD cases rattle within – Social Distortion, Smashing Pumpkins, Nine Inch Nails. Above the CDs: comic books. Batman stares from the top, with Killer Croc in a headlock. Beneath that, a glimpse of Jean Grey from the X-Men. Miriam spies the bindings of paperback books she nabbed from the used bookstore down in Sunbury: Poppy Brite, Stephen King, Robert McCammon, *Catcher in the Rye, Slaughterhouse Five.*

"This is trash," her mother says. Thumbs laced together. Worrying a piece of butterscotch candy between her teeth, rattling it from molar to molar. Worrying being the operative term: She only eats sweets when she's agitated.

Miriam doesn't know what to say. She can only swallow hard and ask, "How did you find them?"

"The smartest girl in the room is never the one who thinks she's the smartest girl in the room," her mother says. "Thought you were clever. Didn't you? You know what I found? I was walking underneath the attic and saw something on the pull-down cord. A little smudge of something red, something sticky. Jam. Strawberry jam. And I said to myself, 'Well, who is it that eats toast with jam every morning before school?' It's not me. I don't like sweet things. And there's only one other person in the house. So I wondered, 'What would my little Miriam be doing up in the attic?' And I found these. Under a box of old clothes."

"I'm sorry, Mother."

"You've been hiding things from me, Miriam. You've been lying to cover up this filth. This is not God's work in this box. This is not how your mother raised you." She picks up a pile of pop culture, lets it fall back through her hands into the box with a thump and clamor. "Sex and perversion and horror. All of it."

Miriam wants to stand up and say none of it is hurting her, none of it calls her stupid or fat or questions whether or not she's going to go to Heaven. Each song of an album, each page of a book, every panel of every comic, they're all doorways, little escape hatches where Miriam can flee the sad shadows of this life.

She wants to say worse things, too – mean things, sharp words, insults like little knives. Cunt, whore, bitch, fuck you, fuck everything, her mouth brimming with foulness the way a soup can bulges with botulism. A little voice inside asks: *What would Uncle Jack say*?

But that thought and all the others die back like dead vines.

She's not the type to talk back. She's a quiet girl. A well-mannered mouse who dreams of being a rat.

"I really don't know anymore," her mother says, shaking her head, the candy clicking against her teeth, the cloying butterscotch breath turning Miriam's stomach. "I don't know how you're going to turn out. I don't think well. I think you're a bad girl destined for bad things. A worthless girl. Bringing nothing to God's creation but misery and mayhem. What do you say?"

"I'll be better. I'll get better."

"We'll start tonight. Bring that box. Take it outside to the stone circle. I'll meet you out there."

And an hour later the box sits in the circle of stones – an old planter her mother has forsaken in order to make it a fire pit during fall and winter, and that's how it's used tonight. Her mother empties a can of lighter fluid. Flings a match.

Bright light. Hot wave. A plume of fire that dies back.

It burns. Black smoke from melting plastic. It reeks. Words and images caught on the heat waves, lost and gone but not forgotten.

Miriam thinks idly about shoving her mother into the fire. Like shoving a witch into her own oven inside the kitchen of a candy house.

But she doesn't. Instead she just cries, feeling worthless like her mother says, and she goes inside to pray for God to make her a better girl.

FORTY
WICKED POLLY, WICKED POLLY

The taste of dust and mud on her tongue.

Pressure. Her skull in a vice. She can almost hear it cracking like a frozen lake beneath her feet.

Her hearing roves wildly between ringing and pulsing: a high-pitched whine that segues into the sound of a blood river rushing behind her eardrums.

She plants her hands beneath her – and a sharp pain bites into her palms. She drops back to the ground, head against earth, not even sure where she is.

Deep breath.

Head turn. Cheek on cold dirt.

Where is she?

She sees rock walls. Wooden shelves bolted to them. All empty. Above, a bare bulb hanging from a fraying cord, casting a diseased glow but not much more.

Cellar. She's in some kind of cellar. Dirt floor? It's a root cellar.

She turns her head the other way, and then she sees the other girl.

Annie Valentine.

Annie's huddled up against a bare spot on the wall. Head down on her knees. Pale naked body shivering. Body striated with dirt and bruises.

And sores. Some fresh. Some not.

Her hair, grungy and sweat-slick, hangs down over her legs like the strands of a filth-caked mop.

Miriam rolls to her side. Her head feels like it's inflated to the size of a balloon (*a red Mylar balloon*), and the ringing in her ears spikes sharply.

With her hands in front of her, she can see: Two Xs. Carved into her palms.

Slowly, glacially, she sits up.

She feels along her bare feet. One X on each foot. Blood dry. Wounds puffy.

She, too, is naked. No pants, which means no phone, no knife. Behind her, an old water heater on cement blocks. Beyond that, another smaller room – an antechamber filled with what looks to be remnants of old coal.

Opposite that: rickety steps up, lead paint flaking off like strips of leper skin. The door at the top is shut. A line of light frames the edge.

That door is surely locked. But that doesn't mean it can't be gotten through.

"Hey," Miriam says, her voice a tattered remnant. "Valentine."

The girl looks up but says nothing.

"Where are we?" Miriam asks. "Are we in Keener's house? How long have you been here?"

Still nothing.

"Do you know anything?"

Annie Valentine is worthless. She's been trauma-bombed, her mind a chalkboard wiped clean of its writing.

"There's two of us," Miriam says. "We can fight him." Right now she doesn't feel like she could fight off a drooling baby, much less a serial killer with a fire axe, but this is all they have. "The two of us together can get out of this. Okay? Look at me. Please. Valentine. *Look at me.*"

The girl looks toward her but it's like her gaze is sliding off the edges, slipping on the ice of troubled thoughts. Her stare is dead, empty. It's driftwood.

Miriam stands. The process is slow and wretched.

Her feet touch the floor and she has to stand on the balls of her feet to avoid the pain of her injured soles.

A head rush – the pain churning into her skull – almost brings her low again.

Miriam does a spot check. Feels her body – no cracked ribs, no additional cuts. No sores like Valentine has, which makes Miriam wonder.

She feels down below. Between her legs. No blood, no pain. She's woozy and right now the whole world feels like it's gone ass-up, but she takes the small elation this news gives her.

Her head, though – her pink-and-bleach hair is matted to her skull with a lacquering of dried blood. This injury sits on the opposite side from her bullet furrow, (which is now mostly healed over, though the hair still hasn't grown back).

A matching set.

She hopes the autopsy technician will note that.

Don't think like that.

You'll get out of this.

Move. Look. Find.

Above her head, the floorboards groan and bang – footsteps. Keener's up there. Something heavy – a piece of furniture – drags across the wood with a grinding stutter.

Hurry.

She hobbles into the old coal room. No heater here, but she can see the concrete pad where one once sat. A pair of cellar doors looks old, weak, just a series of half-rotten wooden barn-boards lashed together. But when she tries to open them they don't budge, and she hears a metal clanging on the other side.

Miriam leaves behind footprints in coal dust, the soot grinding into the slashes on the bottoms of her feet. *If Keener doesn't kill you, an infection from this will.*

Back into the other room. She creeps up the steps, trying to be silent – an impossible task. The stairway shifts, squeaks, moans like an old woman on her deathbed. Miriam drops to her hands and knees.

At the top of the stairway, she stares through the bright crack under the door. It's there she sees her exit. The dimensions of the cellar and what she saw when she was in the junkyard make this a one-bedroom cottage at best, and the door she sees must be the doorway out.

It's a wooden door with an old warped glass window. Beyond it, a screen door.

Through the window, she sees that night has fallen.

But her view is suddenly blocked.

Two black pillars, two dark boots.

Keener.

Keys rattle. She hears a padlock thunking dully against the door as she hurries down the steps – almost slipping and falling and breaking her damn fool neck in the process.

She stands by Annie Valentine, who's begun to rock back and forth. The sound coming out of the girl's throat is that of a wounded animal, its leg caught and mangled in a trap.

"I'll get us out of this," Miriam says. She hurries into the coal room. Grabs a palmful of coal dust from the ground. Goes and stands beneath the bulb. She steadies herself, a near-impossible task – her whole body feels like a little ship on a storm-fucked sea.

Keener opens the door. Walks slow down the steps.

He's got an old wooden baton in his hand, the leather cord wrapped around his wrist. At the end of the baton are two metal probes.

Sparking and snapping.

A 1950's-era cattle prod.

Worse, he wears the mask: the guise of the beak doctor, here to cleanse them. Light smoke drifts from the beak and Miriam catches the smell of burning herbs and flowers – *Wren, Tavena, Valentine, me, strapped to tables, barbed wire gags, heads on the block, tongues in the hand* – and she has to fight back the darkness that threatens to drop her.

The mask's eyeholes are covered in glass. Goggles retrofitted on the outside of the leather and affixed with brass bolts.

Defiant, Miriam blows the coal dust.

It coats the goggles. Keener wipes them away.

He thrusts the cattle prod into her stomach.

Everything lights up. It feels like the bare bulb above suddenly goes supernova: the room hot and white like she's trapped by a bolt of lightning.

And then she's on the floor – she doesn't remember how she got here – her extremities twitching, fingers and toes curling inward.

That wounded animal sound rises in volume, a dread yowl: a cat with four legs broken, a rabbit in the teeth of the fox.

It's Annie Valentine.

Keener's dragging her by her hair up the steps.

The girl's legs kick, and he jams the cattle prod right under her collarbone. Miriam reaches, and finds that all her synapses and circuits are still misfiring. All she can do is curl into a fetal ball.

Keener hauls Annie up the steps, through the door. Slams it. The whole house shakes.

She can hear his footsteps tromping above. The slide of the body behind.

Did he lock the door?

She doesn't hear the lock re-engage.

Miriam tries to find her bearing. Hell, she tries to find her soul inside her body. It's like the strings and tendons that connect her willpower to her muscles, her mind to her limbs, have all been cut or frayed. Her jaw won't unclench. Her fingers are bent so that her hands look like animal paws. Miriam feels like she might piss herself.

It's then she sees Annie Valentine. Sitting where she just was.

Curled up.

Staring off at nothing.

How?

Was all that a dream? Is she just waking? The Trespasser giving her a vision?

But then Annie's mouth opens, and a raven's head – slick with blood and mucus – slides forth from her lips, and squawks at her. That wasn't the Trespasser before. This is.

"No t-t-trespassing," Miriam babbles. She laughs a little. But the laugh melts away and turns to crying. Tears clean dirt from her cheeks.

"The river is rising," the raven says.

"F-fuck you."

"You've got work to do."

"Did I st-st-stutter? I said, *fuck you.*" Everything is spit and snot and tears.

"He breathes in the smoke of those flowers because he does not want to be tainted by your impurity." The raven cocks its head this-a-way and that-a-way. Like it's studying an escaping worm. "He believes you are not only sick but a sickness, and he is the surgeon cleaning the world's wound of your foulness."

Miriam wipes her face and hisses. "That's helpful. And since three times is a charm: fuck you."

"The river is rising."

"Fuck. You."

"You've got work to do."

"Fu–" But before she can get it out, Annie Valentine and the raven are gone.

Upstairs, though, the real Annie Valentine screams.

A scream swiftly muted. It turns into a gurgle.

Footsteps cross the floor above.

Is she dead?

Then Miriam hears him start to sing. She can't make out the words, but she hears that grim, sing-songy quality. The song of "Wicked Polly" again?

The mockingbird's song? Or the song stolen from the swallow so that it can no longer sing?

Get up.

She tries to move. Her body is not cooperating. An elbow slips out from under her.

Get up!

Her legs feel like meat without bones, tendons like blown elastic. She can't get them to comply. They move, but not as she wishes.

GET UP.

Miriam rolls over. Hands beneath her. Knees, too. Prop up. Body a bridge.

She sees the water heater.

Propped up, like her. Not on hands and knees. On short cement blocks.

Miriam crawls over. Wraps her hands behind one of those blocks. Pulls.

It doesn't budge.

Pull, pull, pull–

The porous cement bites into her palms, and she feels fresh blood from the slash-marks in her hands opening up. It lubricates her grip and that's not helpful, not at all–

You stupid twat, if you can't pull this out everybody dies. Valentine.

Tavena.

Wren.

You.

How many others?

Above, the song continues. The smell of ashen roses clings inside her nose. She hears him crossing back the other way. Probably with the axe.

She loops her right arm around the block, squeezing it under the water heater. She knows it could crush her arm if she does this too slow.

She squeezes her eyes shut.

Finds herself praying. Not to God. But to the Trespasser.

Miriam gives it her all – puts all her energy into the shoulder, tugs the arm. The concrete block scrapes against the bottom of the heater, which suddenly tilts and dips –

But does not hit the ground and does not make a sound. The other blocks support it.

She lets go a relieved breath, almost cries. *At least one thing went right.*

And now, Miriam holds the concrete block

Hefts it with both bloody hands.

It's time to kill Carl Keener. Time to silence the Mockingbird's song.

FORTY-ONE
TURN FROM YOUR SINS, LEST YOU DESPAIR

The door swings open. It's blessedly silent, as if doing Miriam some kind of favor, a favor of objects granted by the parliament of doors.

An absurd thought. But that's how everything feels. Crossed wires. Synaptic misfires. Skull pulsing so hard it feels like her heart is now in her head.

The cement block, the gray streaked with red, *her* red, sits comfortably in her grip.

Ahead of her, the door. The exit.

She could just go.

Go and leave and come back another day.

Or don't. It doesn't matter.

These girls don't matter. Miriam is a selfish creature. Designed to survive. The cockroach. The crow. The hungry vulture.

Miriam goes to the door.

Stares out. The hard rain is hissing. Urging her outside.

Cleansing. Baptismal. A hymn sung by the heavens.

To her right, here somewhere in this house, another song. Floating. Shrill and trilling. With it, a chorus of whimpers, the miserable cries of Annie Valentine.

That, and the mockingbird's own ditty.

"Your counsels I have slighted all, my carnal appetite shall fall..."

Miriam turns away from the door. Her path chosen.

She creeps deeper into the house. A house without decoration. Water-stained wallpaper. Mid-century furniture gone to pot. Not dirty like she expects. Clean. No television. No books. Unadorned by anything: an eerily sterile environment. As though anything else would be an affront, would be a corruption, a filthy poison. Her mother's voice rises to greet her–

You've been lying to cover up this filth. This is not God's work in this box. This is not how your Mother raised you.

The room beyond the living room – what a normal family might use as a den or a sitting room – tells a different story.

Lights dim. Tarp on the floor.

An old wooden doctor's table.

A small card table. On it Miriam sees an array of objects. Some she doesn't recognize, some she does: her clothing, her bag, Katey's phone.

A coil of barbed wire sits in the corner and, atop it, a pair of wire cutters.

Annie Valentine is strapped down. The wire wound around her mouth.

And there stands Carl Keener.

Facing away from Miriam, toward the girl. His right bicep is wrapped in dark, wet gauze where she stuck him with the blade.

He holds the axe with one hand. With the other, he grabs a Zippo lighter from the card table. Flicks it open, gets a flame. Lifts it under his mask's beak.

She can hear the crispy sizzle of flame consuming dead flowers.

He inhales it, then exhales – two oily plumes of smoke like the smoldering breath of a conquering dragon.

He sings:

"When I am dead, remember well, your wicked Polly groans in Hell."

He raises the axe.

"She wrung her hands..."

Miriam creeps forward. Raising her own weapon, the cement block, high above her head. It's a cave-woman's weapon, no finesse, only brutality.

"And groaned and cried..."

You have work to do.

"And gnawed her tongue before she–"

Miriam smashes the cement block hard against the back of Keener's hooded head.

He staggers forward, using the base of the axe to prop himself against the doctor's table, preventing his fall.

Miriam brings the block back again. She feels slow, like her whole body is caught in molasses, a mosquito stuck in cooling amber. But where she is slow Keener is fast, and he brings the base of the axe handle in a wide arc, connecting with the side of her face, opening her cheek. She reels.

The block falls from her grip, and she staggers against the doorframe.

Stars–

Exploding–

Dark shadows like birds between the bursts of hard light–

Keener's hand winds around her throat.

She smells burning funeral flowers. A fog of rose. A fume of carnation. Little embers burning bright beneath the leather-punched noseholes.

Keener rears back a fist. Snarls.

Hits her once. In the mouth. Rocks her head against the frame. Everything hurts and everything tastes like a mouthful of copper.

He rears a fist back again.

A phone rings.

Katey's phone.

It's enough. He flicks his gaze toward it, startled, irritated, confused. His grip on her throat relaxes.

He breathes in the smoke of those flowers because he does not want to be tainted by your impurity.

Miriam gets her own grip–

On his beak.

She plants her numb and bloody mouth against the two noseholes of his plague doctor mask, draws the deepest breath she can muster, and blows all her air into those two cavities.

Oxygen stirs the embers to fire and blasts a searing whirl of ash into his mask. She sees orange cinders like fireflies swirling behind the glass and suddenly he's flailing, knocking over the card table, screaming inside the beaked leather hood, trying desperately to pull it off his bare shoulders–

And when he finally does, there stands Miriam.
With a pair of wire cutters.
She plunges them into his throat.
Again.
And again.
Until there remains no throat to ruin.

PART FOUR
THE MOCKINGBIRD ECHO

Hush little baby
Don't say a word
Mama's going to buy you a mockingbird
And if that mockingbird won't sing
Mama's going to buy you a diamond ring.

Child's song

FORTY-TWO
MISSED CALL

Don't tell anyone I was here.

Louis, please... come get me.

You're safe, now – safe.

Hurry.

Don't tell.

Hurry.

Midnight in the harsh light of the hospital. Antiseptic stink. Making it smell so clean somehow makes it smell all the filthier.

She's not in a room. There's no need to be. For her, it's all here in the ER. This cubicle isn't much more than a closet. When the attending examined her, he sat down on a blue medical waste bin like it was a chair.

They tell her she has a concussion. No brain bleeding. Just beaten up pretty good. They took out a tooth, too. In the back. So she doesn't look like some kind of hillbilly whistle-britches.

No fracture. And to her surprise, no stitches. Instead, something called Dermabond. "Skin glue," the attending said. The cuts on her hands and feet and face are smeared with yellow-brown iodine. Reminds Miriam of being a child. Holding a grasshopper and the bug spits a brownish goo. Some kind of defense mechanism.

"Hospital again," Louis says. His heavy hand rubs circles around her back. His hand feels good. Warm. "You have to stop making a habit of this."

"I hate this place," she says, her voice throaty and rough, like she's been eating fiberglass insulation with a whisky chaser. "This is my last time." But she wonders: *is it really?"*

He kisses the top of her head – where no wounds wait. She can't tell if it's brotherly, fatherly, or the gentle kiss of one lover to another.

She doesn't give a shit. It's nice.

"Your call saved my life," she says. "And the girl's."

"What do you mean?"

She tells him: If he hadn't called, Keener wouldn't have been distracted. That moment was critical. Even that half-second gave her the upper-hand.

Louis cups her chin in his hands. Pulls her face toward his.

"Are you okay? That was pretty... messy back there."

It was. Her blood flecked on the walls. Annie's blood dripping to the floor, purple dots on a blue tarp. And Keener...

He stands behind Louis. Tall and mean. He's not real. Miriam knows that. But he looks as he did back there, at the house. Throat a pile of red ambrosia salad. Miriam doesn't remember how many times she stuck him with those wire cutters. Not enough to take his head off. But not far from it.

The manifestation of the Trespasser tilts its head back like a Pez dispenser, speaking out of the ruined esophageal hole.

"Go get 'em, killer," the throat-hole burbles.

She hears the excitement of wings. Then Keener is gone.

"I'm good," she says. Once the phrase that plagued her was *it is what it is*. Now, though, she feels like it has become *I am who I am.*

Go get 'em, killer.

"You sure you don't want to speak to the cops?"

Miriam called Louis first. She called the police once he got there – but she called anonymously.

"Real sure. I've been at too many crime scenes already. Eventually they're going to think that's a bit strange. I don't need cops sniffing around and making trouble." *Especially if this is who I am and what I do.* "I feel bad, though. Just leaving that girl behind."

"That's all right. The police will help her out."

"Still. Her being alone like that. Even for five, ten minutes. In that house. She's already messed up. Physically. Mentally." Mind like a plate of scrambled eggs."

"She'll find peace. You saved her life. Give yourself that. I've been there, remember." He kisses her cheek. She's not sure what it means. "*And* you saved those other girls, too. I just wish you would have looped me in."

"You were gone. You seemed to want to be gone." *Maybe I wanted you gone, too, if only for a little while.*

"I won't let that happen again. I'm here to protect

you. You've got your mission, and I've got mine. My wife..." His voice trails off.

She can't imagine what he's thinking. Something about how he lost one woman and now might lose another? That's not healthy, him tying his dead wife's memory to her. A psychological boat anchor like a boat anchor. But healthy or unhealthy, Miriam likes the feeling. She's sinking into it. Drowning, maybe, but the drowning feels good.

"We'll figure out all the other stuff," Louis says. "Just know that I have your back. From here on out."

"Thanks," she says. She offers him a smile.

There's a commotion. Down the hall. A familiar voice rises, a voice slightly panicked.

Katey appears at the door. Out of breath.

"Oh, Lord," she says, flying into the room and wrapping her arms around Miriam.

Miriam grunts and clears her throat and gives an awkward hug back.

"Kind of sore all over," Miriam mumbles with a wince.

"Sorry, sorry." Katey backs away. Gets a good look at Miriam. "I'm glad you called. And I'm glad you're okay."

"Here's your phone," Miriam says, grabbing the cell off a nearby counter near a jar of swabs. "Saved my life."

"Louis came to me, desperate as a starving dog," Katey says, "said he looked up and down, went to your old motel, tried calling your old cell, and couldn't find you. Good thing he decided to check in with me." She frets at Miriam like a mother monkey picking mites off her baby. "Heavens, you got banged up pretty good."

Miriam shrugs. "At least I didn't get stabbed in the boob this time."

"At least you made it out *alive*."

"Keener sure didn't." A sick swell of pride rises inside her. Like a red balloon inflating. Floating above her head.

"And that other poor girl. Amy Valentine?"

"Annie. Yeah, I don't know if she'll ever be the same."

The look on Katey's face strikes Miriam then. The way her brow furrows, the way her lips move to form words that don't yet come. When they finally do, Katey says, "You sure you're okay? You have a concussion. Is that right?"

"I know what year it is. And I know how many fingers and toes I'm supposed to have. Why?"

"Then that wasn't a funny joke."

"Joke. I wasn't making a joke."

"That girl, Annie Valentine. She's dead, Miriam. It's all over the news."

FORTY-THREE
BLACK VALENTINE

They find a room nearby. A proper hospital room. An old guy sleeps in the bed like a broken doll, a ruined puppet with his leg lifted and his hip propped up.

In the corner, a TV. Miriam hobbles over, grabs the remote off the old guy's nightstand, flips on the tube. The patient mumbles but doesn't stir.

She flips, flips, flips.

There.

And she doesn't believe what she sees.

It's a whole scene. A whole fucking nightmare of a scene.

Cops. News vans. A helicopter. All over Keener's property.

Which is, in fact, on fire.

The house burns despite the rain. So too do various pockets of the labyrinthine junk-land. Fire and black smoke bellow from a shipping container, a few cars, and the long decrepit bus.

She tries to put it together. *Maybe the girl flipped her shit. Maybe whatever tiny little thread was holding her sanity together just snapped and she went and found a… a gas can and started burning everything.*

But then they say they found two bodies.

Carl Keener, fifty-six. Body burned up.

And Annie Valentine, eighteen.

They found her outside the house.

Shot in the head.

Miriam grabs the waste can, throws up atop the remnants of hospital food.

Maybe she found a gun. In the house.

Killed herself.

That's what it has to be.

Something pecks at the back of her mind. A bird catching a bug.

A phone rings.

When Miriam pulls her head out of the trash, Katey is there. Holding the phone. "It's for you."

Miriam takes it. Clears her throat. "Hello?"

"You said to call you if anything strange is going on," Wren whispers.

Miriam clears her throat, wipes her mouth. "What? Tell me. Are you all right?"

"I'm fine. I snuck out to use the hall phone. The guards haven't seen me. This isn't about me. It's about you."

"What are you talking about?"

"Someone left something under my door. A white piece of paper with something… something written on it."

"What does it say?"

"It says, 'Wicked Miriam, turn from your sins lest

you despair, or the Devil take you without care'."

An ice-pick of fear drives sharp and cold through Miriam.

"Go back to your room," she hisses. "Go. Now."

"I'm… a little scared."

Miriam draws a deep breath. Tries not to puke again.

"Lock your door. I'll be there soon. I promise."

FORTY-FOUR
A BAD TIME FOR CONFESSIONS

The cab of Louis' truck feels tight, like Miriam's stuck in a body bag that's been dragged under dark water. The rain cascading down the windshield does little to help. It's not just because they've got one more passenger – Katey, who sits behind them on the bunk – but because Miriam can't parse what's happening. Too many questions. This mystery a clock with broken parts.

Annie Valentine's death. Self-inflicted? Maybe. Her sanity was a doll without stuffing, and Miriam feels a twist of guilt for leaving that poor, empty girl behind. And her sores: Those weren't fresh. Couldn't have been from Keener. Meth addict? Maybe. That might explain the suicide.

But the paper left under Wren's door...

Turn from your sins, lest you despair.

The Devil take you without care.

Keener's song. "Wicked Polly."

Except here it's "Wicked Miriam."

Someone knows. Could it have been Keener? She was unconscious long enough for him to go back to the school. If he's been watching Wren all this time, premeditating her murder all the way back to now – it tracks. Maybe.

Still. Something doesn't feel right.

Peck, peck, peck.

Miriam turns on the radio. Scans stations, listening for news.

"Phils are out of it this year but with all that pitching power–"

"–rain intensifying for another four days as we catch the edge of Tropical Storm Esmerelda–"

"And now a jazz selection from Mumbai Xochitl as part of our Sounds from the Global Café program– "

She turns the radio off. Rubs her head. It feels like her sinuses are wadded up with bloody cotton. The Dermabond pulls her face tight. Tugging and biting and burning.

"Maybe we should have stayed at the hospital," Louis says. "They wanted you to stay overnight. Keep an eye on that concussion."

Miriam grunts. "Fuck that noise. It's not that bad. In fact–" She taps out a cigarette, opens the window and lets a blast of cool night time air wash over her. "This is just what the doctor ordered. Spoonful of sugar." *And 37 types of carcinogenic chemicals. Yummy.*

"There's something I have to tell you," Louis says.

"This isn't the time for confessions."

"Maybe it is."

Katey watches the exchange. Miriam sighs, lights the cigarette with her injured hands, blows a plume of smoke outside.

"Fine. Then I get to confess first." Before Louis can interrupt she blurts it out. "I had… something go on with one of the teachers. The coach. Or sensei. Or whatever the hell you'd call him."

Katey is the first to speak. "Beck Daniels?"

"I… I know him. I met him. Once." Louis straightens in his seat. "Delivered some gym mats."

"We didn't fuck," Miriam says.

"All right."

She can see his hands tighten hard around the steering wheel. Were the wheel a man's shoulders, that man would fall to the floor with shattered collarbones.

"We fought. Literally. And then – we collided together and we almost – but we didn't and – you know what? I should have just kept this to myself. Like I said, this is a bad time for confessions."

Louis draws deep breaths through his nose, like he's trying either to calm down or to build up enough psychic energy to kill everybody in the truck with his mind.

"I belong with you," Louis says suddenly.

"What?"

"I've got a job. And it's to protect you." Another deep nostril-flaring breath. "I saw something."

"You saw – what? Louis? What did you see?"

"A bird. A crow."

Miriam tenses up.

He tells her everything. Not just one crow, but a whole road full of them – but only one that mattered. The crow that spoke with Miriam's voice. And then, from his eye socket, the feather. The muddy strands of hair.

"The Trespasser," she says aloud without meaning to. Her inside voice let out of its cage.

That means the Trespasser is real. Not kept to the prison of her own mind. Not merely an expression of her subconscious.

"I've been seeing the Trespasser for a while now. I always thought it was just me, just a thing that's in my head, but–"

"It still could be," Katey says. "Maybe what Louis saw was you... well, for lack of a better word, transmitting. Putting out a beacon."

"That message is why I raced here," Louis says. "Katey might be right. Besides, The Bird *did* speak with your voice."

Up ahead, the gates to the school.

Nobody mans the booth this late – it's already 1 AM. Katey hops out, though, and heads to the stone pillar sporting the Caldecott Crest. She pulls back a brick to reveal a white-button touchpad.

A few button-pushes later and the gate drifts open.

They head toward the school. They pull up out front, and Louis kills the engine, but Miriam touches his hand.

"No – you stay in the truck. Stay here just in case we gotta bolt. Katey's going to take me in because she has keys."

Katey jingles a key ring and offers a sad smile.

"I'm coming in," Louis growls. "I just got done telling you: I'm here to protect you. I can't let you go in alone."

Miriam half-laughs. "It's a girls' school. A school full of *girls*. Okay, sure, one or two of them might know how to carve a shiv out of a bar of Dove soap but, *by and large*, I think I can take them."

"Whatever psycho left that note for you could still be in there."

"Dude, we're trying to go in there and not attract attention. I don't call you Frankenstein because of your taste in platform shoes. *You're huge*. We'll be fine." She says it, and she hopes she means it. It's not that she doesn't want to attract attention. It's that the truck cab-as-confessional has made her a bit uncomfortable. She needs the space. He does too, she figures.

He doesn't smile, but he nods. "Fine. Don't linger."

"I won't."

She thinks to kiss him on the cheek but then isn't sure – is that a mixed message? Does she even know what kind of message she wants to send?

Instead, she salutes him.

Then she winces and says, "I don't know why the fuck I just saluted you."

He stares at her like she's a total moon unit. Which she probably is.

Red-faced and confused, Miriam goes to join Katey at the entrance.

FORTY-FIVE
THE HALL OF RED DOORS

The girls' dormitory is a wing off the main house. Right now the main house is dark, all lines and shadows, but Katey knows where to go. As she stands by the door, going through the key ring, feeling each one by one, a sudden beam of light appears from the upstairs balcony.

Miriam grabs Katey by the elbow, and pulls her down behind a wooden side-table sporting a coffee percolator and ceramic teapot.

The beam intensifies. A shadow steps up to the balcony, then begins walking down the steps toward the lobby. The light bounces until it reaches the bottom. Then it drifts back and forth, searching, searching. *Like the beam from a lighthouse.*

A radio squelches, and the shadow speaks.

"I swore I heard something. Yeah. I'm in the lobby."

Miriam knows that voice.

Sims. AKA Roidhead.

A voice chatters from the radio, but Miriam can't make it out. The other guard? Horvath?

"Yeah," Sims says. Pause. "No, I don't see anything. Uh-huh, I'm heading back to finish rounds. And you better not have eaten my sticky bun again."

Miriam's worst instinct is to blurt out a joke about two men eating each other's sticky buns, but for once wiser heads prevail. She feels a small surge of pride. *Aw, baby's all grown up.*

Sims retreats back up the steps.

Katey lets out a held breath and says, "I'm not sure we should be doing this."

"We have to. Something real fucking goofy is going on, and I wanna know what it is. Please?"

Katey nods. Goes back to the door.

Finds the key. Opens it.

Inside is a stairwell. All dark wood and dusty ochre carpets. Brass wall sconces sport white electric candles.

Katey whispers, "Up here is the Dorm Mother's desk. Miss Betty. She walks rounds sometimes so I'm going to go distract her, just in case. Lauren Martin's room is on the third floor – room 322. You good?"

Miriam's not good. But she nods anyway.

And then Katey's off to the races, and Miriam's taking the carpeted steps two by two until she reaches the third floor. She pops open the door and peeks out: nobody. She creeps through.

It's a hallway of red doors. More cherry wood, more moldy-oldie carpets that might as well be from a Victorian brothel, more of those brass sconces. Beneath the doors: a dark line. The girls are all asleep.

Miriam darts along, looking for 322.

The Rolling Stones in her head.

I see a red door and I want to paint it black.
There. Wren's room.
She raps lightly on the door.
The door flings open–
Hands grab her and yank her into the dark.

FORTY-SIX

WHAT FATE WANTS, FATE GETS

Miriam's hip slams hard into the corner of a dresser, rattling its contents. She's already reaching in her pocket for the knife when a pair of flashlights clicks on beneath a pair of chins.

Lauren Martin and another moon-faced girl. She reminds Miriam a bit of the chunky one from *Facts of Life*.

"Hey, psycho," Wren says.

"Hi, psycho," the other girl says.

"Okay," Miriam says, pointing at the roommate, "*you* don't get to call me that unless you want *me* to call you Fatalie-Natalie. You dig?"

"You suck," the porky girl says.

"You don't even know me, *Fatalie*."

"Guys, shut up!" Wren hisses. "Miriam, this is Missy. Missy, this is Miriam. Shake hands and be nice."

Miriam sticks out her tongue, but she offers her hand just the same.

Missy, flashlight still under her chin, goes to shake Miriam's hand–

The vision plays fast.

Missy's lost weight. No longer the pudgy girl with the Karl Malden nose, Missy has thinned out, stretched long on the antique doctor's table.

The song begins, "One Friday morn, Polly took ill–"

Burned out walls.

The man with the swallow tattoo and the plague mask.

Funeral flowers, smoldering, smoking through nose-holes.

The Mockingbird Killer sings.

Missy struggles, crying, teeth scraping against barbed wire, flakes of rust snowing on her dry tongue.

The axe rises.

The axe falls.

Her head does not come off entirely. The spine is severed but the rest of the meat must be cut away by wire cutter.

The tongue comes out. Clip clip.

The song ends.

The Mockingbird laughs. Trill, trill, warble, trill.

–and Miriam again hip-checks the dresser as she pulls away from Missy, her hand radiating pain from the X carved there and the deeper weirder pain of knowing that all this isn't over, that Keener isn't gone and the Mockingbird lives and girls are still going to die. And it's then she sees the ghostly skulls in front of both the girls' faces before the projections dissolve away to nothing.

"Oh, shit, shit, *shit,*" Miriam mumbles, holding both fists to her face and biting her knuckle so hard she thinks she might draw blood.

How?

How?

Carl Keener. Not dead? She killed him. She didn't

just kill him – she turned his throat into a sloppy hole. His body grew cold as she waited for Louis, as Annie Valentine sat trembling on the doctor's table, the wire pulled from her face, the leather straps unbound from her hands and feet.

And yet, there he waits. In the future.

Reborn.

How could Keener come back to life?

Suddenly nothing is certain. Everything is spinning like a top.

Miriam's own life has never been rock-steady, never a solid bedrock of sanity, but the one thing she could count on was the truth of her visions. And she thought, after saving Louis, that she could save others.

Was she wrong?

Was that a one-and-done deal?

Fate, it seems, has learned her tricks. It has moved to oppose her.

Her mother's voice: *It is what it is…*

I didn't save you," Miriam says to Wren, nearly breathless.

"She really *is* psycho," Missy mumbles.

Wren punches the other girl in the arm. "Miriam. What are you talking about?"

"I didn't stop anything. You still die. I killed Carl Keener – I really fucking killed him – but he still kills you. And I don't know how."

Annie Valentine with a bullet in her head.

The fire, burning down.

It hits her suddenly: In all the visions, the house and the bus have been burned. As the killer went to work on the girls, he did so surrounded by the charred walls of the house or the half-melted seats of the bus. But the fire just happened. *After* Keener's death.

Possibly as a result of it.

Keener isn't the only killer. He can't be.

Suddenly there's a pounding on the door.

She hears Sims's voice from outside. "Come out, Miss Black. I know you're in there."

Damnit!

Miriam snatches Missy's flashlight and points it at the window. The dark lines of iron sit beyond the glass. *Can't get out that way.*

Wren pipes up. "There's no one in here! We're trying to sleep!"

"We have cameras. You're not fooling anyone."

Missy buries her face in her hands. "We're *so* going to get kicked out."

Wren punches her again.

"Stand back," Miriam says to the girls. "Go! Go to the window."

What choice does she have? She opens the door.

Sims stands framed by the doorway. At first Miriam thinks he's got a pistol drawn but then she sees the truth: It's a Taser.

She *hates* those things.

"Come out of the room," he says. "Slowly."

"Okay. Okay. I'm coming, I'm coming."

She takes a step forward. Then flicks her gaze over his shoulder.

"Oh, you had to call your partner? Horvath, I take it?"

Sims looks.

It's a lie; nobody's there.

But it's enough.

Miriam flings the flashlight like a fucking tomahawk – it pivots through the air and cracks Sims between the eyes. The Taser goes off but Miriam's already out of its way. She slams hard into him, knocking him into the red door across the hall.

Then she bolts. But he's on her like flies on shit. She can feel his heavy steps shaking the whole dormitory floor. She has to escape. Has to. This is no time to be caged, no time for cops or bureaucracy or any of that.

Because the Mockingbird still lives, and as long as he lives, Wren Martin and those other girls are sure to die.

FORTY-SEVEN
THE RUSTLE OF WINGS

It's hard not to make noise.

The plan was to do this whole thing on the down-low, the QT, the *No, officer, I wasn't breaking into a girls' boarding school to – hey, are those handcuffs?*

But that plan flew out the fucking window.

She rounds the corner, sees a small table with a fake Chinese cloisonné vase on it – and she pulls the whole table over with a clatter.

Ahead is the opposite stairwell.

She reaches the door. Throws it open, darts through it.

Then – stops and waits, hiding behind the inward-opening door.

When she hears Sims come careening toward it, she smashes it closed at the last minute just as his head crosses the threshold.

The door smacks into his cue-ball skull, sending him tumbling onto his ass.

Then she bounds down the steps, leaping the banister as soon as she can do so without breaking an ankle.

Every footfall sends jolts of pain across her soles and up her legs. By now she's sure she feels blood soaking her socks from the cuts on her feet but there's no time to think, no time to stop.

From third floor to second, down to the first – already she hears him above, heavy feet plodding *thumpthumpthumpthump*, and she knows this guy's not going to give up.

He's full of Red Bull and steroids, this fucker, and worse, he has an axe to grind. Sims isn't going to give up this chase. And it's not like she can go toe-to-toe with this guy physically. Before, maybe, if he wasn't expecting it.

But now? When her hands and feet are cut up? And her head's like an overinflated kickball and it feels like her brain's rattling around her skull like the dice in a Yahtzee cup? Not a snow-cone's chance in Hell.

She has to find a place to hide.

The door ahead is marked by a plaque engraved with: CLASSROOMS.

Much better.

Shoulder first, she throws herself through the door and into the classroom wing. There the darkness is lit only by red emergency lighting.

And immediately she sees a familiar sight: the cafeteria.

There? She doesn't know the layout. Where to hide?

Nearby, though... the gym. A big room. Plenty of places to hide: bleachers, whiteboard, behind big-ass medicine balls. Maybe even Beck's office.

She keeps her head low and hurries along the wall (almost cross-checking a water fountain) just as she hears Sims throw open the door not twenty feet behind her.

A flashlight beam sweeps the halls.

The gym doors are ahead.

The flashlight beam roves towards her.

Only one shot at this if she moves now.

Miriam pops her shoes off, leaves them where they stand, and she runs on the balls of her feet – *pad pad pad pad ow ow ow* – as the beam drifts toward her–

She reaches the double doors to the gymnasium.

No need to fling them wide. Just open a crack. Just like before.

Slide in. Like a shadow.

She lets the door ease shut just as the flashlight beam finds it.

She prays Sims didn't see that.

Miriam darts into the wide-open dark. Again a red emergency light helps illuminate the room, and suddenly she realizes: That light is above an exit door.

Escape.

She reminds herself to find the resting place of the architect who built this school and lay flowers and whisky upon his grave.

Miriam darts toward the exit, but then sees something–

Off to the far end of the gym, another light. White light. Framing the half-open door of Beck's office.

Huh.

She turns back toward the exit and a shape looms – suddenly, strong hands capture both of her wrists and pin them together, and she's about to cry out, but it's then she smells him: the simple scent of soap and sweat.

Beck Daniels.

"Miriam?" he asks.

"Beck. Jesus. Beck."

"What are you doing here?"

Avert! Misdirect!

"What are *you* doing here is the better question. It's like 2:00 in the morning, dude."

"I did katas until midnight. Then I was trying to get caught up on paperwork. I thought I heard someone come in here."

He lets go of her hands. His hands find her hips. She feels suddenly, strangely safe. Her hands find his lean, strong chest.

Her wounded palms come away damp with his sweat. She ignores the stinging. Pain fades.

The doors to the gym swing open behind them.

Sims.

Shit.

She turns to face him just as he flips on all the lights – bright, garish overheads that rip the darkness from the room and leave Miriam feeling like she just got caught staring at the sun." to "Miriam reeling. Blinded as if staring too long at the sun.

The rent-a-cop comes charging into the room like he's SWAT, already jacking a second cartridge into the front of the Taser. Dark spots swim in front of her eyes.

"Back away, Daniels!" Sims shouts, face red, the veins

on his forehead like exposed tree roots. "She's dangerous. She tried to hurt two girls in the dorm."

Beck holds up his hands, bumps hard into Miriam, but then pulls away from her. She sees a flash of red as her eyes start to adjust. "Miriam. Is that true?"

What?" she asks. He continues to back away toward Sims. She pleads with him. "No! No. I told you – I'm here to *save* them. For fuck's sake, Beck, you don't know me very well but you know this mall cop wannabe has it out for me. Christ, c'mon."

Sims takes a long look at Beck. "Beck – you're hurt."

As her eyes start to finally adjust, she sees.

Beck's got a white T-shirt stretched taut over his chest.

And that white T-shirt is wet with red. Blood soaking through.

Her hands are red, too. What she felt wasn't his sweat.

And the blood on his chest, it forms an image–

First she thinks it's her own blood, but…

Oh, god.

Becks backs up and stands behind Sims, and Miriam shakes her head, reaches out and cries, "Sims! Jesus. Get away from him!"

But it's too late.

Beck flicks his wrist down and reveals the blade of a knife, a spring-blade knife, *her* knife. He grabs Sims by the forehead, and in one motion draws the head back and slashes a vent in the guard's throat.

Air and blood gurgle together, spattering on the gym floor.

The sound echoes.

The body drops.

Dead by her knife. Beck must have stolen it when he bumped her.

But this isn't how Sims dies–

He dies by a heart attack. At his weight bench. In eleven years.

Everything goes topsy-turvy. Can she trust what she sees anymore?

She can't trust her visions. Can't trust that she has the right man.

Carl Keener wasn't the only killer.

"The swallow," she says, her voice small – each word feeling cracked like a delicate teacup, each on the word of breaking. "On your chest."

The red on this chest bleeds through the fabric in an all-too-familiar pattern: the razor curve of the wings, the sharp tines of the tail, the head and beak thrust upward as though in flight. Spreading bigger, wider, dripping downward.

He lifts his shirt, smiling.

The tattoo is fresh. *Tonight* fresh. Beads of blood rise along the margins of the tattoo and smear like the juices drawn out of a T-bone as it starts to grill, oozing across the plate.

"You fucker," she spits.

"Now, now. That's not very lady-like." He takes a step toward her. Drops the knife on the still-twitching body of Sims. "Neither was killing Sims. Messy business."

"I hear there are cameras in here."

"Who said they were on?"

Another step closer. She retreats one step.

The exit.

Get to the exit.

There: the parking lot. Louis. The great egress.

"You're sick," she says. Another step back.

He steps forward.

They continue this dance. She's close now. Ten feet. No more. Maybe less.

"Come on, Miriam. We're birds of a feather – if you'll excuse the pun."

She manifests false bravado. Puffs out her chest. "I will not excuse a pun. Lowest form of humor, dude. You should be ashamed."

"Always quick with the wit. It's your defense, isn't it? Little girl doesn't want the world to know how sad she is, how damaged. Your words, your attitude, all a big misdirection. A magician's trick."

"Fucking die."

"But we're the same. We both kill for purpose."

"I'm not a killer."

Five feet.

"Carl Keener would beg to differ. You did a number on him."

"You and Keener working together? Are you the one who shot Annie?"

He just smiles.

Almost there.

Get ready.

"There's so much you don't know," he says.

"Here's what I know," she growls through trembling lips. Tears burning hot at the edges of her eyes. "I know you like to hurt girls. But those days are done. Maybe

I am a killer. Maybe that's who I've become, or maybe it's who I always was. Keener found out. And you'll find out too."

Now run.

She pivots, crosses the last couple feet between her and the door, between her and *freedom*–

–she slams into the door–

It doesn't open.

She shoulders the emergency bar.

Nothing.

She screams. Pulls on it. Kicks it. Jacks her body into it again and again. Still doesn't open. She sobs. Puts her head against the door – cold metal against warm skin. Hears Beck clucking his tongue behind her.

"I locked it, of course. Fire hazard, I know."

Her hands ball into fists.

She tries to kick off from the door like a swimmer. She plans to run toward his office where maybe, *maybe* he's got a gun stashed somewhere, a gun he'll one day use to parachute his monstrous brains out of his fucking skull–

But Beck has other ideas.

He moves fast. Spins her, shoves her face first against the wall. Two pistoning rabbit punches against her kidneys steal the strength from her legs.

Before she falls, he catches her.

He turns his arm into a triangle, a crushing vice with her neck at the nadir, and he begins to choke.

She swats backward, rakes his face. Struggles. Kicks.

The world goes blue at the edges. Then black.

She tries to call for Louis.

Tries to say something, anything.
It's all just a whispered whimper.
"Go to sleep," he whispers. Kisses her cheek. "Shhh."
She does as she's told.

FORTY-EIGHT
THE PROTECTOR

2.30am.

Louis doesn't know what to do.

He thinks, *I could run them off the road.* Ram them. The Mack would handle it. It would crush the bumper and push the rear of the car into a hard spin.

But Miriam's in there. The little girl, too. Wren.

Twenty minutes ago he'd just been sitting there in the parking lot. He thought about leaving the engine to idle but eventually he just turned it off. It was frustrating just *waiting* for something to happen. While worry gnawed at him like a starving rat.

And then he saw.

Then, at the other end of the lot, a black car pulled up. Mercedes, by the looks of it. Nice, too, an S-Class, brand new.

A man – hard to see who, but Louis could see that he was young, strong, with a shock of dark hair and a white T-shirt stained with something dark.

He came out holding Lauren Martin the way you might carry a barrel or a beer keg: both arms wrapped tight around her middle, pinning her arms. Louis couldn't tell whether she was gagged. Her head lolled. She was knocked out.

Or dead.

The man tossed her in the back of the Mercedes.

And then he went back inside.

Returning moments later with a new body. This one carried over-shoulder, like a rolled-up rug. And it was then that Louis saw the flash of bleach-white and hot-pink and knew exactly who the man was carrying.

Get out. Stop him. Kill him.

But he'd be too slow. It would be too late. And he had no plan.

You have to have a plan if you're going to save her.

You lost your wife. Don't lose her.

They pulled away. Louis followed.

Now he drives. Keeps the black car ahead far enough so that he can see the pinprick tail-lights ahead, glowing red like demon eyes.

What to do?

Stay calm, he thinks. *Just follow.*

Don't lose them.

See where they're going.

Then call the police.

The Mercedes crosses an intersection. A four-way stop framed by a thicket of trees. The car doesn't stop. Just coasts through.

Louis thinks to do the same–

The world lights up. Red and blue. A cop car comes gunning in from the east, and Louis thinks, *Here comes the cavalry.* But the car slams to a stop in the center of the intersection, and Louis has to punch the brakes.

The truck brakes lock up. Wheels skid. The Mack grinds to a stop mere feet from the cop car. *What the hell?*

A cop gets out of the driver side. He's squat, thick, built like a fire hydrant. Bushy black horseshoe mustache framing an acid scowl.

He's got his gun out – a Colt Python by the look of it, a .357 with a vented barrel and a shiny nickel finish that captures the strobing lights.

The cop points the weapon at the windshield and fires.

Louis tilts hard to the right, diving across his front seats as a hole the size of a golf ball punches through the glass. He hears another two shots and suddenly the truck shudders and tilts forward.

He shot the tires.

Then: footsteps off to the left of the truck.

Louis quick shuts off the engine and snatches the keys.

The driver-side door flings open, and the cop fires a shot into the cab. But Louis has already popped the opposing door and is clambering out the other side on his hands and knees, palms stinging from the bite of gravel.

He gets his legs under him, starts to stand –

And there's the cop. Already around the front of the truck.

Gun leveled at Louis's head.

Louis holds up one hand. The other hand – holding the keys to the Mack – dangles by his side.

"Why?" he asks. Desperate. Confused.

The cop seems to consider this. "Because it's what I do."

With a fat thumb, the cop pulls back the hammer on the revolver.

Louis's thumb has its own mission.

He presses the alarm button on the key fob.

The truck lights up like a tree at Christmas. The horn honks and the alarm woops and wails.

Distraction. That's how Miriam fights, he thinks. It's enough. The gun goes up and fires–

But Louis is already under the cop, plowing forward like a linebacker and slamming him to the ground.

Wham.

The gun cracks Louis along the side of the head.

But he's not having any of it.

Anger swells up inside of him. It's like a dam breaking. He doesn't know what's happening but he knows this cop is *in his way*. Preventing him from finding Miriam. Worse, the cop is a part of it. He has to be. How could this assassination attempt be any other thing?

Louis grabs the cop's wrist with one hand.

And with the other, he forms a fist – the truck key sticking out between the second and third knuckle.

He pops the cop right in the mouth.

It cuts the cop's lower lip – splits it in half, leaving behind an inch-deep V-shaped cleft from which fresh blood swiftly flows. The cop gags and coughs.

Louis wrenches the gun from his hand and staggers backward to stand.

The cop sits forward, pressing his sleeve against the key-split lip. He looks up to see Louis pointing the gun at his head.

"One-eyed man points a one-eyed gun," the cop says,

mumbling around the cut. Probing it with his tongue and wincing. "Between the both of you, you've got one good set of peepers, at least."

"Tell me what's going on." Louis thumbs the hammer back.

"You'll never know the scope of it."

"I'll kill you."

"Will you, now? See, I don't think you have it in you. I don't think that's who you are. I know killers." He smiles, spits blood against the pavement. "That little girlfriend of yours, she's the real deal. But you ain't shit, Hercules. A big gentle giant. With piss-poor depth perception."

The gun shakes.

Show him, Louis thinks.

Show him what you're made of.

The cop sneers.

Louis pulls the trigger.

INTERLUDE
UNCLE JACK

Jack's got a cigarette pinched between his teeth, and he sometimes picks tobacco bits from inside his lip and flicks them off into the grass.

"Here," he says, pushing Miriam's cheek so it's pressed against the cold blue steel of the barrel. "Look down the gun. Match up the sight at the end to the little – you know, the little notch right here at the back sight. Close your one eye. Go on, close it up."

She does – squeezes that one eye shut real tight and glances down the sights. The robin hops into view. Stabbing at the ground with its beak. A wan little worm flung up and down.

"Target acquired."

"The bird?" she says. "I'm supposed to shoot the bird?"

"Uh-huh. Now, what you wanna do is this, you want to take a deep breath and then let it out – I saw this in a movie, it's a sniper thing – and then you exhale so that your heart slows down real good, and you don't pull the trigger, I mean, you don't jerk it, you just – well, you just squeeze it real gentle-like, as if you're trying to pleasure your–"

Biff!

The bird tumbles to the side. Feet sticking up in the air.

Miriam shrieks. Throws the gun against the lawn and hops up over the rock they were leaning against and hurries over to the bird.

The worm lies nearby, still alive.

The bird's dead. A few drops of blood wet the grass.

Jack sucks on the cigarette hard enough she can hear it sizzle. He claps her on the shoulder, laughs like a hyena.

"Goddamn. You popped that robin right in its head. She ain't going home to her babies anytime soon, is she?"

Miriam looks up. Cheeks wet. "Babies?"

"Sure. Shit, I dunno." The robin isn't even a female, and it's too early in the spring for the robin to have bred. But what does Miriam know? She's only twelve. "All I'm saying is, this one's not heading back to the nest." He flicks the butt of his cigarette into the woods. "Nicely done, killer."

"I'm not a killer!"

"That dead bird says otherwise."

She stands up. Wipes tears away. "Don't say that."

"The hell's your problem? That was an ace shot, little girl."

Miriam sticks out her lip. "I'm not a murderer. And I'm not a little girl. You say mean things."

"Okay. Uh-huh. Fine." He starts to walk back to the rock.

But she runs around the other side and beats him to it. Picks up the rifle again.

He whoops. "There you go! Now we're cooking with gas. Let's go shoot something else. Whole shitload of squirrels around here, that's for damn sure."

Miriam fishes in her pocket for a pellet while he's lighting another cigarette. She cracks the barrel open, tucks the pellet in its hole, and then snaps the barrel shut.

When Uncle Jack looks up, he's staring down the barrel.

"Say it," she says, still crying.

"Say what?"

"Say I'm not a killer!"

"Put that damn gun down. You're gonna get someone hurt."

"Say it!" she screams.

But he doesn't care. He marches toward her and reaches for the gun. But she backpedals and–

Biff!

Jack's suddenly hopping around like a bee-stung rabbit, clutching his knee, the cigarette falling from his lips as he howls. He pulls his hand away – the denim at the knee has a little ragged hole in it, the pellet wound looking like a little popped tick.

Miriam runs away into the woods.

Jack cries after her, "Better not tell your mother about this!"

FORTY-NINE
BIRDS OF A FEATHER

Tap tap tap.

Miriam struggles to find air. Submerged in shadow.

A thundering rush of noise, like white water, like the crash of the ocean surf or the muddy churn of the Susquehanna.

Tap tap tap.

And above it all, that noise.

Tap tap tap.

Hands hold her beneath dark water. Cold water.

She reaches. The shadow has shape. Her fingers curl around it. A rope.

It slips from her grip and again she's gone beneath the surface, sinking once more into those wintry depths – the sound of the water mimicking the sound of the blood in her ears, a sound like someone breathing sharply through clenched teeth as a drum beats in the distance.

But there: the rope once more. And she grabs it and pulls, pulls until every synapse in her brain fires in a twenty-one-synapse-salute, white lancing needles of light arcing through the know-nothing void–

Tap tap tap.

Her eyes bolt open.

Above, a square of gray light. A smeary water-slick square.

Rain thunders against the skylight.

A raven stands in its center, the glass separating Miriam's world – a world that feels oddly warm, curiously cozy – from the cold rain of the outside.

The bird bangs its black beak against the skylight glass.

Tap tap tap tap tap.

Then it takes flight, a flurry of inky wings gone in the downpour.

Miriam sits up. It takes all her energy to do so. Pain shoots through every limb and muscle. Everything feels like a bolt tightened too hard. All her screws, stripped.

What she sees, she does not expect.

She's on a bed. Queen-sized. White sheets and a white down comforter – she knows it's down because one of the feathers pokes through and sticks her in the hand.

A hand swaddled in gauze. She pushes her feet from the bottom of the blanket and sees those, too, are gauzed. Fresh gauze. Not from the hospital.

A fat-bellied iron pellet stove sits in the corner, a fire glowing bright behind its door.

A nice rug. Dark walnut wainscoting. Everything, clean lines. Not a speck of dust. The one outlier is the painting that hangs opposite the bed.

It's one fucked-up piece of art.

An old man – naked, by the look of it, his shriveled wormy genitals barely covered by a sweeping black cloth – holds a screaming infant in his hands, a boy, and he bites the child's breast, a swatch of the boy's flesh in his teeth.

"It's the original." A woman stands in the doorway.

Her.

The nurse. No – not just the nurse. The matron of the school.

Eleanor Caldecott.

"What?" Miriam asks, her tongue sharper than she'd like. But she's a tooth rubbed raw of its enamel, a fraying exposed nerve. Everything hurts, and it feels somehow pertinent to hurt everything right back.

"The painting. It's Peter Paul Rubens' original *Saturn Devouring His Son*. Better than the Goya, I think. The Goya is, to me, derivative."

"Well," Miriam says, taking a thumb and rubbing circles in the space between her eyes. "Whoever painted it, it's really quite lovely. And by 'lovely,' I mean it makes me want to throw up all over these very nice sheets." *Thread count: three million*.

"I could have it covered up," Caldecott says, bringing over a tray.

"Don't make the effort. I'm just being melodramatic." Suddenly, a familiar smell sneaks up her nose and activates all the pleasure centers in Miriam's brain. Bacon. Eggs. Coffee. *Breakfast*. "If that's bacon, then I am prepared to hug you, and I assure you, I am not the hugging type. For bacon, however, I will radiate a force field of pure unadulterated love."

The nurse – dressed not in her school garments but rather in a simple white blouse and ankle-length black skirt – sets the tray down. "Enjoy the food, Miss Black."

Miriam wastes no time. She can't remember the last time she's eaten a proper meal. The bacon goes into her mouth with a gulp of coffee. Best thing she's ever tasted. Her knife and fork scrape against the fine china. She chews noisily. Makes *mmm, ah, oh* sounds.

"You were hungry." Caldecott watches her.

"Starving. *Starving.* It's been a… bad couple of days." She swallows a throatful of molten hot eggs, not caring that it scalds her windpipe all the way down. "So what? You found me on the gym floor and now I'm your patient? Do all your patients get the royal treatment?"

Eleanor smiles. "You're not my patient."

"Well, what am I, then?" Coffee. *Coffee.* Best thing ever. If only she had a cigarette. And a little Irish whiskey to pour in there. That's how she knows she's not dead: If this were heaven, she'd have those things right at hand.

"It remains to be seen what you are," Caldecott says. Rather icily, to Miriam's ear.

"Oh yeah?"

"You will have a choice this morning. We make our own choices in this world, and it will fall to you to make yours."

"Choices," Miriam says, rolling that word around her mouth. Suddenly the breakfast doesn't taste so good. She almost laughs, and even almost laughing hurts her whole body. "Lady, we don't get as many choices as we think we do. The world doesn't work like that."

"It does for you."

"Does it now."

"And it does for me, too."

Miriam's about to ask just what the hell that's supposed to mean, but then someone else appears at the door.

No.

She grabs the knife – just a butter knife, but a knife all the same – from the tray, gets her back up against the headboard, and hisses like a cat. Miriam waves the silverware in front of her like a weapon. Making sure he sees it.

"Come near me and I start stabbing."

Eleanor Caldecott doesn't seem fazed. "So you remember my son, then."

Beck Daniels stands in the door. Clean shirt. No blood. Smiling softly, like nothing's wrong, like he didn't just beat the piss out of Miriam and choke her out on a gymnasium floor. After he murdered a security guard with her knife.

"Miss Black," Beck says, offering a gentlemanly head nod.

"Your *son,*" Miriam seethes.

"Hello, Mother," Beck says.

"Good morning, Beckett." Eleanor turns to Miriam. "We don't share the same last name. Nor do we publicize the fact that we're related."

"It's a *secret,*" Beck says, finger to smiling lips.

Miriam feels like an animal trapped in a corner. Desperate for an escape route. Beck stands between her and the door. She's got no way to Batman up to the skylight. A window sits off to her right.

That might be the way out.

The knife pivots in her hand. She turns it from blade-out to blade-in so that it's less about the *thrust* and more about the *stab*. Miriam makes a show of it. She has to.

Her fingers tighten so hard around it the blood drains from her knuckles.

"She's a fighter," Beck says to his mother.

"She's more than that," Eleanor says.

Miriam snarls. "I'm in the room. I can hear you."

"Look at the way she holds that butter knife," Beck says, pointing at her.

Eleanor nods. "And she's eyeing up the window."

"Fuck the both of you. Twisted fucks."

"Miriam," Eleanor says, "I understand if you're upset. Anybody would be. You've been through a lot. Before you make any ill-considered moves, I feel obliged to mention two things. First: We have the girl. We have Lauren Martin."

Miriam's bowels clench.

"I'm willing to discuss the girl's fate with you, but only if you're kind enough to hear me out. And that brings me to the second thing: If you do something drastic now, you may not be afforded the privilege of discovering what's really going on. What's really going on. And we will not be able to guarantee the safety of Lauren Martin. Further, you won't be privy to my offer."

"Stick your offer up your son's ass. Preferably with a fist wrapped in barbed wire."

"You won't sit for a story, then?"

Miriam says nothing. She just hunkers there against the headboard like a feral child.

Eleanor smiles. "I'll take your silence as acquiescence. Let me tell you about the time I was raped by Carl Keener."

FIFTY
ELEANOR'S STORY

I was not a good girl.

My parents came from wealth. My mother had ties to the steel industry and, before that, shipping. My father came from the Ivy League and flourished there, learning and teaching across an array of subjects. I was expected to make someone a very happy husband, and at the time it was de rigueur to attend a woman's college – to learn how to be refined, intelligent, a capable wife for a deserving man of proper breeding.

But I was not a good girl.

Yes, I was on the sailing team. The equestrian team. I did theater and sang in choir. I also drank a lot. And smoked marijuana. I tried LSD and magic mushrooms, and though I did not try it, I knew girls who procured heroin from black gentlemen in the ghetto.

I was what one would call a "loose woman."

I was a disappointment to my parents. A fact of which I was quite proud. I had no interest in appealing to them. My mother was a secret drunk. My father distant and icy. I had no brothers, no sisters, and so all the attention fell to me, and I was happy to abuse the spotlight in whatever way I could.

Word got around. As it does with girls like me. I did things.

I had pregnancy scares. Had abortions.

I got blackout drunk one night and almost fell off the roof of one of my classrooms.

Another night, I raced around town with a pair of boys from one of the Catholic colleges. They were drunk. I was stoned. They were driving a cherry red Buick Riviera. They took a curve the wrong way and flipped the car down an embankment – over and over and over again. The one boy broke his collarbone, the other his leg. I had only bumps and scratches, a few unsightly bruises. Bruises perfect to show my mother.

Word got around.

One night I was in the basement of the Troxell building. Our dormitory. I was down there in one of the supply closets, waiting for a group of girls to come meet me with – well, I don't quite recall what they were bringing me. Drugs of some kind. I had a little cabal of girls, you see, who would do what I wanted. But these girls were late. No matter, I thought. I was having a fine time by my lonesome, drinking rye whiskey from the bottle and smoking cigarettes and just not giving one care in the world.

The door opened, and there he stood. Carl Keener.

He was my age, roughly. Two years older.

He had dark eyes, like smoldering coals. He was strong, wiry, with a strong jaw and a cruel smile.

I'd seen him before. He was the night janitor. On loan

from Naval Supply. He had, unbeknownst to me, gotten into some trouble there – fights with senior officers and other indiscretions – and they decided to loan him to the college for a few nights a week. That was a practice, back then – naval officers were thought to be good, honorable men. More to the point, they were thought to be safe around fragile, impressionable girls.

I told him to get out. I didn't like him. I didn't like the way he looked at me.

He said, no. No, he wouldn't. He wanted a drink, he said. And a Pall Mall.

And then I thought – well, what's the harm? Wouldn't it make Mother burn if she knew I was cavorting with a common janitor, naval officer or no?

We sat and drank there in the supply closet, our backs to the metal shelves, the smoke between us an eye-blistering haze, and I said that it might be time to air out the closet and go for a walk.

He said, "No, I want to stay here. With you."

Then he planted a rough hand on my hip. I wriggled away but the closet was barely big enough for the both of us – and he was between me and the door.

He did it again. And I let him. Just to see.

The hand crawled up my side. A rough touch, like a clumsy child petting a disinterested cat. The way he laughed: a low chuckle, like he was in on a joke that nobody else understood. His hand did not linger on my chest – to my surprise.

Rather, it went to my neck. And tightened. Not enough to choke me but enough to make the blood throb in my head.

And again I told him, no. It was time to stop.

I tried to push past him, and he picked me up and slammed me back.

I started to cry then. No matter what I'd done so far, I'd never had anyone be like this with me. Boys had become improper with me before. But they backed off when they thought I'd scream or realized I wasn't playing some foolish girl's game.

I pushed him again and his response was to–

Well. He grabbed a fistful of my hair and smashed the back of my head against the metal shelves. Bottles of floor cleaner and rolls of brown paper towels fell to the ground. I started to cry out, and he punched me in the mouth.

He… turned me around. Pressed my face against the shelves. The edge of the shelf bit into my lips, cut my cheeks.

Carl took a swig from the bottle – a long swig, finishing it off. Then he hit me in the back – between the shoulder blades – with it.

Then he lifted my skirt and…

It was over faster than I probably realize. In some ways it was worse than I could have imagined, in some ways better. It hurt, but only a little. He was rough, but not so rough anything was damaged. The pain was inside. Not just physical pain but rather the pain of knowing that this was where my life had led me. The pain of realizing that I was a girl of good breeding and fine stature and my choices put me in a supply closet with a thick-skulled, dim-witted brute – a cruel man of the sort to pull the wings off flies. He was slow and mean and it seemed we deserved each other.

The girls who were supposed to meet me finally did. They found me alone in the closet. Curled up on the ground. Mouth bleeding. Head bleeding. Bleeding down there. Half naked. Traumatized.

The girls did what they could. They took me to the nurse. The nurse got the assistant dean involved. No police, of course. Back then, that simply wasn't proper.

I told them about Carl and they would have fired him but it didn't matter – he never came back to work after that night.

The administration contacted my family.

My father, then teaching at Princeton, came home.

They pulled me out of school for the rest of the semester.

Then came the discovery: I was pregnant.

My father, who I loved as much as I hated, told me then that the Caldecotts do not abide slights against our bloodline, nor do we absolve anyone of their responsibility to our family.

Carl Keener, he said, had a responsibility.

My father and my two uncles went and found Carl. They waited for him to leave NAVSUP and head off to his new job – as a janitor at another school north of Chambersburg – and they threw a bag over his head and tossed him into the trunk of Father's Lincoln. They brought him to the estate – this estate – and they beat him half to death. Then they beat him another halfway. And halfway again. Zeno's paradox writ in blood and bruises – I remember my father saying, if you beat a man halfway to death every time, you will never quite kill him.

I don't know how they entreated the Navy to stop looking for him. Money, I assume. That and Carl had a list of offenses dogging his every step – fights with other sailors and harassment accusations. They were happy to be rid of him, I suspect.

We kept him.

Like a pet.

A damaged pet.

He lived in the greenhouse. Tending to plants.

And we were married two nights before I gave birth to my first son, Edwin, in that very same greenhouse.

FIFTY-ONE
BAD TOUCH

Miriam's thumb runs along the edge of the butter knife. It's not sharp. The faint serration might hurt somebody if she had time to hold them down and saw away at their body like they were a piece of steak.

Just the same, she holds it out in front of her. Twirling it.

She needs them to see she has it.

Rain continues to hammer the skylight.

"What a beautiful tale!" Miriam finally says. "*So* heartwarming. Nice twist ending, too. I give it five-stars, two thumbs up, and a bunch of wiggly toes. I'm sure the movie version will star Sandra Bullock and, I dunno, Billy Bob Thornton as Big Bad Carl Keener. But here I am thinking, gosh, this story isn't done. Can't *possibly* be done. A great big gulf lies betwixt 'and then my brain-damaged rapist and I got married in a greenhouse' and 'now he kills eighteen-year-old girls dressed like a monstrous bird-man'."

"Yes," Eleanor says, knitting her hands together. "The story takes a curious turn. For that, I suspect we should walk. I'm sure you want to see Lauren, make sure she's well. She's in the greenhouse, on the far side of the house."

Miriam's throat tightens.

You could just stab her now.

No. Not yet.

"Is Wren okay? She'd better be okay, because so help me–"

"As I said, she is well. And she can continue to be well if we all play well together. I can show you."

"Yes. Show me."

"First," Eleanor holds out her hand. "The knife."

"Mother," Beck says, stepping into the room, snapping quick into an alarm state. Eleanor offers only the gentlest of head nods and he freezes.

"It's fine, Beckett. Miriam understands that the knife isn't going to do much good. It's just for show."

Shit. Does she know?

She can't.

Miriam eases the knife forward. Blade first. Watches Beck watching her – a falcon atop a telephone pole watching a mouse cross the road beneath. She's not sure who's who, here – *which of us is the falcon, which of us is the mouse*?

She sees Eleanor smiling. It wouldn't take much to punch this knife into her throat. But then what? Beck's the bigger problem.

Besides, this affords Miriam an opportunity.

Miriam doesn't just drop the knife into Eleanor's hand.

She places it there.

Palm touches palm, fingertips touch fingertips, skin on skin, and–

Darkness, howling darkness, cold waters, mud and silt and screaming. Everything is breaking glass and a radio dial turned to a dead station, bad sounds in an empty void, like sleeping at the heart of a tornado or falling to the bottom of a rushing river at night. Everything is nothing and nothing is everything and–

–Miriam gasps, tries to breathe, can't. Her throat feels closed. Her lungs feel pancaked. Her eyes water as tears push at their edges.

"Yes, I thought so," Eleanor says. Calm. Cool. As though this is expected. "Give it a moment."

And then, she's right – all it takes is a moment. Miriam's lungs inflate like a balloon against the nozzle of an oxygen tank. A great heaving wheezing breath – cold and bright and powerful – enters her body.

"What did you see?" Eleanor asks. Genuinely curious. Leaning forward in her chair as one might do when watching a scary movie.

"I saw..." She thinks to lie. Thinks, *Tell her she dies by your hand, chopped in half by a fire axe and thrown into a wood chipper*. But the truth comes out. "I saw nothing. I heard sounds. Awful sounds. But I saw absolutely nothing."

"That troubles you, doesn't it? You're used to seeing things. Things well beyond the purview of others."

"You don't know me."

"But I do. I have the gift, too."

"It's not a gift."

"Oh, but it is. Sometimes to fix something you must first break it. Power and wisdom are born of trauma and – well. I'm getting ahead of myself. Walk with me and my son. I'll tell you the rest."

FIFTY-TWO
TO THE GREENHOUSE

As they walk through the house, Eleanor moves beside Miriam. The woman has a kind of resplendent, queen-of-the-castle vibe – she seems to glide along, a swan atop a placid lake aware of both her beauty and her authority. Nothing like the nurse Miriam had seen back at the school. There she seemed small. Servile. A part of the whole.

But this is her place. Her rules. Her family.

Beck walks behind. Miriam can feel his eyes on her shoulder blades, searing in like two cigarette burns. Any move she makes, he'll be there.

Miriam doesn't waste time. "You're psychic, then."

"Yes. As are you."

"Not like me." Miriam chews on the inside of her cheek. "How'd you know?"

They stand at the top of steps twisting downward to the foyer. Where the Caldecott School is all about its Victorian trappings, the house instead carries a distinct retro vibe. Mid-century modern is in full effect.

Everything with clean lines, rounded corners. Lots

of windows, gray light streaming in through the rain-battered glass. Frugal arrangements of ferns and orchids – by the sidebar in the foyer, by the pair of vintage easy chairs, by the door, in the corners.

"I was left with something that night Carl and I found each other in the supply closet," Eleanor says.

Found each other, Miriam thinks. *What a delicate understatement.*

"I discovered that night that I could touch people and see not only who they'd become but also the chain of consequence and causality cascading outward – as though each person's life was a stone thrown into a pond. I could see the ripples. For every choice, a new ripple, a new disturbance of the water. It was fascinating. And horrible. All at the same time."

"And with me you saw nothing."

"Just darkness and clamor and the sounds of churning dark waters."

That sounds about right.

They descend the steps, Beck only a few behind. Miriam thinks to make her move but – no. She needs to see Wren first.

At the bottom of the steps, a familiar face meets them.

Edwin. The Headmaster of the Caldecott School.

It's now that she sees: He reminds Miriam of her own mother. Small, pinched, buttoned up so tight. He's got a cup of coffee. Steam rises from it like ghosts from a grave of dark earth.

"Ah," he says. "The disruptor."

"So, you're part of this, too," Miriam says.

"Family must stick together."

"That makes you a killer."

His eyes smile, though his mouth stays a sneering line. "What is it the girls sometimes say? *Takes one to know one*. Isn't that it?"

"I hope someone poured drain cleaner in that coffee."

He takes a long sip. "Always a pleasure. Must get to school and tend to the mess you left behind. Naughty girl, killing that security guard. Found him dead in the gymnasium." His eyes twinkle suddenly, as though he's hiding something and loving every moment of it. "If you'll excuse me?"

Then he walks away.

Images of the guard's body flash in Miriam's head along with the lightning outside.

Eleanor pulls her along. "Don't fret about him. For now, let's talk about Annie Valentine."

Miriam's body tightens. "The dead girl."

"Yes." They walk down a hall into what must be another wing of the house. Miriam sees a drafting room with an old architectural table. Across from it is a library two stories high, the only way to get at all the books being a ladder against the shelves, a ladder with wheels for feet. "Can I tell you what I saw when I met Annie Valentine five years ago?"

"Can I stop you?"

Eleanor stops. Faces Miriam. "Miss Black, you can stop this conversation any time you'd like. Just say the word and we can conclude our business and I will reluctantly bid you farewell."

"Bid me farewell. A euphemism. For chopping off

my head like you're a fucking Al Qaeda operative. Do I have that right?"

Eleanor says nothing.

Beck tenses.

Miriam's hand itches, fingers tucking into a fist.

But she lets it go. "Yeah. Great. Tell me all about that poor dead girl."

FIFTY-THREE
IF ANNIE WERE ALIVE

At age eighteen, Annie Valentine is a drug addict. Methamphetamines. A boyfriend gets her hooked on it a year before she graduates from the Caldecott School.

At age nineteen, Annie finds that she's pregnant. The father could be one of several men. The pregnancy is a troubled one, because Annie chooses not to give up or even mitigate her addiction. When the baby is born ten weeks early, the child has a low fetal heart rate and has to be kept in the hospital – but eventually the child, who Annie names Alicia, stabilizes and can go home with her mother.

At age twenty, Annie decides she needs a man in her life. She chooses a weak man ten years her senior, a man desperate for love and the need to do anything for it. He is himself not addicted to crystal meth, but he does have too much to drink on occasion. His name is Byron, and he believes – like many in bad relationships do – that he can fix Annie, that he can rescue her from her own worst inclinations. After six months with her, Byron becomes addicted to methamphetamines.

At age twenty-one, Annie is with Byron at a local motel, looking to score. Alicia, not quite two years old, is at home alone. Alicia has not yet learned to walk as she is slow in her development, but she can most certainly crawl. And crawl she does: over to the cabinet beneath the sink where she finds a bottle of old drain cleaner. She opens it. She drinks it. She dies in pain on the kitchen floor. Annie and Byron don't find her for a full day because they forget to come home and check on her.

At age twenty-two – on her twenty-second birthday, as a matter of fact – Annie is in the hospital. Byron, now clean of crystal meth but sodden with alcohol, beats her. He breaks her jaw. Shatters part of her eye socket. She leaves him.

At age twenty-three, Annie gets clean.

At age twenty-five, Annie relapses.

At age twenty-six, Annie incorrectly believes she has been cheated by her dealer, a woman named Hypatia. Annie's mind can no longer produce the chemicals that stimulate pleasure in the human brain, and all sense has gone from her. She believes Hypatia stole her money and did not give Annie the drugs, but the truth is Annie received the drugs and consumed them already. The delusion persists, and Annie breaks a mirror hanging over Hypatia's couch. She slits the woman's throat with a shard of mirror. Annie goes to jail for a very long time.

At age twenty-eight, Annie beats another inmate to death with a lunch tray.

At age twenty-nine, Annie gets hooked on a new drug invading American life – starting first at the prisons. Krokodil, a derivative of morphine. Called that – Krokodil, or "crocodile" – because of the way it ruins the skin of the user, giving it a scaly appearance.

At age thirty, Annie suffers gangrene from Krokodil use. They have to amputate her left leg to the knee. Complications arise during surgery. Annie dies in great pain at the prison. Only her mother misses her.

FIFTY-FOUR
ATROPOS IN THE GARDEN

By now they've come to the greenhouse, though they have not yet entered.

They left the house by a side door and walked beneath a trellis verdant with wisteria, the vines gone dry in autumn.

Before they exit, Eleanor nods to Beck, who pulls an umbrella from a nearby stand and holds it above their heads as they cross the ten yards to the greenhouse door.

They pause there as Eleanor finishes her story. The tale of Annie Valentine, drug addict, bad mother, and, one way or another, dead girl.

"You can see all that," Miriam says – not a question – as she stands there, fidgeting. "You can see how her life unfolds."

"It is my gift."

"I thought you couldn't see how they die."

Eleanor sighs. "Not always. Not often. In this case I was able to see the consequence through the mother. She dies a year later, you see."

"Let me guess: of a broken heart?"

"A broken liver, actually. Overdose of medication. Lipitor. It shuts down her liver and her kidneys and that is that. Another broken doll and shattered teacup in the wake of Annie Valentine. And that is why I see it."

Miriam shivers against the cold. Out beyond the trellis she sees the gray nothing of pounding rain. The smudge of distant trees. Above her head, water filters down through the old vines and the trellis top, forming puddles at her feet.

She doesn't want to talk about this anymore.

"I want to see Wren."

She moves toward the greenhouse. Eleanor touches her arm.

"It's through her that I saw you, Miriam. You are a part of her life. You are just one more piece of her wreckage. Because of her, a piece of you will one day go missing." Eleanor's voice grows quiet. "We're not so different, you and I."

Beck shifts closer. Water thumps dully against the umbrella.

The old woman's grip on her arm tightens.

"We're very different." Miriam says, but she doesn't want to think about it. *Don't look at this one too close. You may not like the answer.*

"Are we? Fate has a path. You step in. You change lives by ending lives. Don't you? That's what I do. What *we* do. As a family. We see those girls twisting in the wind – poisoned girls, damaged girls, *ruined* girls. Girls who will themselves become ruiners.

Their lives are hurricanes and tornados, sweeping up everything in their paths and throwing them back to earth so hard they shatter."

"Get your hand off me. I said I want to see Wren."

But Eleanor continues, eyes wide with the fervor of her beliefs. "Annie Valentine's death is a pure thing. A good thing. And good things, truly good things, don't come without sacrifice. Hers is a garden of hate: Leave the ground barren and only barren things grow. A dead child. A dead mother. So many others. Remove her from the timeline–" Eleanor forms scissors with her two fingers – *clip clip clip*. "–and the garden grows."

Miriam tries to pull away, but the old woman has a grip like pliers. Eleanor's breath is fragrant with rose hips.

Burning roses and carnation, wisps of smoke from the mask's noseholes.

Eleanor's eyelids flutter, almost as though she's caught in the throes of an ecstatic revelation. "It's like cancer, you see? Sometimes to save the body you must cut out the disease. Remove an organ. Sever a limb. Annie Valentine and all the others – *all the others* – were malignant. Tumors deserving the knife."

"Or the axe."

At this, Eleanor smiles.

Then she turns and, with a small brass key, unlocks the greenhouse door. From inside Miriam smells a hothouse breath of turned earth, fertilizer, and the heady scent of wet leaves. Sees the splash of green punctuated by pockets of bright flowers. Orchids and tea roses and birds-of-paradise.

In the center of the long hothouse is a tree – a ficus tree with three separate tapering trunks winding together into the branches.

Wren sits next to the tree. Her hands are bound in polished cuffs. Another chain links those cuffs to a rusted eyebolt in the greenhouse floor.

Her chin dips. Eyes half-lidded. Bottom lip wet with saliva.

"You drugged her," Miriam says.

"To keep her quiet," Beck answers. "She's... a bit mouthy."

Miriam hurries to Wren, kneels next to her. The girl's eyes try to focus on Miriam, but the pin-prick pupils wander the empty space around her. Like Wren's seeing more than one. Two Miriams? Three? An infinity of her?

The scariest thought of all.

"Shh," Miriam says, pulling the girl close. She's not good with affection but the girl needs something. As the heavy rains pummel the windows above their heads, Miriam continues to shush her and rub circles in the girl's back. Her shoulder grows wet from the girl's drool.

"Mom," Wren mumbles.

Miriam shivers. It's like she can feel her ovaries tighten, breaking off a decade's worth of ice and snow. It's a terrible feeling. It takes everything she has to swallow back a pained cry and to dam up the tears that want to fall.

She eases Wren back against the tree and stands. "What do you want from me?"

Eleanor eases toward her. The beneficent smile on her face gives her an eerie, grandmotherly glow. All around her, the verdant plants – life spilling out of pots and boxes and over table edges – call to mind the Garden of Eden. A place where a woman made a choice, a choice predicated on a lie.

"I want you to join our family," Eleanor says.

"You've gone off your meds. You're monsters."

"We're healers. Aggressive as excision. As radiation or chemotherapy. Aggressive as bloodletting leeches. But healers just the same."

"That's what it's about, isn't it? The whole... ritual. The Medieval doctor's get-up. The mythic underpinnings. The table. The fact you're a nurse. You've fallen in love with the idea. You're huffing your own crazy vapors like all the old oracles. Except you've taken the oracular thing one step further. You get your hands dirty. You *make* things true."

"And what is it that you do, Miss Black? A life for a life. We both step into the stream and let our bodies change the direction of the water – we redirect fate. By ending some lives we save so many others."

Miriam feels the Xs in her palms itching. She needs to do something. Soon.

But not yet.

"You could just kill them. The bad girls. But oh, the theatrics. You don't only put a bullet in their heads. You make a... presentation out of it. A ritual for all the bullshit gods and non-existent goddesses to see."

"Ritual is necessary," Beck says.

Eleanor says, "My gift is from the divine. We must celebrate it in all its aspects. I'm surprised you don't feel the same way. Don't you believe in things greater than yourself?"

"I don't believe in freaky folk songs and fucked up medical masks."

"The song is our prayer. It's an old song. Carl's mother used to sing it to him." Eleanor offers a strained smile. "The mask is both symbol and function. The beak doctor's mask was the face of the bird – the plague affected mammals, you see, but not birds. And so with the herbs in the beak the doctor was protected from catching the plague. The plague was more than just sickness back then. It was thought to be a mark of sin. A punishment by God."

"Fuck. Who taught you all this?"

"My father was an academic. What can I say? His florid imagination was infectious."

"These girls. Why not just... help them? Offer them a chance? You say you have the power to sway fate – so why not show them how to be better people? Instead of torturing them. *Killing* them."

"That *is* what we do," Eleanor says, as though Miriam should have this figured out already. "It's why our schools exist."

Oh, god. "Schools. Plural?"

"We have four schools in three counties. Caldecott. Woodwine. Bell Athyn. And Breckworth. Three through dummy corporations, but I serve on the board of each school, as does my son Edwin."

Miriam doesn't want to ask. Doesn't want to know. She already feels sick to her stomach. But that urge to know, *to see*, is present – the same urge that makes her put skin to skin so she can see the most intimate and troubling moment of a person's life.

And so she asks, "How many? How... many girls? How many *victims*?"

Eleanor says to Beck, "Show her."

Beck waves her on.

He leads her past the ficus. Down a row of white orchids, flowers like white spiders.

At the end of the row, a metal cabinet. Rust at the hinges and edges.

Beck puts his hand at the middle of Miriam's back (*not the small of her back, thank all the gods*) and his touch makes her feel queasy and unstable, like she's tuning in to some nauseating frequency.

He pulls a small key. Unlocks the padlock. Opens the cabinet.

Inside?

Jars.

The cabinet is filled with jars.

Five shelves. Easily a dozen on each shelf.

Each containing cloudy fluid. Turbid, like brackish pond water.

In each, something that looks like a slug or a sea cucumber. Lean at one end. Fibrous at the other, like the root of a stubborn weed.

Tongues.

In each jar, a girl's tongue.

She wrung her hands and groaned and cried

And gnawed her tongue before she died.

Miriam doesn't want to do it, but she has to.

She plucks a jar from the top shelf. Nothing identifies to whom it belongs. No tape. No name. No date. The jar shakes in her grip. Bubbles long-clinging to the mouth meat flutter to the top.

"What do you do with the bodies?" she asks, though she's not sure she wants to know.

Beck reaches over into a pot where a bromeliad the color of fire blooms. He fishes out a fistful of earth and holds it in front of her.

Moist earth, rich as pipe tobacco but speckled with white – like shards of finely shattered pottery – tumbles to the earth.

No, no, no, no.

"We compost," he says.

Black dirt. Bone shards. Headless corpses feeding lush plants as fertilizer.

"So many dead girls." Tears creep down her cheeks.

"They needed to die. You'll see that."

"I'm not like you."

"My father proves otherwise. You're a killer, Miriam."

Go get 'em, killer. You have work to do.

An eye for an eye. A tooth for a tooth.

A life for a life.

You are who you are.

"So be it," she says, and she bows her head.

Then she whips the tongue jar around and smashes it against Beck Daniels' head. The stink of formaldehyde blooms fast, and he staggers to the side. Bits of glass stick in his temple, his cheek, that prodigious jaw. An archipelago of shards around his eye socket.

Run!

She shoves past him–

But his knee comes up and nails her, a hard hit to the kidneys. She falls forward, cracks her head on a table edge. A pot spins off the side. Dirt – *grave* dirt, the dirt of dead girls – rains down on her.

She tries to get up, but he grabs her and throws her down.

Pins her.

Flips her over.

His hands close around her neck.

Blood pulses in her cheeks, lips, eyes.

He bangs her head against the concrete. Once, twice. Shotgun blasts of stars.

Her palms slap against the ground. She slides one hand beneath her as his thumbs press hard against her windpipe.

She feels the waistline of her jeans, fingers searching blindly along the small of her back.

Where is it where is it where is it

Beck leers above. Glass glittering in his face. Blood oozing to the edge of each shard, dripping down on her face – *pat pat pat*.

Darkness rips away the light.

Her hand, still searching.

Then–

She finds it.

The fork.

She made a big deal about that butter knife from breakfast. Waving it this way and that. Beck's earlier words echo in her head.

"Your words, your attitude, all a big misdirection. A magician's trick."

Misdirection, indeed.

They watched the knife. They missed her tucking the fork into her pants.

Her hands curl around the utensil.

She brings the fork up hard–

And jams it deep into the soft meat of his armpit.

Release. Light pushes back the darkness as his hands loosen. Miriam gets her knees up against his midsection, extends her legs, pushes him off her as he howls in rage, pawing at the fork like a bear.

Miriam finds her feet beneath her.

Still woozy.

Will-o-wisps still dancing in front of her eyes.

A small gust of pride swells within her: *Second sonofabitch I dispatched with a fork.*

She bolts. She knows that staying to fight Beck is a losing battle. A broken jar and a forked armpit will slow him down, but he's easily the superior fighter. And going toward Eleanor – she's an old woman and Miriam's sure she can take her but doesn't want any surprises.

That means going out the window.

Miriam gets a running start.

Foot up on one table–

Launches herself at thePlexiglass.

Her shoulder hits it. The window bends inward,

pops out of its frame, and takes her with it. Suddenly it's all wind and rain and the great outdoors.

Miriam runs.

FIFTY-FIVE

THE DEVIL DRIVES A BLACK MERCEDES

Louis shivers in the rain, the cop's gun tucked in his waistband.

Everything here at the school is lit up like a carnival. Red and blue lights strobing, disrupting the wan light of morning. He hides behind an alcove corner, peering out, unsure what to do, where to go. His head is a dozen cats running in a hundred directions – he doesn't know how to find Miriam, doesn't want to talk to the cops because if one of them is in on these murders then *many* might be, doesn't like being this close to a parking lot full of cops with a stolen police revolver in his pants. He's paralyzed. *Some protector.*

Water rushes down the school gutters, overwhelming the drains. The streets are wet at the sides, and soon those deep puddles will meet. It won't be long before all of it floods. The rains are endless and without mercy. Hurricane Esmerelda is here – and she's showing her teeth.

By now, some of the cop cars are leaving. Soon they'll all be gone.

A shadow falls over him and above him, the airy *fwump* of an umbrella unfurling. It's Katey.

"Louis, I'm so sorry." She's been crying. "I left her alone and then... The next thing I knew, all hell was breaking loose. This is my fault."

"Your fault." He almost wants to laugh. "Katey, I told her I'd protect her. That my job was to be there for her. This doesn't look like that."

He called Katey from the guard gate – Homer let him use a landline wired to the booth. Louis' cell phone remains back at the truck. Lost now, probably.

"They say..." Katey's voice drifts away.

"What?"

"They say she hurt one of the security guards in there. Real bad. Slit his throat ear to ear."

Louis feels drunk. Like his center of gravity is a tiny boat on a rapid river.

"She killed him?"

Katey shakes her head. "He's not dead. Not yet. Critical condition but somehow he's still alive. I guess you can survive having your throat slit if it isn't too deep. If it doesn't hit an artery." She sniffs. "But they say he's barely holding on."

"Miriam didn't do it. Or if she did, she had good reason."

The wind picks up, casting stinging cold rain underneath the umbrella. Louis doesn't even notice it.

"They took her, Katey. Took her and the other girl."

"We need to tell the cops. Soon they're going to look at the tapes. And want to talk to me. Might as well get ahead of it." She pats his chest.

"No. They're in on it. Don't tell them anything."

She pulls away. "Now you're sounding a bit paranoid."

"One of them came at me. I was following after this black Mercedes, and a cop car came hurtling through the intersection and blocked me. Next thing I knew, he started shooting at me."

And now I've got his gun.

And it has only three bullets left in the cylinder.

"Black Mercedes," she says. Blinking. Thinking. "Well – no. No, that can't be right."

"What? What is it?"

"It doesn't seem like it should even matter but… the headmaster, Edwin Caldecott, he drives a black Mercedes."

"Is he here?"

"No, he never showed up this morning–"

Then Louis hears the sound of tires splashing through deep puddles.

Katey says, "Speak of the Devil, and the Devil shall appear."

Louis turns.

Sure enough, the black Mercedes. Coming up the drive. Soon it will pass directly in front of them.

That's the car.

He's sure of it. Sure as he's been of anything. He feels that certainty crawling around in his marrow like a canal of hungry worms.

"Katey, I'll have to talk to you later."

She says something in response but it's swallowed by the storm.

Louis reaches for the gun and steps out in front of the Mercedes.

It's time to find Miriam.

FIFTY-SIX
HIDE & SEEK

She doesn't know how long she's been out here.

She doesn't know where to go.

All she knows is the rain. And the lightning and the thunder. And the time passing. Time that might be minutes. Time that might be hours.

The Caldecott estate is sprawling. The house. The greenhouse behind it. A large pond with a white gazebo nesting on an island at its center. Tennis courts. Pool. Barn. Four-car garage. Another smaller barn. A shed, smaller yet.

The one place she wants to run – the driveway, the one that will presumably take her to the road – is around the front of the house. She tried to run that way but heard voices. She went the other way.

You need to get back.

Find Louis.

Find Wren.

Then kill these monsters.

Now she's at the back of the property. She found a small springhouse of crumbling wood and crooked stone over a spring that has run dry.

Here she waits. With the cellar spiders and centipedes. Behind a warped wooden door that rattles and bangs any time the wind kicks up.

Around the property are woods. She could just run wildly through the trees in the rain and the muck. But where would it take her? She's not even sure she has it in her to run that far, that fast.

And the last thing she wants to do is break her goddamn ankle in a muddy hole. Drown face-down in a puddle fifty yards from the Caldecott estate.

That leaves the driveway.

There's probably a gate.

And a camera.

It's time, then, to look for a weapon.

All she has here is the circle of flat stones surrounding the dry spring source (now just a moist dirt pucker like a cancerous asshole). She tries to pick one up, but they're mortared together. The shed, then, she thinks. The shed will have something. A shovel, rake, hedge trimmers, pool skimmer, wasp spray.

She's about to open the door and peer out–

But then, a sound.

At first she thinks it's just the rain. Leave a fan on in a room or listen long and close to a hard rainfall and you'll hear things: murmurs and footsteps and voices calling your name.

Then it comes again.

"Miriam!"

Someone calling her name.

Except–

Not just someone.

Louis.

It can't be. It's not possible.

But again: "Miriam. *Miriam.* Where are you?"

The voice is close. Not a shout, not a holler.

My protector, she thinks. She fiddles with the iron latch on the door and a warm, strange tide of comfort washes over her. She's warm despite stepping out into the cold rain once more. With Louis on her side, she knows she's guarded, protected, shielded from evil.

She steps out onto the loose stone pavers, clambers up over one of the small grassy berms bordering the springhouse. Her feet barely find purchase over the wet grass and smeary earth.

Miriam hisses his name. "Louis! *Louis,* over here."

She pulls herself over the top on her hands and knees.

And there he stands.

Not Louis.

The cop.

The one from the Keener's junkyard. With the handlebar mustache. Short and stout – not like a little teapot but rather like a thick-shouldered pit bull.

Miriam is on her hands and knees before him. *You fell for it again. The Mockingbird.*

The cop's got a gun in his black-gloved hands. A small pistol – a .380 maybe. Walther PPK. Water beading on the oiled metal.

"Please," she says. But she already knows he's foe, not friend.

He laughs. Coughs. Rain cascades over the brim of his cop hat.

Then he says, "Miriam, Miriam, it's me, it's me."

And he says it in Louis's voice.

Of course.

"You're the Mockingbird," she says. All the energy and hope is sucked out of her as the wind casts needles of rain against her cheek. The grass is slippery between her fingers.

"We're all the Mockingbird. Whole family of 'em." He chuckles. "Your man should've killed me when he had the chance."

He slams the gun into the side of her head. A head already wracked by the pain and daze of a concussion.

Miriam rolls over.

Fetal position.

Everything hurts.

His fat little hand gets a grip on her hair. A good grip. He twists his wrist so that he winds the hair around his hand, closing his fingers.

He begins to drag her past the springhouse. Caveman-style. Through the rain and the mud. Not toward the house.

Toward the pond.

FIFTY-SEVEN
BLOOD & FEATHERS

The pond's edge is naught but gray clayey sludge. Miriam's knees sink into it as the cop wrenches her arms behind her back, snapping a pair of cuffs tight, too tight. Her chin falls to her chest. She can barely keep it up.

The pond water shakes and shudders, pocked with rain so hard and so heavy it looks like a hail of pebbles pelting the surface. She cranes her head – dizzy, vision blurry, wondering how much more punishment her poor ruined pumpkin of a skull can take – and can barely see the gazebo at the center.

Behind her, the cop checks his clip, draws back the action, fires a round.

Her ears ring from the shot.

She thinks, *I'm dead, he got me. Bang bang.*

The stink of expended powder worms into her nose.

He didn't shoot her. Just fired up into the air.

A signal.

"Here they come," he says.

Miriam barely manages to turn her head. She sees two figures crossing toward the pond from the house. Beck holds the umbrella over his mother's head.

His shirt is soaked with blood on the side.

Eleanor steps up next to Miriam. Light as a feather. She doesn't even seem to sink into the mud. Clucking her tongue, the old woman bends her knees and crouches down next to Miriam.

Miriam notices the rain no longer pounds her hair into her scalp. Beck hunkers on the other side of her, holding the umbrella up over her. *Ah*.

"I find you very disappointing," Eleanor says.

"Sorry, Mom," Miriam croaks.

A voice hissing at her ear. Beck's. "Be *respectful*, Miss Black."

"*Fork you,*" Miriam hisses. Then she laughs so hard she coughs, almost tumbles forward into the water. It's still a great joke.

"You're going to die here today," Eleanor says.

"I thought you wanted me to join your little family."

"It seems we're past that."

"Yeah, I'm kind of a *lone wolf* type. I'm also not a psychopathic fuck-faced monster like you lot of lunatics." She hacks again. Spits. *Ptoo*. There's blood in her saliva. "So. There's that."

The old woman sighs. Looks to her son. "She won't be your bride, then, Beckett. I know you had a romantic connection. I'm sorry."

"Oh, I'd say that connection is broken," he says.

"Bride? You really thought–? Jesus, you fucking people. So what's the plan?" Miriam asks. "You gonna do me here? Where's all the pomp and circumstance? The doctor's table and the fire axe and that fucking creepy song you sing? Don't I rate a bad girl's death?"

Eleanor smiles. Strokes her hair. "You do, dear. But we don't have time for that. Find some peace that your death will be quick. A mercy the other girls did not and will not have, I'm sad to say."

A small column of fire, a sirocco of bitter and petty rage, rises inside Miriam's heart and she licks her lips and says, "Your husband? Carl? That fucking mutant gurgled so loud when he died. You should've seen his throat, Eleanor. When I was done with it, it looked like a road-killed possum. Like an animal on a highway. Hit again and again, tires pulping the fur and the blood and the *bones* until it's just a pile of red nasty shit."

"You think to shock me," Eleanor says. "I hated my husband. He served a purpose for us, a purpose that my sons will now pick up."

"Oh, but you love your sons."

"Of course. With all my heart."

Fine. She didn't like that story? *How about another, you old bitch?*

"I saw how your son Beckett is going to die," Miriam says. Grinning now, ear to ear. "He shoots himself, Eleanor. Blows his mind out the back of his head and paints his office walls with brain salad. Boom."

"That's a lie," Beck seethes. "I'd never–"

"Shush," Eleanor hisses, a new serrated edge to her voice. "I won't hear any more of this. Beckett, let's go–"

"It's the guilt!" Miriam yells over the downpour's din. "He can't hack it. Can't deal with what you made him."

From behind her she hears Eleanor's icy proclamation. "We're going inside. I don't want to be here for this. When we're gone, kill her. Weigh her down. Dump her into the pond." To Beck she says, "Earl will handle this. Won't you, sweet Earl?"

The cop says, "I will, Mother."

"Can't hack the grisly bit?" Miriam shrieks as Eleanor leaves. "You're soft, Eleanor! That's where Beckett gets it! *You fucking witch!*"

A hard pressure at the base of her skull appears: the gun.

The cop – Earl – takes a knee next to her but keeps the gun at her head. "You shut your bitch whore mouth. You say one more thing about my mother and I won't make this quick. I'll blow your fucking feet off. I'll shoot you in the knees. In the hands. In the elbows. One bullet from the side will erase your jaw. But you'll still be alive. Bleeding and screaming. But alive."

Miriam whispers, "Mommy's boy. But I guess she doesn't feel the same about you, huh? You're just the fucking clean-up boy, aren't you? Mommy's least-favorite little shithead."

Earl grunts in rage, then clips her again on the side of her head. She doesn't go down this time. Her knees are mired in the mud.

Answers that question. The thought swims laps in her dizzy head.

The cop stands up. Gets behind her.

Begins to hum that song, "Wicked Polly."

Miriam looks over her shoulder.

She sees two figures under one dark umbrella.

They're at the house.

At the side door.

About to go inside.

This is it, she thinks.

Makes sense. What put her on this path was a gunshot to the head, and now that's how it ends. Such lovely symmetry. Like two grisly book-ends.

It's then she hears a flutter of wings.

Real wings? Or an illusion? She sees, or thinks she sees, a fat-bellied crow fly through the rain and over the pond water, landing at the apex of the gazebo. Miriam can barely see the bird – just a black dot, a shadow on an X-Ray.

But that changes when the rain stops.

It doesn't stop falling. Rather, it stops in mid-air.

Slashes of rain like gray threads. Paused. Frozen in time.

A dream. An hallucination. An impossible reality.

She sees the bird better now. Black eyes, shiny like buttons.

The bird speaks. *Of course it does.*

"Before Julius Caesar died," the crow says, voice booming loud and rippling over the water and the land like the report from a rifle, "he had a dream. A dream of flight. A dream in which he was a bird soaring high in the sky above the seven white hills of Rome. His soothsayer, Titus Vestricius Spurinna, warned him of his coming death and said that it would be presaged by a king-bird flying into the halls of power with a sprig of laurel in its mouth, but the bird would be pursued by a flock of blackbirds and those blackbirds would attack the smaller king-bird and tear it pieces then and there – and it came to pass as the haruspex suggested."

"I'm done with the fuckin' bird thing," Miriam says. "Seriously. Don't you have any other symbols in that bag of tricks?"

The bird clacks its beak together. *Clack clack clack.* "Poor Miriam. Railing against that which she understands but does not want to admit. Like Caesar. Even after the signs and portents, old Julius told the haruspex that her words were lies and he could not die, oh no, not him."

"I'm tired. And in pain. Just go away."

"You die today. Here and now." The bird adjusts its wings. "This is the moment fate has marked for your death. Which would be something of a failure, don't you think? Those girls. Not just Wren. Nor Tavena. But so many others. The Caldecotts continue. They'll have children of their own. The snake eats its own tail. An endless parade of pain, a procession of misery."

"Someone else will have to step in. I'm done."

"If not you, then who?"

"Fuck you. Fly away."

"You called me a symbol," the bird says. "Who said I'm a symbol? I'm as real as you. Real as the gun at your head. Here. Look."

It feels like Miriam's consciousness is dragged swiftly from her body and run through a gauntlet of thorns–

And suddenly she can see herself.

Kneeling at the pond's edge. The stocky cop behind her, gun frozen.

Miriam tries to move. She hears the rustle of wings.

Her wings.

She's out of her body. And into the crow's.

And then–

Whoosh.

She's back. Staring at the gazebo and the dark raven atop it.

"Just tell me what to do," the crow says, "and thy will be done, poor Miriam."

Time unsticks itself.

The rain once more hammers the pond.

Thunder rumbles.

The cop clears his throat.

She feels the gun press tighter.

Miriam looks to the crow atop the gazebo. Whispers, "Please."

Feels a part of herself slip away.

The bird takes flight.

"Now the Devil take you," Earl growls.

A dark shape moves fast. A flurry and flutter of wings.

The pressure of the gun barrel is gone. Earl screams. Miriam cranes her neck to see just as the gun goes off by her ear – another ringing, this time so loud it drowns out even the sound of the rain.

All Miriam can see of Earl's face is the bird – black

oily wings flapping. He cries out. Bashes at the bird with the gun.

The beak pecks. *Stabs.* Into his mouth again and again as he screams.

The bird pulls away, talons leaving claw marks on Earl's chin.

His mouth is a red crater, a blood-slick gopher hole–

The bird has bits of his tongue in its mouth. Like strips of stir-fry beef. *A spring robin with a wriggling worm in its mouth.*

The crow flies.

Miriam seizes her opportunity. She awkwardly buries the fronts of her feet into the mud and pushes off like a swimmer, barreling forward into Earl's knees. He tumbles over her, splashing into the pond.

On her side, she tries inching her way up the bank but the grass is smeared with mud and she can manage no purchase.

A hand grabs her ankle.

Earl rises back out of the water.

And begins dragging her toward it.

She kicks her legs. He turns her over so that she's facing him.

He scowls, his teeth filthy with blood-black clots. Grabs her by the shirt. Points the gun at her face. And she thinks, *Why? You stupid bird, what good did any of that do? He has no tongue but he's still got the gun and I'm dead either way.*

In her mind, she hears an answer. *Because it bought you just enough time.*

But just enough time for what?

A gunshot.

Earl's head jerks hard to the right.

He falls across her legs. Dead weight. Rolling into the water.

"I don't understand," she says to the sky, rain washing away her vision and filling her mouth as she speaks.

Big hands find her. Haul her back up the bank.

And a one-eyed truck driver stares down.

"Louis," she says.

"I told you I'd protect you."

"Maybe next time show up a little earlier. This fashionably late shit is for the birds." But then he's gone again. Pulling the cop's body up out of the water. She sees the black hole in the side of Earl's dead face. Sees that Louis has a gun – a fucking hand-cannon, actually – as Louis comes back to her, the handcuff keys swallowed by his massive mitts.

Louis stares down at the body. "Should've shot him when I had the chance. I had him, Miriam. Had him laying there. But I turned chickenshit. Shot the ground beside his head… and, and, and I ran away."

"It's okay," she says. A few moments pass between them as the rain falls. "Louis, I think I telepathically commanded a bird to do my bidding."

"Oh." He gets her hands free and the blood rushes back to her limbs.

"That cop. He's not the only one," she says, gasping.

"I know."

"They've got the girl. Wren."

"I know."

"Will you help me save her?"

"I will."

"Then get me that fucker's gun. We're going to need it."

FIFTY-EIGHT
CHOOSER OF THE SLAIN

"I'm happy you're here," she says as they creep back into the house. They slip in through a side-door: the laundry. Shelves of towels and front-loading machines stand silent.

The whole house is silent.

"Shhh," he says.

They enter back into the hall. Pass by an old gilded mirror. Miriam sees her face. She looks like hot microwaved death. Bruises and scabs and swollen protrusions. First from her encounter with Keener. Then from the brothers Caldecott: Beckett and Earl. She can even see the crusty scar where the gunman's bullet dug a ditch in her head – but that wound is nothing compared to all the others.

"How'd you get here?" she whispers as they creep toward the foyer.

"I saw it was the headmaster's car that brought you here, so I put a gun to his head and made him drive me. Then I shoved his ass into the trunk."

"Edwin's *here*?"

Louis nods, Colt Python in hand.

"Bring him in," she says.

"I don't want to leave you."

"I'll be okay."

"Wait for me," he says, and she nods.

It's a lie. She's not waiting for him. This is on her, not him.

Louis hesitates. But he finally nods, buying what she's selling. They reach the foyer, and he heads out the front door.

Leaving Miriam alone in the house.

Alone with a pair of monsters.

"Earl's dead!" she yells out. Voice echoing. "But I guess you know that. That's why you're hiding."

Still nothing.

She thinks she hears something upstairs, a creak of a floorboard.

Beck's dangerous. He's like a coiled viper. Hard to see. Fast to strike.

"You wouldn't believe it, Eleanor," Miriam calls. "I cut out his tongue before he died." Not a lie. Not exactly. "He got what was coming. He's been the one covering up all your dirty business, isn't that right? Edwin helps case the girls. Carl did the killing. And Earl made sure the girls were just *missing*, not murder victims. But Beck... he's your baby. With Daddy dead, he's the one who picks up the axe. Who sings the Mockingbird song."

Eleanor appears.

The old woman is upstairs, walking along the balcony's edge, one hand running along the banister. Miriam tracks her with the pistol.

"They're good boys," Eleanor says. Rattled. Trembling.

"Why is it that you hate girls?" Miriam asks. "You don't look for trouble in boys. You don't kill anybody with a dick. Just young girls. Bad girls."

"Because girls are poison. Whores if you let them be that."

"Like you? Harridans and whores like little Ellie Caldecott?"

"I went by Ella, if you must know."

"Send Beckett out," Miriam says.

Eleanor smiles.

It's then Miriam realizes she's been played. Played by her own damn game: Eleanor's been distracting her.

A flash of movement comes from Miriam's left–

Beck.

She pivots her hip, raises the .380–

But she's slow. And he's got a fireplace poker.

The iron bar *whangs* against the gun and knocks it out of her hand, leaving her palm and fingers stinging with the reverberation. The pistol spirals across the floor and lands under a stocked art deco sidebar.

Beck starts bobbing erratically – it's hard to get a bead on him. He drives a heel punch into her solar plexus. The wind sucks out of her lungs. He grabs her head, goes to slam it into his knee–

Miriam's not having any of that. She forms her hand into a point and jams it high up into his armpit, right where she scored the blow with the fork.

He grunts but is otherwise unmoved.

Fuck.

Two hard punches to her side. He stomps down on her foot. Throws her to the ground. Her shoulder cracks against the floor.

On her hands and knees, she scrambles toward the sidebar – the gun sits beneath it, still wet from the rain.

But Beck has other ideas. He grabs her by the waistband of her pants, and as he pulls her toward him he drives wide-elbowed hammerblows into her kidneys. Again and again. He's better than her. In every way.

She's dead.

Unless–

What is it that Beck teachers? Sensei Beck. Ninja Warrior Beck.

He teaches girls how to fight back.

To fight dirty.

Repeat after me: Eyes nose throat groin knees and feet–

Miriam rolls over. One hard kick with her boot lands square against his knee. The pain is evident on his face – eyes wide, epic jaw in a rigor-mortis flinch.

He growls, hauls her back to her feet–

"Eyes," she says, and then spits in his eye.

"Nose." She slams her head against it, feels it give way. He grabs her by the chin but she's wet from the rain and squirms out of his grip.

"Throat." Again she forms her hand into a sharp point and jabs hard against his throat. His breath is a keening wheeze.

"My favorite," she says. "Groin."

Knee up into his junk drawer. A gleeful strike.

He gasps and she shoves him backward.

He staggers. Tries to get his bearing. Bangs his butt against the wall. Rebounds and comes at Miriam–

–time collapses into staccato moments, a ragged drum beat–

–the door opens, Louis hauling Edwin inside–

–she reaches under the sidebar, finds the prize–

–Louis calls, "Miriam!"–

–the gun is small but heavy in her hand–

–bang–

–a red rose blooms on Beck's chest–

–Edwin screams for his brother–

–the swallow on Beck's chest bleeds out, shot through the eye–

–and he falls, face forward, onto the foyer floor.

Smoke drifts lazily from the barrel.

Edwin crawls over to his brother. Sobbing into the man's hair. Holding him. Hugging him. Miriam storms over.

She levels the gun at Edwin. "Give me your hand."

"Go to hell, wretch," the headmaster gasps.

She clocks him across the top of the head with the gun. "Fuck it," she mutters, and she grabs his face with her hand–

She sees.

Sees the tableau of his death play out in front of her.

That sonofabitch.

"It figures," she says.

"Leave him," Louis says. "Let's call the police."

"The police?" She laughs, but it's a mirthless, acid bark. "Do you know how he dies? He dies at a fucking *ski chalet*. I don't know where. Colorado. The Swiss

Alps. It doesn't matter. He dies an old man by a crackling fire as two grandchildren play at his feet. *This* evil prick, who helped his monster mother and fiend-fuck father hunt and torture and kill young women, gets away with it. And keeps on killing, for all I know."

Louis eases closer. He's holding up those enormous hands of his in a gesture of peace and calm. It isn't working.

"Miriam, he's defenseless."

"Tell that to the dead girls. You didn't see their tongues. Jars upon jars of them. Five dozen dead girls."

Edwin swallows a hard knot, wrings his hands together. "I'll do better. I'll be better. Your friend is right. Let me live. Please – "His lips connect by a slick string of saliva. His nose runs. His eyes glisten.

The gun wavers in her hand.

Louis says, "This isn't justice. This is revenge. This is murder."

"It… is what it is."

"Miriam, this isn't you–"

"You have no idea who I am."

She pulls the trigger. She shoots Edwin through the heart. Just like his brother. He collapses atop Beck.

Blood pools beneath them.

Louis says nothing – but a terrible sound comes from him, a great heaving gasp like he can't believe it.

Miriam feels the pulse-beat drumming at her neck.

"I'm going to get Wren. And then I'm going to kill Eleanor Caldecott."

She doesn't wait for him. She doesn't stop to soothe

him. There's no time.

Miriam marches forward through the house. Winding her way back to the greenhouse, where the rain once again pummels the Plexiglas, where the cabinet of tongues and the plants fed by dead girls await.

Wren is gone.

FIFTY-NINE
THE ABYSS BETWEEN THEM

Outside, Miriam stands in the driveway.

Watching the taillights of the black Mercedes as it barrels down the drive toward the front gate.

Through the back windshield Miriam sees a shock of white hair. Eleanor's driving.

No sign of Wren, but smart money says the old woman has her.

"She took her," Miriam says to Louis as he steps out into the rain. "She still has Wren."

"Is it over?" he asks. He wants it to be. She can hear that in his voice.

Things have changed.

No time to worry about that now.

"No!" she says. "No. I still have to finish this."

"What else is there to do? Just stop. Take a breath and stop. Let someone else handle this part." He's pleading with her. Like he's trying to talk her off the ledge, away from the edge. "We don't even know where they're going."

"No. I know where they're going."

And she does.

Eleanor's taking Wren to finish what she started.

The river is rising, Miriam.

They're going back to the school.

SIXTY
RIVER'S EDGE

The Caldecotts have other cars in the garage. At first she can't find keys, any keys, and the whole house is there – a giant manor where keys could literally be anywhere, and with each moment gone is another chance for Wren to get dead. But then Louis calls out that he finds a set of keys – kitchen, junk drawer, of all places, fucking rich people – and they find the keys start a silver BMW sedan.

The drive is long, or so it feels. Rain pounding on the windshield. Louis does the driving; Miriam doesn't even have a license. He guns it. Shaky hands, but steady foot.

They get to the school. Homer's smart enough not to ask any questions. By now he doesn't want to know any more than he does, so he just lets the gate swing wide.

As they pull the car forward, Miriam sees Eleanor Caldecott.

She sits by the river's edge, Wren lying still beside her.

The Susquehanna is a tumbling channel of muddy

water already spilling over the banks on the other side. The river has almost crested the top. It won't be long now. The rain is merciless and without measure.

Miriam tells Louis to stay by the car.

He doesn't argue this time.

She crosses the lawn, the earth squishing beneath her feet. Gun in hand. Pointed at Eleanor. Just in case.

Wren isn't moving.

Oh, god.

"Eleanor," Miriam calls out over the guttural river rush.

The woman looks nothing like her graceful self. She is now a sodden old woman, her silver hair draped over a thin skull. Her once-elegant clothing lays plastered against her narrow frame and long lean bones.

"Miss Black," Eleanor answers. Not bothering to look.

"Wren," Miriam calls out. "Wren. It's me. It's Miriam."

But the girl is just a lump. Lying there on her side.

"You think you're different," Eleanor says, her voice quiet enough that the words are almost lost. "You think you're not the same because you have righteousness on your side. But one day they'll come for you, Miriam Black, and then you'll see. You'll see what it's like to be persecuted for your unswerving faith in who you are and what you do. Then you'll understand."

"Eleanor shrugs."

"She's not dead. She's drugged."

Miriam casts a look toward the school. She sees one last cop car in the parking lot – lights off, nobody else to be seen.

"You're here to kill Wren. And maybe Tavena White."

"You know about Tavena."

"I saw. Yes."

"I didn't get to her. The girls are locked away in the dormitory. Her actions will poison the world, I'm afraid. You know what she does one day? She steals from a preacher, and when he catches her, she kills him. With a letter opener. She stabs him thirty times. A community leader, dead by her hand."

"And what does Lauren Martin do?"

Eleanor turns then to face Miriam.

Her face is a mask of satisfied peace.

She smiles softly. "She does nothing. Because she dies."

Dies? Not dead yet?

"Wait!" Miriam cries out. But it's too late–

The woman grabs Wren, and together they tumble into the rising river.

SIXTY-ONE
RISING

The waters are dark and cold and as soon as Miriam leaps into their glacial embrace they grab her with terrible hands and drag her forward and pull her down.

She can see nothing. Hear nothing. *Feel* nothing.

Blood-colored mud. Bruise-colored water.

It's then she knows what a terrible error she made. The waters are moving too fast. She tries to swim but it's like falling through space – it seems to make no difference at all. Finding Wren and Eleanor is an impossible task.

This is where you die, she thinks. *Here it is. Your final destination.*

You deserve it. Don't you?

You're no different than Eleanor Caldecott. She's right.

You murdered her son.

In the coldest of blood. There he sat, weeping over the body of his brother – dead thanks to you – and you shot him. No due process. No jury. Just you and a gun and the rage inside you that told you such a monster should not be allowed to live.

Is that who you are now?

The battlefield crow? The chooser-of-the-slain?

How are you different?

Answer that and you may live.

An echoing sound, a voice distorted.

It's a baby crying.

And then a body swims up next to her. A corpse, its dead cheeks fattened by river water. A woman, stringy seaweed hair floating behind her. Louis' wife. In her arms she cradles a dead baby, a bloated flood-choked cherub.

My baby, Miriam thinks.

A twinge in her womb. Like an old woman's tweezer fingers pinching closed her ovaries, pinchity-pinch. A quick twist and they're shut forever. *No baby for you, Miss Black.*

The urge strikes her – *just open your mouth. Breathe in. Take a big gulp. Snort the waters of the mud-gush Susquehanna until it clogs your throat and your lungs. Then you can rest. No need to answer such hard questions.*

Louis' dead wife is gone.

So too is the baby. Her own nameless baby.

Another face floats up.

The face of Eleanor Caldecott. Eyes wide. Mouth open.

Is she real?

Real or no, she's certainly dead.

Miriam reaches for her. Feels the clammy flesh. Pulls herself along the body as the river carries them both. And finds that her bony wrist dead-ends in an arthritic claw grabbing hold of yet another bony wrist.

For a moment the waters clear and Miriam can see Wren – still caught in Eleanor's undying grasp.

Miriam tries to pry the dead fingers from the girl's wrist, but she can't get a grip. And then the bodies are pulled away as a branch comes out of nowhere and separates them. Miriam swims back toward the distant pale shape, reaching, reaching, no longer certain she can hold her breath, lungs straining and burning, her whole chest and throat and face on fire.

But it doesn't matter. She just has to push a little longer.

Just to get Wren out of the water.

If nothing else, to save the girl and lose herself.

It's in that breathless misery that the answer to the question blooms bold and furious in her mind's eye. It's all she needs.

She kicks her legs and swoops her hands and swims forward, once more anchoring herself to the old woman's carcass. She gets underneath Wren and, carrying all the girl's body, wrenches her frame and kicks at the corpse so that the two are suddenly disconnected.

She has Wren.

But to what end?

How to escape the river's embrace?

The answer: a shape like a shark swims up from underneath, carrying with it a cluster of filthy, greasy bubbles.

Miriam feels arms enclose around her. The world goes upside-down. River water rushing. In her nose, her eyes. Stinging. Swallowing gulpfuls.

And then a sudden surge forward–

Miriam sees Eleanor Caldecott's corpse one more time.

But this time, it's staring at her and smiling.

The corpse raises one bony finger to its lips, as though to say, *Shhh.*

The corpse is gone.

They break surface.

Miriam's up on the bank. Pulling Wren up, too. Miriam's coughing and choking as she rolls the girl over. Two fingers under her neck – there lurks a pulse. Faint like the feeling of an eyeball rolling beneath the lid, but *it's there.*

And then Miriam looks around.

"Where's Louis?" she asks. But the girl's unconscious.

A shape like a shark.

Arms enclose.

Oh, no.

Oh, to all the gods and fates, no, not like this.

Caldecott's voice echoes – watery and distant as if from the deep. *You are just one more piece of her wreckage. Because of her, a piece of you will one day go missing.*

Louis.

Then – downstream – a splash.

A shape, gray through the rain. Grabbing fistfuls of mud and grass. It's him. It's Louis. She runs to him. Pulls him up. Falls atop him and clings to him like she's still in the river and needs him to save her from drowning.

PART FIVE
THE ROAD AHEAD

"Prophet!" said I, "thing of evil! –
Prophet still, if bird or devil!
By that Heaven that bends above us –
By that God we both adore –
Tell this soul with sorrow laden
If, within the distant Aidenn,
It shall clasp a sainted maiden
Whom the angels named Lenore –
Clasp a rare and radiant maiden,
Whom the angels named Lenore?"
Quoth the raven, "Nevermore."

"Be that word our sign of parting,
Bird or fiend!" I shrieked upstarting –
"Get thee back into the tempest
And the Night's Plutonian shore!
Leave no black plume as a token
Of that lie thy soul hath spoken!

Leave my loneliness unbroken! –
Quit the bust above my door!
Take thy beak from out my heart,
And take thy form from off my door!"
Quoth the raven, "Nevermore."

And the raven, never flitting,
Still is sitting, still is sitting
On the pallid bust of Pallas
Just above my chamber door;
And his eyes have all the seeming
Of a demon's that is dreaming,
And the lamp-light o'er him streaming
Throws his shadow on the floor;
And my soul from out that shadow
That lies floating on the floor
Shall be lifted – nevermore!

The Raven, *Edgar Allen Poe*

SIXTY-TWO
RED WREN

With money that's not hers, Miriam buys a burner phone – a prepaid cellular phone fresh from Wal-Mart – and uses it to dial the hospital.

They put her through to Wren's room.

"Hey, psycho," Wren says. She's sounding pretty good.

"Still charming as ever," Miriam says.

"Sorry." She sounds like she means it.

"No, it's cool. I like that about you. You remind me of me."

A pause. Just Wren's uncertain breathing. Finally, she says, "They said I was a bad girl. That's why they wanted to kill me."

"They did. They thought you were going to turn out to be a real bad apple and so they figured on killing the tree before it could drop the fruit. Ugh. Metaphors. You know what, fuck metaphors. They thought one day you were going to grow up and be a bad person and hurt other people."

"Will I?"

I don't know, Miriam thinks.

But that's not how she answers.

"You won't if you don't want to. Fate isn't written," she says. It's not a lie, not precisely. "This life leaves room for choice, but only if you want it real bad."

"I want to be good."

"Then be good."

"Will you help me?"

Miriam sighs. Sucks on her cigarette. Blows smoke. "I'll be back for you in a few years. Check on your smart-ass, make sure you're not a total shit-bird."

"Thanks." She sounds like she means it. Miriam's not used to such raw sincerity. "Thanks for that and for saving my life."

"Ain't no thing."

"There are cops outside my room."

"I know. That's why I'm calling you instead of visiting."

"I told them you were one of the good guys."

"Not a bad girl?"

"Not a bad girl."

Another drag off the cigarette. "Thanks, Wren. I'll catch up with you one day. Keep your grapes peeled."

"Bye, Miriam."

Click.

SIXTY-THREE
FUNERAL FLOWERS

The flowers – paid for with stolen money – arrive at Katey's doorstep around noon. Roses and carnations in a silver wrap. She fetches them only minutes after discovering in the bathroom mirror that her eyes and cheeks are a bit yellow – jaundice, by the look of it. An early sign of pancreatic cancer, or so she read.

With the flowers, a note:

Dear Miss Wiz,

I won't be seeing you again. Gotta bust ass out of here before the cops find me. I've heard by now that the guard lived – who knew you could survive having your throat slit? Just the same, things are a wee bit complicated and I don't feel like sticking around to get tangled up in all of that.

I don't know who else to talk to about this – I know, I know, Louis, but that's a whole other kettle of fucking fish right there – so I'm talking to you.

Eleanor Caldecott told me I was the same as her.

And fuck me if I wasn't starting to buy that line of thinking.

But then, down in the dark of the river I had a – well,

what alcoholics call their moment of clarity. Eleanor Caldecott was willing to die to make sure that Wren died, too.

I was willing to die to make sure that Wren lived.

Two sides of the same coin, maybe, but different sides just the same. Or maybe I'm just fooling myself. Maybe I'm no different.

But I like to think I am.

And that means I have work to do.

Maybe we'll meet again someday. In the here or the after.

Die well, Katey Wiznewf…howeverthefuckyouspellyourlastname.

Hope you meet Steve soon.

Peace in the Middle East,

Miriam Black

"Most people just write a card," the delivery guy says.

Katey looks up at him, wiping tears out of her eyes.

He's a big fellow. Round. Like a teddy bear. Kind of a buckethead, but adorable in his delivery outfit. Clean and pressed.

A tag pinned to his button-down shirt says: Steve.

"Steve," Katey says, laughing. The laughs start out small but soon go tumbling into a whole crazy cacophony of laughter – so that she's laughing and crying not at the thought of dying but at the madness of it all.

"Are you okay?" he asks, offering her an old-fashioned paisley handkerchief.

The laughter dies down. "Steve. I'm going to need you to come inside and have a cup of tea with me. You good with that?"

Steve smiles. "I'd love a cup of tea."

"And maybe a trip to the Caribbean?"

"I'd love a cup of tea first."

"Tea first it is, then."

INTERLUDE
TRAILER PARK

They lie together, Miriam and Louis.

"How's your eye?" she asks.

"You mean the eye that isn't there anymore?" he says. "It itches."

"I bet."

"How's your…"

"Boob? Tit? Bazonga? You mean where that fucker stabbed me?" She bites at her thumbnail, suddenly wishes she could smoke in here. "It itches."

They laugh.

"Guess we're just two itchy people," Louis says.

Miriam thinks, *But I got itches you can't scratch.*

That's not what she says, though.

She says, "I'll scratch your itch if you scratch mine."

"You sure you're feeling up to it?"

Her hand slides down to his jeans, eases past the waistband like a snake sliding under a closed door, and she puts her chin up on his shoulder. "The question is, Mister Darling – *are you*?"

SIXTY-FOUR

LETTING GO, AND OTHER DICK MOVES

She finds him in the parking lot of the motel. A low fog clings to the ground and above the sky is a hazy white smear that's eaten the sun. Louis kneels down by the first slashed tire of his truck, head on the rim, rubbing his temples.

The day after the fracas at the Caldecott estate, he had two new truck tires delivered to him and put on right at the intersection where he left the truck, and before the police came sniffing around he and Miriam hit the road. They traveled about a half-hour south to Mechanicsburg.

"Dangit. I just got these fixed," he says. He bites his knuckle so hard it leaves pale indents.

"Somebody slashed your tires," she says.

"Yeah."

"That was me."

He turns. "Ha ha, Miriam. Now isn't the time."

"I also stole a bunch of money from the glove box. A couple hundred. About half of what you had sitting there. I know, I know. Dick move."

Crestfallen, he stands. "Wait. You're not kidding."

"Nope."

It's then he gets it.

"You're leaving me behind."

She hesitates but finally says, "Yeah. Yes. I know. I'm sorry."

"I'm your protector."

"And you did that job crazy good. Look. See? Still alive." She pats her chest as though to confirm she's not a ghost. "But I saw the look on your face. When I shot the headmaster. That's no small thing, Mr. Darling."

"I can get past it. I killed someone, too."

"I know. And that's fucked up. That's not who you are but this is who I am. Once I thought I was a good girl but it ended up I was a bad girl. Then I thought that fate was what fate was but then I learned there was one way to change it. I thought I was a thief. But as it turns out… I'm a killer." She looks up at the sky, sees geese overhead heading south. "I'm not going to be responsible for turning you into me."

"It doesn't have to be like that," he says.

"Oh, but it does. Like Popeye says, I yam what I yam."

"Why the tires?"

"Because I knew you'd come after me."

He shrugs. "I still will."

"Don't."

"You are who you are, and I am who I am."

"You won't find me. This is the end of our road."

She walks over, and stands small before him.

"I could grab you," he says. "I could just… reach down and hold you here. Forever. You wouldn't be able to get away."

"I'd like that. I would. But you'd be better off jumping on a grenade. Instead, let's just do this." She gets on her tippy-toes and kisses him. Long, slow, deep. The kind of kiss where you can feel little pieces of your soul trading places as mouths open and breath mingles.

He reaches for her but she pulls away.

"Bye, Louis."

"I'll find you."

"No, you won't."

But she's not so sure.

SIXTY-FIVE
ON THE ROAD AGAIN

"Stop here," she tells the driver. He's a cantankerous old git, a slack-jawed denture-wearing pucker-eyed motherfucker named Albert. His wife died a year and a half ago, and now he travels the country doing what he and his wife always said they'd do as a joke but never did – find all those crazy roadside attractions like the world's biggest ball of yarn and the house where everything sits at crazy angles and haunted hotels and gravity hills and all that silliness.

He picked her up thumbing for a ride outside the Roadside America exhibition, an 8,000 square foot building depicting the United States in miniature. The sign announces that they have over 10,000 little trees, over 18,000 light bulbs, and 22,000 feet of electrical wiring.

It's probably the only attraction in Shartlesburg, Pennsylvania, a town whose name Miriam finds so funny she, well, nearly sharts every time she hears it.

Albert was coming out of the epic miniatures display when he saw Miriam hitchhiking. He asked her where she was going and she told him.

He's a nice guy. Chatty as a squirrel. Which is okay by her. She likes to talk, too, but for now she figures it's time for her to be quiet.

Albert dies soon. In thirteen months.

It's evening when it happens, and he's standing in front of a giant tree-stump – a sequoia or a redwood – carved into the face of a bearded man that calls to mind a real Paul Bunyon type. A sign next to it indicates it's the face of John Muir, whoever the hell that is. And as the sun goes down, Albert takes out an old photo of his wife, as he's wont to do, and he turns the picture toward the big stumpy head (so she can see it) and then he clutches his chest and dies.

Dead before he hits the ground.

The picture blows away on the wind.

For now, though, he's very much alive.

"You good, little missy?" he asks. That's what he calls her. Little Missy.

She gives him a wink and a thumbs-up.

"Stay frosty!" he yells at her. "I'm gonna have one of your ciggies while you're gone! You gotta pay the hitchhiker toll!"

She's glad he only means a smoke. He cackles as she walks up to the house.

The walkway remains ruined beneath her feet.

Pots still shattered. Steps, too. Above her head is a crow perched on the edge of the gutter, shuffling from foot to foot. She tries to think her way into the crow's mind, tries to get the bird to do something, anything – *lift a wing, clack your beak, take a shit* – but all the bird does is take flight and disappear into the trees.

Whatever. Stupid bird.

She knocks.

Eventually, Uncle Jack answers.

"You," he says. Dubious.

"I want Mother's number. And her address. In Florida."

"I'm surprised."

"Me, too. Just go get it, willya?"

He returns, puts the paper in her hand. Fort Lauderdale.

Fine. Good. Her heart races.

"Thanks, Jack. See you when I see you." *Which will probably be never.*

"Later, killer."

She turns toward him. She expects him to be smiling at her. Maybe holding up a dead robin and a loaded pellet rifle. But he's already gone, back in the house.

Miriam hops back in the car with Albert.

"Where we off to?" he asks.

"Just head south," she says.

And that's the direction he goes.

ACKNOWLEDGMENTS

Sounds so soft, so limp, so passive – "I acknowledge you" is the barest, smallest thing we can offer someone, isn't it? It's hardly a head-nod, a shrug, a fluttery gesticulation in one's general direction. So, assume that these are not acknowledgments but, rather, Awesome Freeze-Frame High-Fives of Awesomeness. With bacon and whisky and unicorn dreams.

Awesome Freeze-Frame High-Fives of Awesomeness to go:

Stephen Blackmoore and Stacia Decker for helping kick this book into high gear.

The fine feathered folks at Mysterious Galaxy for helping *Blackbirds* fly.

The clanking doom-bot geniuses of Angry Robot for putting Miriam Black into your hands.

My wife and son for supporting me and not kicking the crazy pantsless writer out of their house.

And all the people who read *Blackbirds* and wrote reviews and told me how much they dug it.